BABY I'M YOURS

CARRIE ELKS

Harper Hayes was running late again.

Okay, so it was only five minutes, and she was making it up to them by carrying in a whole cardboard tray full of barista-made coffees – the reason for her tardiness. But it was only her ninth week on the job, and her attempts to make the best impression were definitely falling short.

The door to the workshop was closed. Harper frowned, trying to decide whether to risk sloshing the drinks as she pushed on the handle with her elbow, or to take the extra time to put the tray on the floor, open the door, pick it up again, and...

The door flew open, the edge slamming into the tray she was still holding. She stumbled back as the cups flew everywhere, coffee spraying across the walls, the floor, and most particularly on Harper's white embroidered dress.

Almost immediately, she dropped to her knees, attempting to pick up the fallen cups and stop the coffee from pouring out of them. The floor was a puddle of brown liquid, and the whitewashed walls resembled some kind of collaboration between the artist Jackson Pollock and Starbucks.

She didn't want to look at herself, at the dress she'd made from a vintage fabric she'd discovered in a flea market in upstate New York, or at whoever had opened the door and was silently surveying the caffeine massacre she'd created.

Whoever it was cleared their throat. Harper slowly lifted her head, her pink-tipped blonde hair falling wetly on her shoulders. She didn't recognize the woman at all. In her stark black suit and pulled back hair she looked strangely out of place in the costume department.

"Miss Hayes?"

"Yes?" Harper half-frowned as she nodded at the woman.

"You're late. The meeting started twenty minutes ago."

Harper blinked. "What meeting?"

"Didn't you get the text? All members of the costume department to attend a meeting in the boardroom. Eight-thirty sharp," the woman clucked. "You're the only one who isn't there."

Harper managed to pick up the last of the cups, and put it back on the tray. "I didn't get a text." Unless it came in the last twenty minutes, when she was in line at the coffee shop, smiling at a little kid who was drinking a baby chino in his stroller. She grimaced, pulling her phone from the tiny grey purse slung across her body. Sure enough there was a text from her head of department.

"You should probably head over there now."

Harper nodded. "I will. Just as soon as I clean myself up." She smiled at the woman who didn't smile back. "And call the janitor."

The woman let out a sigh. "I'll call the janitorial staff. Go straight to the boardroom before it's too late."

"Too late?" Harper tipped her head to the side, trying to work the woman out. "For what?"

But the woman had already turned and walked back into the department, slamming the door behind her and turning the lock. For a second Harper stared at it, as though by some miracle she'd developed x-ray vision and could see through to the design tables and shelves with reams of fabric of every description. Behind the workshop was the wardrobe itself, though it was a paltry description for something so huge. Rack upon rack of covered costumes, some dating back to the heydays of the 1920s and 1930s when Hollywood was all about glamor and glitz, with clothing to reflect it.

Two months into working here and Harper was still star struck. Even walking through the security gate gave her a buzz, making her grin at the thought of how many famous actors had stepped on the same ground as her. On her first day she'd been taken on a tour and seen the sound stages, the outdoor sets, along with the huge office building housing the massive administrative staff who were the engine behind all the movie magic.

Her co-worker had explained they were often called out while the cameras were rolling to deal with wardrobe malfunctions and repairs. It was their job to get to the set as quickly as possible to assist the team already there, with the right tools, colored threads, and accessories needed. And though the movie she was assigned to was still in pre-production, she couldn't wait to see the designs they'd been working on brought to life.

The excitement and adrenaline were everything she'd been looking for when she had made the move from New York, where she'd been working in the costume department on Broadway. Along with her side hustle of selling one-off, handmade clothes on Etsy, this job ticked off every requirement in her creative box.

"What the heck happened to the floor?"

Harper turned to her left to see three of her co-workers

walking up the hall. Damon, Marcia, and Bree had been working here for years, but had welcomed her into the department with open arms.

But right now they looked anything but welcoming. Damon's expression was the kind of dark clouds you never saw in the California sky, and Marcia looked as though she was about to cry.

"Is the meeting over?" Harper asked, biting her lip. She was going to have to kiss some major ass over this. "I was about to join you but..." she trailed off, inclining her head at the pool of coffee at her feet.

"Yeah it's over." Damon's voice sounded as dark as his expression. "And we're over too. Kaput. Fired."

Marcia gave a little sob.

Harper blinked. "You are? Why?" She'd only been here for a short time, but that was enough to see how skillful they all were.

"No, you don't understand," Bree said. She was the oldest of them, having worked in different studios across Hollywood for the past thirty years. "*We're* fired. All of us. They're closing the department."

Harper froze like a statue. The sound of her pulse rushed through her ears. *Two months and two days.* That's how long she'd been here. Two months, two days, and a whole load of debt from moving to L.A. just to work here.

"We have ten minutes to pack our things and leave." Bree checked her watch. "Make that nine." She pushed at the door to their department, grimacing when it didn't budge. "They've locked us out, those rat bastards."

"Bree!" Marcia said, tears still pouring down her face. "You don't swear."

"I don't get fired either," she muttered, rapping on the door. "And somebody had better let me in. My sewing box is in there. I'm not leaving without it."

It was as though Harper was in a see-through plastic box, the sound of their conversation muffled by the thoughts whirling around her head. She was fired. The thought of it made her feel sick. Along with the thought of her cramped Melrose apartment that took up more than half her wages, and the small red Toyota she'd just taken a loan out for.

And as she looked down at the coffee on the grey tiled floors, which was also covering the front of her pretty dress, she found her eyes stinging with tears.

What the hell was she going to do now?

"What do you mean you're fired?" her best friend Caitie asked through the phone. "I don't understand. You only just started working there. Oh honey, I wish I was there to give you a big hug."

After collecting their things from the workshop, Harper's colleagues had decided to head straight to a bar, unruffled by the fact it was nine in the morning, and the only bars open were the ones that hadn't yet closed from the previous night. They'd invited Harper, too, which she'd thought was very kind of them, but she'd declined. As welcoming as they'd been, she wasn't even part of the team yet. Getting drunk and commiserating with them felt distinctly uncomfortable.

Instead she'd driven straight home to her second floor apartment and taken a shower to wash the coffee from her pink-tipped blonde hair. Then she'd put her dress into a mixture of warm water and baking soda to soak it, though from the way the coffee stains had set to the fabric she knew it wasn't going to work.

And now? Now she was on the phone with her best friend, the only one who would know exactly how she felt. Harper and Caitie had been friends since their first week of college in New

England, having been assigned as roommates as freshmen. From the moment they'd met, they'd hit it off. Where Caitie was serious and ambitious, Harper was full of fun and mischief, though both of them had excelled in their studies. They were the ying to each other's yang – no wonder they'd stayed roommates when they arrived in New York to begin their working lives, then made the cross-country move to California together. But while Harper was in L.A., Caitie had moved to her small hometown of Angel Sands where her boyfriend lived.

It wasn't an exaggeration to say Harper missed her best friend like crazy.

"The studio has gone bust. They're under new administration," Harper explained, repeating the details Bree had told her. "They're still trying to keep it going, but they're outsourcing everything they can, including the costume department."

"But you'll get severance pay, right?" Caitie said.

"No." Harper sighed. "I'm not entitled to anything under my contract. And California is an at-will state, so I'm completely out of luck." She was trying to keep the panic out of her voice, but it was a close-run thing. All she'd been able to think about since she'd arrived back in her apartment was that she didn't even have enough money for next month's rent.

She bit her lip in an attempt not to cry. It had seemed like such a good idea to move to California. While she'd loved working on Broadway, the thought of being employed in a huge department in Hollywood sounded amazing. When Caitie had been offered a contract in California, and fallen in love with a guy from her hometown, it all seemed to gel.

And now here she was, with nothing. It scared her to death.

"You'll get another job," Caitie said, as though she could

read Harper's mind. "You're so good at what you do. Any studio would be delighted to have you. And in the meantime you could do more Etsy work, or take on freelance somewhere. I bet there are lots of places recruiting in LA."

"You're right." Harper nodded, even though Caitie couldn't see her. "It'll be okay. It always is."

"I hate to hear you so down. It's not like you at all. I wish I was there right now." Caitie took a deep breath. "I could drive up this weekend if you like? We can buy a few bottles of wine and drown your sorrows." She sighed. "Oh damn, I can't. There's the opening party for the hotel on Saturday." Her voice rose up. "Okay! I've got it. You can drive down here and come to the party. It's going to be amazing, and it'll take your mind off everything in L.A. And I'll get to give you all the hugs I want to. It's perfect."

"I don't know." Harper pulled her bottom lip between her teeth. "Maybe I should stay here. I've got a job to find." Though the thought of driving down the Pacific Coast to Angel Sands was enticing. Since the first time she'd visited the small beach town with Caitie, it had cast its spell on her. She'd felt a little envious of her friend growing up in such a close-knit community.

"We can look at things together," Caitie said, sounding sure of herself. "Make some plans; I'm the queen of lists, remember?"

"I do." Harper bit down a smile, thinking of the pages of lists Caitie had created before their move to California.

Thank goodness for best friends. The anxiety that had been tugging at Harper was lifting. She'd never been one to dwell on things for too long, and she didn't worry about things unnecessarily. Life had taught her that when things went wrong she somehow survived.

And this blip would be no different. She'd get through it

the way she always did, and if she could come out smiling, that would be all the better.

She'd drive down to Angel Sands and feel the sand between her toes, the surf wash over her feet, and let the warmth of the sun chase all the gloom away.

And until then, there was always that bottle of wine in the refrigerator to keep her going.

2

Dr. James Tanner pulled his green scrubs off and threw them into the basket beside the lockers. His muscles felt taut and achy after six hours of surgery. Today was a thirteen-year-old girl with scoliosis who required a spinal fusion to straighten her curved spine.

It was a long and intricate surgery involving continual monitoring from the neuro team to make sure he didn't impair any nerves running down the spine, as well as the rest of the orthopedic team, and an anesthesiologist who ensured the general anesthetic the patient had received didn't run out before he'd finished operating.

Now that it was over and the patient was in recovery, he could feel every inch of his body complaining. It didn't matter how often he lifted weights or ran to keep himself in peak condition, leaning over a surgical gurney for hours with only the smallest of intricate movements always kicked the hell out of him.

He grabbed his towel from the locker and headed to the shower, slinging it around his neck as he reached in to turn the heat all the way up. By the time he stepped inside it was steamy, the hot water stung his body, and he closed his eyes as he embraced the pain. He rolled his neck, his shoulders, moved his fingers to ease out the stiffness, before he scrubbed his skin clean of any bacteria he might have picked up.

When he emerged from the misty cubicle, the pain was beginning to subside. He almost missed it. The pain was preferable to the thoughts and memories he'd rather not have.

The grief that never seemed to disappear, no matter how long it had been.

"Hey, man, how did it go?"

James looked up to see Rich Martin walk in. They'd been at medical school together and then become residents together at the Saint Vincent Memorial Hospital. While James specialized in spinal surgery, Rich was an attending physician in the ER.

"It was good." James grabbed his street clothes from the locker and dried himself with the towel, catching the rivulets of water cooling on his skin. "No problems with the surgery and she woke up nicely. I'll check on her before I leave." He nodded at his friend. "How was your shift?"

"Crap. We lost a patient." Rich pulled open his own locker, the door clanging as he did. "Seventy-two-year old man. Heart attack. Crashed twice." His Adam's apple bobbed as he swallowed. "Should have been able to save him."

James pulled his shirt over his short, dark hair. "Sorry, man." He knew how that felt. The hope, the desperation and then the darkness. Every death felt like a personal injury, something you carried with you no matter how much you tried to rationalize it.

Not that it was anything compared to the pain waiting for him at home. The empty room, the empty beds, the plain dark hollowness that always greeted him. Maybe that was why he spent so much time at the hospital. It was preferable to anything else.

"I'm going to shower it off." Rich inclined his head at the bathroom. "You heading to the party on Saturday night?"

"Party?" James frowned. "What party?"

Rich let out a deep laugh. "The party of the year. The big opening of the Silver Sands Resort. We all got an invite, remember?"

James had a vague recollection of seeing something, but no doubt it had ended up in the trashcan along with all the other invitations he received. He shrugged. "Probably not."

The Silver Sands Resort was down the coast from James' cliff top house, on the outskirts of the small town of Angel Sands. He'd lived there for years, ever since he'd proposed to Sara, and in spite of everybody's entreaties, he'd refused to move after she'd passed.

Why would he want to? That place was all he had left.

It had also afforded him a close-up view of the renovation of the Silver Sands Resort. Originally built in the 1920s, in its heyday the sprawling beachside hotel had been the hideaway of many Hollywood actors and actresses. When James had first moved to town it had been derelict, but for the past two years Carter Leisure had been renovating it back to its former glory.

And now it was ready to open – and Angel Sands was about to have the party of the year.

"Why not come? You're not on shift, are you? And there's free drinks all night for everybody. I hear half of Hollywood's coming down to celebrate." Rich winked. "You might get lucky."

James shook his head and laughed. He wasn't looking to get lucky; hadn't felt anywhere near lucky for years. Luck was something he used to have, along with a wife and child that had lit up his life. But it all disappeared in a heartbeat.

"Maybe I'll just get lucky with a bottle of Jack instead." James raised his eyebrows. "You can have all of Hollywood to yourself."

"Nah ah. I'm not letting you off that lightly. Come on, get out and show your face for once. How long's it been? Three years?"

"Something like that."

"I'll pick you up at eight," Rich told him.

"I won't be ready."

"Yeah you will. We'll hit the party for a couple of hours. Get our free cocktails and nose around the place. And if Jennifer Lawrence wants me to spin her around on the dance floor..." Rich grinned. "I'll ask her if she has a best friend for you."

"Don't do me any favors."

"Eight sharp. And it's black tie."

"Sounds wonderful." James lifted an eyebrow. But maybe the thought of going out was preferable to the idea of staying at home all night. It didn't matter how many glasses of whiskey he drank, the ghosts and the memories always remained. At least when he was out he didn't have to think about them. "I'll think about it."

His home was a brick-and-glass, one-story building on the edge of the cliffs overlooking Angel Sands. He pulled his Mercedes onto the sandstone driveway leading to the low profile bungalow, pressing his foot on the brake and sliding the stick into park.

A car was already there. An old Toyota he never could persuade his parents to replace, no matter how many times he offered to pay for the upgrade. As soon as he climbed out of his own car, his father opened his own car door, smiling in greeting as he reached into the passenger side to grab something.

"Don't shoot the messenger," he said, his eyes warm as he surveyed his son. "But your mom's worried about your diet, so she made you a casserole."

James's lips twitched at the size of the dish. It could easily feed four and still have food left over for the next day. "What does she want me to do, explode?" A smile broke out on his face as he took the dish from his dad and bumped him with his shoulder. "I'll call later to thank her."

"That would be good. She worries about you." His dad didn't add that he worried, too, though it was obvious from the way he was looking at James. Checking him up and down, making sure he was well, the same way he used to after a Friday night football match.

"You want to come in?" James asked his dad, inclining his head at the front door. "I can put some coffee on."

"No no. I need to get back. Your mom made another of those casseroles for us." Even though he refused the invite, his dad didn't seem in any hurry to leave. He leaned on the post below the porch overhang, crossing his arms as a smile played around his lips. "How was work?"

"Pretty good. I had a six-hour spinal fusion. Checked on the patient before I left and she's doing well. Should be up and walking in a couple of days."

His dad's eyes gleamed. "It never fails to amaze me what you can do with those hands. You have your mother to thank for those. And all those piano lessons she forced you to take."

"Yeah." James smirked. "I'm really thankful for those."

"And are you taking care of yourself?" his dad asked. "Getting out and seeing people?"

"Is this you asking or is it mom?" James could hear her now, telling his dad exactly what questions she needed him to ask.

"We worry about you, son. It's been almost three years." His dad cleared his throat, shifting from one foot to the other. "I know you miss them. We all do. You're not the only one who lost people they love that day."

James felt his chest tighten, the way it always did when they tried to talk about that overcast Monday three years ago. It had taken so long to get his thoughts away from that day. Years of therapy to be able to sleep without seeing her drift away from him on that hospital bed. He didn't want to think about it, talk about it, do anything except blot it out of his mind with a tall glass of whiskey.

"I *am* getting out and seeing people," he half-lied. "I'm going to the opening of the Silver Sands Resort on Saturday."

Well that was one decision made.

"You are? That's great." His dad leaned toward him. "Are you, ah, taking anybody?"

"Let's not push things too far, I'm going with Rich. Though I'm almost certain I won't be with him for long. He's heard rumors of Hollywood actresses attending."

"It doesn't matter. I'm glad you're getting out. Your mom will be, too. We want you to be happy. You've got a long life ahead of you. You've beaten yourself up for long enough." He patted James on the shoulder. "I should get back. Your mom was warming up the casserole as I left."

James nodded. "I'll call her later, but tell her thanks for the food."

"I will. And maybe you can come over on Sunday, tell us about the party. That would make us both happy."

"If I'm not working, sure." Not that there would be anything to tell. As far as he was concerned, he'd go, have a few free drinks, and slink off as soon as Rich was occupied by somebody else.

But maybe it'd be better than staying in on a Saturday night; there was only one way to find out.

3

"What's this?" Harper asked, a smile ghosting her lips as she looked around the bungalow. The walls were whitewashed, covered with what looked like expensive one-off paintings hanging in tarnished golden frames. The floors were laid with marble tiles, but the most stunning thing was the bed. A four poster made of intricately carved dark wood posts, with shimmering voile curtains cascading down to the expensive white sheets pulled taut beneath a silver satin throw.

"It's yours," Caitie said, bouncing from foot to foot. "At least for tonight. Breck spoke to his friend Aiden, the hotel director. He was happy to comp you a place."

"That's so sweet." Harper couldn't help but grin. Breck was Caitie's boyfriend and his company had carried out the resort renovations. One of the things she loved about Angel Sands was how everybody knew everybody. The thought that they arranged this for her made her heart swell ten times bigger.

"And we've booked you in at the salon for a facial and blow out. So leave your stuff here and let's go." Caitie reached for her hand, waiting patiently as Harper put down her case and slid her own palm into it. Then they pulled the door closed and headed up the pathway to the main hotel building.

Everything about this place was glamorous. From the perfectly kept gardens – filled with towering palm trees and lush azaleas in vibrant pinks and blues – to the marble statues and sparkling fountains peppering the grounds. Cliffs towered above the resort, the Pacific Ocean in front of it, making it feel secluded and exclusive.

"Rumor has it Marilyn Monroe slept in that bungalow," Caitie said, inclining her head to the low sandstone building they'd just left. "Maybe that's where she met up with JFK."

"It isn't new?" Harper thought they'd razed the old buildings and built new, custom-made ones.

"Nope. The resort is renovated to match the old blue prints. They reused the same building materials where they could. According to Breck, they've updated a few things – added all the modern amenities where they weren't before. But if you look around, it's pretty much the same as it was back in the golden days of Hollywood." Caitie grinned. "Once Marilyn escaped to here, and now you have. It's kind of fitting."

"As long as I don't find a politician in the bedroom, I'll be fine," Harper said, unable to keep the smile from her face. God, she loved her best friend; Caitie always knew how to cheer her up. It used to be pizza and beer when she'd failed an assignment, now it was a glamorous stay in a brand new exclusive resort when she'd just been fired.

"Well, there'll be plenty of politicians tonight. Along with a lot of celebrities, and pretty much all the inhabitants of Angel Sands. If you're looking for your very own JFK…"

Harper laughed. "I don't need any more complications in my life. Let me sort out my job first, then I'll look for a guy."

She slipped her arm through Caitie's as they reached the

iron-and-glass oversized doors leading into the main foyer. A bellhop, perfectly dressed in light blue livery, pulled them open and gestured them in. "Good afternoon, ladies. Welcome to the Silver Sands Resort. Please come inside"

As they stepped through the doors the sound of a string quartet echoed out. The four musicians were in the corner, perfectly dressed in black tuxedos and dresses, looking every bit as glamorous as their surroundings.

And as the sweet melody caressed Harper's ears, she felt all her worries melt away. "Thank you," she whispered to her friend, pulling her in for a hug. "This is perfect."

Caitie hugged her back. "It's a pleasure. I've got a feeling this is going to be a night neither of us will forget."

By the time Harper had finished in the salon, it was time to get dressed. When she got back to the bungalow nestled in the trees, she found Caitie waiting for her with a glass of champagne, along with her sister-in-law, Ember, and her friends, Ally and Brooke.

She'd met them before when she'd visited Angel Sands, and they welcomed her like old friends, giving her hugs, commiserating with her about her job – and most importantly – making sure her wine was topped up.

"Another job will come along," Ember told her. Caitie's sister-in-law was full of warmth – made warmer still by her pregnancy. She was almost four months along and glowing with it. "Look at Ally. When her dad sold the beach café she thought she was out of a job. But then she met her new boss and fell in love. One door might have slammed shut, but the new door was so much better."

"You make it sound so easy," Ally said, raising her eyebrows. "It wasn't quite that simple. It took a broken ankle and having to stay with him and his daughter for weeks before I realized there was something between us."

Ember rolled her eyes. "She's so unromantic. But all I'm trying to say is that when we reach our rock bottom the only way is up; and quite often the climb is a beautiful one."

Harper smiled at her. "I hope so. It has to be better than the hole I'm in now."

"You're not supposed to be thinking about that tonight," Caitie reminded her, topping up her champagne glass. "Tonight is about glamor and beauty. Let's not talk about holes."

Brooke's phone buzzed. "It's also about actually getting to the party," she said, her lips curling up as she glanced at her screen. "Aiden wants to know where we all are. The guys are getting jittery."

A moment later, Ally's phone buzzed, followed by Ember's and Caitie's, and they all started to laugh. "I think that's our signal," Ally said, shaking her head with amusement. "Let's head over before they send out a search party."

Ten minutes later they were walking into the ballroom of the Silver Sands Resort. It was already full-to-bursting with glamorous guests; the women clad in sparkling dresses, the men dashing in their jet black dinner suits. On the stage an old-fashioned swing band was playing, the singer crooning softly into the microphone as a few couples danced in the center of the room. As they made their way across the shining tiled floor, Harper recognized a few faces. Actors and politicians, mingled with reality stars and sports personalities. The buzz in the room was electric, and she couldn't help but feel it too.

"There they are," Brooke said, pointing over at a group of ridiculously handsome men. Harper had to look twice – she knew Breck and his friends quite well, but she'd never seen them dressed up for an event like this before. In their jeans and t-shirts they were good looking enough, but dressed in black suits they were glorious. And attracting a lot of female glances.

"Hey baby," Breck said, sliding his arm around Caitie's waist. "What do you think?"

"It's amazing." Caitie grinned and brushed her lips across his cheek. "You did a wonderful job."

As the contractor responsible for renovating the resort, Breck had worked tirelessly to hit the deadlines the owners had set. One of who was standing next to him – Aiden, Brooke's fiancé.

Harper watched as her friends embraced their men. Ally and her boyfriend, Nate – the gorgeous owner of the Déjà Brew chain, and father to a teenage daughter, laughed together, as Lucas, Caitie's firefighter brother, swept Ember into a big hug. Aiden ordered them all another round of drinks, then kissed Brooke and told her how beautiful she looked.

It was impossible not to smile at their obvious adoration for each other. But Harper's heart clenched a little, too. Because that feeling of belonging with someone, of always having them by your side, it was something she'd never have.

Maybe she never would.

"Is this where the single people are supposed to stand?" a deep voice asked her.

She turned with a grin to see Griffin and Jack standing next to her. Griff was the captain of the whaling ship that sailed daily in the summer from Paxton's Pier, and along with Jackson, an owner of an up-and-coming tech company, they'd grown up with Lucas and Breck, and were still their best friends.

"Griff." Harper smiled at him. "I didn't recognize you. You scrub up well." It was an understatement. Griff usually preferred to dress down, and was known to have a very distant relationship with his razor. He was the most laid-back person Harper had ever met. When he wasn't working, he was usually surfing. The man lived for the Pacific Ocean.

Griff looked down at his dinner suit. "Thanks. I asked if I could get away with jeans, but apparently the answer was no."

"Brooke was just worried about you smelling of fish," Jackson said, grinning at him. "And anyway, you've only worn that suit at Lucas and Ember's wedding before. Now you're getting your money's worth."

Griff pulled at the collar. "Yeah, and I'm counting down the hours until I can get out of it."

"Stop griping and start drinking," Lucas suggested, handing them both a beer. "Can I get you anything?" he asked Harper.

"I'm good." She smiled at him.

As the evening continued, the group became more raucous, and Harper found herself laughing out loud at the banter between the men. She even managed to dance a couple of times – first with Griff and then with Breck, before the music got slower and more romantic.

By ten o'clock all her friends were dancing, their faces illuminated by the soft light of the crystal chandeliers overhead. Harper was sitting at a table in the corner, her champagne glass empty once again, and she could feel the worries she'd managed to ignore for a few hours racing back into her mind.

"You okay?" Caitie asked, as she and Breck danced past her.

Harper smiled. "I'm good. I might go and get some fresh air."

"You want me to come with?"

She shook her head. "No. You keep dancing." She didn't want to spoil Caitie's fun with her melancholy. "I'll be fine."

As she walked toward the terrace, she could smell the

salty air of the ocean wafting in through the open glass doors. Tiny sparkling lights were strewn across the deck and nestled in the foliage of the trees and bushes like fireflies sending out a mating call.

She was about to step out when she saw another door. According to the etching on the glass, it led to a saloon bar. Maybe she'd go grab another drink to take outside with her.

She was determined to have a good time. Tomorrow she'd worry about the mess that was her life, but tonight was all about having fun.

***

"Can I have another, please?" James slid his glass across the dark oak counter. The barman caught it and poured him a double whiskey. James slid a bill back at him – though the drinks were free the tips weren't – and he could just about remember how hard it was to work behind a bar. It was how he'd paid his way through college.

He lifted the glass to his lips and took a sip, feeling the amber liquid heat his tongue. Mellowness washed over him as he swallowed, making his muscles feel loose and relaxed for the first time in forever.

He'd been at the party for a couple of hours. Enough to wander around the grounds, greet old friends, and let himself be seen. Though there had been some sympathy in people's eyes as they asked him how he was doing, he'd managed to keep the smile painted on his lips for long enough that they didn't press him.

He didn't want to talk about how he was, wasn't sure of the answers to their unasked questions. His emotions were mercurial, waxing and waning depending on how long he decided to let himself wallow. Who wanted to talk about that at a party?

He'd last seen Rich about an hour ago, when he'd been dancing on the terrace leading down to the beach with a pretty nurse who couldn't take her eyes off him. She'd tried to introduce James to her friend, but he'd managed to extricate himself.

From the corner of his eye he saw the bar door push open, and the sound of the band wafted from the ballroom, a jaunty Sinatra tune. A woman walked in, her hair pinned to her head in a mass of gold-and-pink waves, her full lips painted perfectly red.

It was her dress which drew his eye – shimmering gold, with printed white flowers. The fabric molded close to her bodice, before flaring out at the waist in a fifties style puff. She looked like Grace Kelly on acid. Nearly everybody in the room turned to look at her. James turned, too, swallowing hard as she sashayed across the marble tiled floor, completely unaware of the effect she was having on the men in the room.

"What can I get for you, ma'am?" the bartender asked, as she reached the counter and perched on a stool.

James waited to hear her voice. He had no idea why he wanted to hear it so badly. Maybe he was waiting for her to sound like Marilyn Monroe, all breathy and completely idiotic. Anything to take away the allure she had.

"A Jack Daniels on the rocks, please." Nope, not breathy at all. But she did sound faintly like Grace Kelly. Her vowels were clipped, her words short. She definitely wasn't from around here. And she couldn't have sounded less like Marilyn Monroe if she'd tried.

James took another mouthful of whiskey. He could feel his heart beat in a way it hadn't for a long time. Years, maybe.

"Jack's a popular drink tonight," the barman said to her, grabbing a tumbler and filling it with ice. "You want another?" he asked James.

"Oh, are you a fan, too?" she asked, turning to look at

him. She was smiling brightly, those scarlet lips curved up at the corners.

His eyes narrowed, as though he was looking into the sun. Her smooth skin contrasted with her dark lips. Her eyelashes were long and curved, framing her perfectly blue irises. If you wanted to nitpick, you could complain her nose had a tiny bump in it, and that there was a scar on the corner of her eye, which seemed to catch the light, but neither diminished the attraction.

"I like your hair," he said, his voice thick.

"Thank you," she said, patting it with her right hand. "I had it done in the salon here earlier."

"Do you work here?" Strange how words were spilling out of his lips. He almost didn't recognize his own voice. It felt so long since he'd voluntarily conversed with a stranger, unless it was for work.

She laughed. "I wish." The barman passed her the whiskey glass, and she took a sip. "But no, I don't live around here. I'm from Hollywood, just visiting for the weekend."

"You work in the movies?"

"Kind of." She shook her head. "Well not any more. It's a long story." She finished her whiskey, and the ice tinkled against the glass as she put it down on the counter.

"Another?" the barman asked, and she nodded.

James wanted to laugh. There was Rich dancing with a nurse from their hospital, when he was sitting opposite a bona fide actress.

"I like long stories," he told her. "And I haven't got anywhere else to be."

She tipped her head to the side, surveying him through those thick lashes. "I'm sure you don't want to hear my tales of woe. This is supposed to be a party."

"I prefer other peoples' woes to my own." He found

himself smiling at her, his eyes crinkling in the corner. God, she was too damn pretty for her own good.

And for his.

She leaned her chin on her hand. "I lost my job. Can't afford the rent. And my best friend moved out and left me all alone." She shrugged. "It's a ten-a-penny story in Hollywood I'm sure, but when it happens to you it sucks."

"Was it an acting role you lost?"

She laughed. "I'm not an actress. I don't think I could be one if I tried. My grandma always told me I can't tell a lie to save my life."

He scanned her with his gaze, trying to figure out what she did, if not an actress. He curled his hand tighter around his glass to stop himself from reaching out to touch her skin. He ached to see if it was as soft as it looked.

Christ, what had gotten into him? He should have taken that cab home an hour ago.

"So what was your job?"

"I'm a costume designer. I design and make the clothes you see on the stage and in movies. My whole department got closed down this week." She sighed. "So I'm jobless, and soon-to-be homeless."

"And yet you're still smiling," he pointed out, nodding at her grin.

"I blame the whiskey. And the company." She lifted her glass. "Cheers."

He clinked his own glass against hers. "Cheers."

"So what are your tales of woe?" she asked him. "Maybe I can lend you a sympathetic ear."

Yeah. No. Now would be a good time to leave, because he definitely didn't want to talk about his issues. He shook his head. "No, you don't want to hear my problems. Let's talk about yours instead. Have you started looking for another job?"

She shrugged. "I'm trying, but with every position that comes up I'll be competing with my old colleagues. And they're all much more experienced than I am, so the likelihood is I'll lose out." She pulled her perfectly painted lip between her teeth, and the action made his body pulse. "In the meantime, I have a little side hustle going. I'm hoping to ramp that up to keep the money coming in."

"What kind of side hustle?" he asked her, leaning closer. God, she was so easy to talk with.

"I design and sell my own clothes."

"Did you make your dress?" he asked, inclining his head at the golden silk bodice.

"Yeah." She blinked, her thick lashes curling down. "I've had it for a while, thought about selling it but I got too attached." Her smile came back, and it was as though the sun had come out from behind the clouds. "This is the first time I've had somewhere nice enough to wear it."

"You look like Grace Kelly." Did he really just say that out loud?

She laughed. "I do? Wow, you sure know how to sweet talk a lady, don't you?" She reached out and touched the lapel of his jacket, rubbing the fabric between her thumb and finger. From anybody else it might have seemed like a bold move, but from her it was natural, almost predestined. "This is nice," she said. "Pure satin. Guys should wear suits like these more often. You don't know what it does to us women."

"Maybe we do," he said, his voice thick. He leaned closer, enough to smell the floral notes of her perfume. His hands were trembling. What the hell was she doing to him? He never trembled – he couldn't. Not with his job. And yet here he was, his skin on fire, his heart pounding, and his fingers aching to touch her so badly it was all he could do to stop himself.

An hour – and two more whiskeys – later, they were still

talking. She was close enough for him to see the dark brown flecks in the vibrant blue of her eyes as she told him a story about a famous actress and a lack of underwear. He laughed and she joined in, putting her hand on his shoulder to steady herself.

He could smell her perfume again, floral and sweet.

"I'm being really indiscreet," she told him, smiling into his eyes. "I blame the whiskey."

"In that case we should get another." A lock of her hair had escaped from the pins. He reached out to push it back behind her ear, his finger trailing down her neck.

She breathed in, her chest rising up, her eyes gazing into his. He was still touching her. Couldn't bring himself to pull away. She was too warm, too soft. Too full of everything he wanted.

"I have a room," she said softly, closing her eyes for a moment. He immediately missed looking into them. "I'm sorry, I don't know why I said that."

Her hesitance was so damn sexy it kicked him where it mattered. He reached out to cup her cheek, desire shooting through him like a bolt of lightning.

Slowly, she opened her eyes, as he inclined his head toward hers, the flat of his brow pressing against her own.

How long had it been since he'd felt another woman's face against his? Forever. Another world, another life.

He shouldn't be doing it now, he knew that. Shouldn't be feeling his body throb to the beat of the music like he was an instrument being played. He traced her collarbone with the tip of his finger and swallowed a smile when her breath caught in her throat.

"You're beautiful," he told her, his voice low and thick. He slid his finger across her bottom lip, gratified at the way her mouth parted at his touch.

It was as though his body was on autopilot, ignoring every

warning his brain tried to shock him back to reality with. He didn't care if it was the whiskey, or the hotel, or whatever else it was that made him act this way. He had to have her or die trying.

He lifted his hand to cup her face once more, swallowing hard at the way she was staring at him. Sometimes you had to ignore the warnings and just do it. Even if you knew you'd regret it in the morning. A smile quirked the corner of his lips as he took her hand and helped her down from her stool.

"Show me your room."

✻ 4 ✺

Harper didn't do this kind of thing. Except here she was, bringing this hot, sharp-jawed, dark-eyed man back to the little bungalow facing the sea.

Of course she knew the risks. She also knew there were panic buttons throughout the bungalow, gleefully pointed out by Caitie as she took Harper on the tour of the place earlier.

She also knew her own gut. And yeah, you could argue that so did the people Ted Bundy managed to drag into his VW Bug, but it had never steered her wrong before.

Still, she found herself typing out a quick message to Caitie as the two of them left the bar, taking the back exit leading straight to the accommodation to avoid the ballroom and terrace full of revelers.

"I'm just telling my friend I'm leaving," she told him, staring up at his warm brown eyes. "In case you're some kind of axe murderer or something."

"Very sensible." He nodded. "Should I tell a friend, too?" He reached out to touch her bare shoulder, as though he couldn't stand not to. She loved the way it sent shivers down her spine.

"Probably." She laughed. "I've watched enough movies to know the villain's always the one you least expect. For all you know I could be some kind of deviant."

"Is it wrong that I hope you are?" His eyes softened as he stared back at her. God his lips looked delicious. "What kind of name would you have? Jane the Ripper? The Preying Mantis?"

Her chuckle cut through the warm night air. "Aren't those the insects who kill their mates after sex?"

"Yep. I can't imagine any insect dies happier than that."

She looked up at him again, and their eyes met, sending another delicious shockwave through her. His hand was still curled around her shoulder as they walked, protective and warm. She could smell his cologne, deep and woody, and see the dark shadows where his beard was beginning to win the battle against his razor.

"I don't even know your name," she murmured, reaching out to trace his jaw.

"I don't know yours."

"Call me Grace," she said, referring to how he'd described her earlier. "And I'll call you Frank."

"As in Sinatra?"

Her eyebrows rose up. "You're wearing a tux, it fits."

Her fingers had reached his lips. They were warm, soft, and she was desperate to feel them.

They'd stopped walking. In the distance, she could hear the sound of music carrying in the breeze, along with the rhythmic sound of the ocean crashing against the shore. But the loudest sound was the pulse in her ears, the rapid thrum echoing in her mind, reminding her how long it had been since she'd been touched. How much she wanted him, needed him. Was desperate to feel his skin against hers.

When he reached out to cup the back of her head, tipping

her face back until her eyes met his, she couldn't think of anything else but her need.

To feel him.

To touch him.

To kiss him.

He dropped his head so his lips were only a breath away from hers. Close up he was overwhelming. Warm eyes, high cheeks, a jawbone that could cut through rock, and lips that might have been too swollen on anybody else, and yet fit his face perfectly.

"Can I kiss you, Grace?" he asked, his voice thick.

"Please," she breathed.

He threaded his fingers through her hair, sliding his other hand down her back to the dip right above her behind. A half step forward brought his body to hers, his hard chest pressing against hers.

"You're so damn beautiful," he murmured, his fingers caressing the sensitive skin of her neck. "I love the way you feel."

"I love the way you touch me."

There was a moment of hesitation. Not from fear or anxiety. But a need to savor the second before their lips touched, before the fire was lit and neither of them were in control any more. She looked up at him, seeing the darkness in his eyes, illuminated by the reflection of the moon over the water. She wanted to bury herself in them, to swim inside his senses the way he was overtaking hers. And just as the second seemed to stretch into a lifetime, he captured her lips with his.

Her toes curled as their mouths pressed together, warm and needy and oh-so-delicious. He pulled her closer, so she could feel the hard planes of his body against the softness of her own, and his need aching between them.

Reaching up, Harper looped her arms around his neck, feeling the roughness of his short hair and the softness of his nape below. He deepened the kiss, the tip of his tongue running along the seam of her lips, until she opened up to him, desperate to feel him against her. Her whole body was on fire, lit up by the closeness of him. One more touch and she thought she might explode.

When he broke the kiss she found herself fighting for breath, light-headed from the combination of lack of oxygen and desire. "We should go inside," she said, her voice rough with need. "My bungalow is over there."

"Come here," he told her, as soon as he'd closed the door behind them. The low lights set into the side of the walls automatically flickered on, their soft glow illuminating her face as she did exactly what he requested. She stopped in front of him, her eyes wide, her lips parted, waiting to see what he'd do next.

Leaning forward, he pulled the pins from her hair, watching as it tumbled around her shoulders in a cloud of blonde-and-pink tendrils. He reached out to touch it, feeling the silky strands slide against his fingertips. "I really like this hair."

He moved his hands down, until his palms slid against her shoulders, feeling their warmth as he rounded them to the top of her arms. "Can I take this off?" he asked, sliding his hand down the back of her dress. She nodded, so he pulled the zipper down, sliding his hands through the gap to feel her shoulder blades, her spine, and the deliciously aggravating dip leading to everything he wanted.

She shrugged the dress off, completely unaffected by the fact she was naked apart from the silky scraps of lingerie. He swallowed hard, taking in her perfectly smooth skin, the rise of her breasts, and the dip of her stomach. Another time, another place and he'd be hesitant, aware this was the first time he'd seen a woman strip for him in years.

But tonight he wanted it all, to touch every inch of her, to hear her soft gasps as he gave her pleasure. Leaning forward again, he kissed her hard and hot, leaving them both breathless when he pulled away.

"Take your tux off," she told him. He grinned at the way she tried to imitate his commands. But he still did what he was told, shucking off his jacket, loosening his tie, unfastening the pearlescent buttons leading down to his waist.

"You like?" he asked as her pupils dilated when he was bare from the stomach up.

"I do," she told him. "I really do."

She stepped forward, pressing her chest against his, and he felt the need aching through him. He slid his hands beneath her ass, lifting her until her legs wrapped around his hips, and carried her over to the bed.

A smile played on her lips as he laid her down, climbing over her, and pressing his lips against her neck. He could feel her pulse throb against his mouth. He licked the point with the tip of his tongue and she sighed.

"Take off your pants," she said, pulling at his belt. "I need you."

God he needed her, too. He unfastened the buckle, and pulled at his zipper, dragging the expensive black fabric down his hips and thighs. She blinked as she watched him, her eyes drinking him in like he was a glass of Jack, widening when she saw the evidence of his need pressing against his shorts.

"Do you have something?" she whispered.

"Yeah." A condom he carried more to appease Rich than with any intent to use it. He grabbed the foil packet from the wallet in his pants pocket, before placing it on the bed next to her. Reaching behind her to unfasten her bra, he swallowed hard as her breasts spilled out.

Leaning forward, he captured a nipple between his lips, tasting her, worshipping her, pleasuring her. And when she arched her back and pulled down her panties, before she grabbed at the band of his shorts, he knew there was no going back.

For the first time in forever he lost himself to the pleasure, and forgot about the darkness in his life.

James wasn't sure when he fell asleep. Not that it was a restful slumber – he'd woken covered in sweat with a racing heart. Blinking the sleep from his eyes, he turned to see her curled on her side. Her pretty hair spread across the white pillow, her lips pursed together as she dreamed deeply.

A feeling of regret washed over him. He shouldn't have done this; shouldn't have opened himself up to a stranger. Shouldn't have let his desires overtake his good sense. Shouldn't have had sex with somebody he had no intention of seeing again.

And yet it had been amazing. Touching her, laughing with her, watching her eyes roll back with pleasure. He'd made her come again and again, just to hear her soft gasps, feel the pleasure of them as they caressed his ears.

God, she was pretty. And funny. And crazily easy to talk to. If he were any other kind of man he'd find it easy to fall for her. But he knew what falling meant. It meant landing on shards of glass and twisted metal, feeling them slice you up until you bled.

It meant pain and hurt and everything else he'd avoided these past three years.

After one last, rueful glance at her, he rolled over and slid his feet out of bed, reaching down to pick up his boxer shorts from where she'd thrown them earlier. He padded across the rug and onto the cold marble floor, keeping his steps light so as not to wake her. He grabbed his pants, sliding them on, and then his shirt, doing up the buttons and slinging his jacket and tie over his arm, turning one last time to look at the angel laying in the bed.

"Thank you," he whispered, pulling on his socks and shoes. He didn't want to leave, but he knew he couldn't stay. Yeah, it would be easy to sleep here for the rest of the night. Maybe wake up in the morning for round three, and take her out to breakfast and shoot the breeze with this woman.

But he couldn't. Because he knew what would happen. He'd hurt her and he'd hurt himself. He was that kind of an asshole, and she didn't deserve that.

He opened the door, stepping out into the silence of the early morning. The sun hadn't yet risen, but there was a threat of it in the air. Slowly he closed the door, checking the handle to make sure it was locked, and walked down the pathway toward the parking lot.

"What do you mean you don't know his name?" Caitie asked as she and Harper carried their cardboard coffee cups to a table overlooking the Pacific, taking a deep breath as she faced the view. Part of her therapy for overcoming her phobia of the ocean was to be exposed to it in small doses. Harper checked to see if she was okay before sitting down to join their friends, Ember, Brooke, and Ally who were already at the table.

"Whose name?" Ember asked as they sat in the two empty seats beside her. "What are you talking about?"

"Harper hooked up with a guy last night, but he disappeared after they... *you know*..." Caitie widened her eyes as though to give them a hint. "And she can't even remember what his name is."

Harper sighed. "I can't remember because he didn't tell me. I called him Frank, he called me Grace." It had been weird waking up to find him gone. She'd felt somewhere between sad and relieved. No embarrassing talk, no empty promises, or scribbled phone numbers they knew would never be used.

And yet she'd felt horribly empty, too.

"Well it's a small town," Ally said, leaning forward. "If he lives around here he probably comes in for coffee. Describe him."

Harper took a sip of coffee, swallowing down the warm liquid. "Um, he's tall. About six two or three. Short dark hair, cheekbones a model would kill for. Brown eyes. He's muscled, too, like he surfs or something."

Brooke laughed. "You've just described half the male population of Angel Sands. Lucas is tall and dark with muscles," she pointed out, talking about Caitie's brother and Ember's husband. "So is Aiden. And I know where they were all night so that rules them out."

"Did he tell you where he works?" Caitie asked.

"No. I don't remember talking about his job at all." Harper wrinkled her nose. "We talked about serial killers and Hollywood and clothes." Why hadn't she asked him about his job? Maybe she'd been too busy wrapping herself around his body to care.

"Maybe he's a cop. Or works for the FBI," Ally suggested.

"Or he's a massive Hollywood star playing a serial killer in his next movie," Ember added with a smile. "What if it was Hugh Jackman or Zac Efron?"

Harper laughed. "I would have recognized them. He didn't seem like he was from Hollywood at all. I know a lot of actors, and he wasn't like one of them." He hadn't cared about his clothes or his looks or anything else. Just her pleasure and her needs.

The thought sent a tingle down her spine.

"Maybe I could ask Aiden. See if he recognizes the description," Brooke suggested. Her fiancé was the Silver Sands Resort director. "This guy must have had an invitation. Somebody knows who he is."

"You could check the security tapes," Ally said, clapping her hands together. "Like in a detective movie."

"Please don't." Harper grimaced. "I don't want everybody knowing I hooked up with a guy whose name I don't know. If he'd wanted me to find him he would have left a note, or at least woken me up before he left." Her stomach dropped. "Let's face it, I was a one night stand to whoever he was."

Caitie slid her hand over Harper's. "I'm sorry, honey," she said. "It sounds like you liked him."

Harper shook her head, refusing to be upset. "It doesn't matter. We had a good time. We were careful." She raised her brows. "No harm was done to any animals."

Caitie burst out laughing. "I'm glad to hear."

"And anyway, I haven't got the time or the energy for a relationship right now. I need to find a job and pay the rent. I don't need any distractions."

"Well, whoever he is, he's the one missing out," Ember said firmly. "You're gorgeous, you're talented, and you're one of the nicest people I know. And as Brooke said, he's nothing special, just another guy like the rest in Angel Sands. If you're looking for somebody we could set you up."

"How about Ethan?" Ally asked, inclining her head at the barista behind the counter. "He's older than he looks."

"He's twenty-one," Brooke said, shaking her head. "And he's got student loans up to his eyeballs." She ran the tip of her tongue along her bottom lip, thinking. "I know. There's a guy at the hotel who's recently divorced. He's the finance director. I bet he'd love to go on a date with you."

Harper shook her head firmly. "You guys are wonderful, but no. Thank you, though. I'm not looking for anything serious, and I'm definitely not looking for a long distance relationship. I saw what it did to Caitie when she lived in L.A. and Breck was here in Angel Sands. If I want a guy – and I don't – I'll find myself one in L.A."

"If you're sure." Brooke almost hid the disappointment on her face. "But the offer is always there."

Harper was certain. Last night had been a one-off; something amazing and embarrassing, and everything in between. This afternoon she'd drive back to LA and forget about it all.

The chances were, he'd already forgotten about her.

5

At first, Harper thought it was a bug. The kind that made you hurl your breakfast in the toilet bowl every morning, then suddenly be hungry for more. The nausea wasn't as bad as it looked; it only lasted a few moments at a time. One minute she'd be sick as a dog, the next she was craving a burger for dinner.

But it wasn't the vomiting that brought her to the drugstore. It was her tender breasts. They ached and throbbed like she was getting ready for a massive period, but her period never came.

So here she was, staring at a shelf full of tests, trying to work out whether she wanted a digital window or a pink stripe, and wondering who the hell bought a three pack of pregnancy tests. As god was her witness, once this one came up negative she was never having sex again.

Maybe she'd become a nun. Did they let nuns dye their hair? She wasn't sure she'd be able to give up the pink tips. Or she could be one of those people who wore purity rings like the Jonas Brothers. Only if they let her be a born-again-purist, though. Otherwise they'd kick her out of the sect.

And while she was on a roll, who the heck thought it would be a great idea to put the pregnancy tests right next to the condoms? Damn taunting little boxes. She started to stick her tongue out at them, then noticed another customer staring at her. Was she talking to herself again?

Harper sighed and leaned forward, picking up a pink box. It didn't matter which one she chose. It was going to be negative anyway. She turned on her heel, lifting her middle finger in a salute to the condom shelves, and made her way over to the registers, opting for the self-checkout in an attempt not to embarrass herself further.

"Frank Sinatra," she muttered. "You have a lot to answer for."

"Seriously?" Caitie said, taking Harper's hands in hers, wide eyed and excited. "Oh my god. How long? When are you due? When did you find out?"

"Nine weeks according to the doctor," Harper told her. The nausea was slowly abating, but she still felt sick at the thought of the positive test.

Not to mention the fact she still hadn't found a full-time job. She'd been freelancing for the past two months, picking up work here and there, making as much money as she could with her Etsy orders, and somehow managing to pay the rent. She was a month behind on her car payment, though, and every time there was a knock on the door she was certain it was a repossession company.

And now this... it was as though life was laughing its ass off at her.

"Oh my god, Harper. You're having a baby." Caitie grabbed her hand, her eyes shining. "A real life baby. Congratulations."

"I'm not sure a celebration is in order," Harper said drily. "At least not from the baby's point of view. She really lucked out, being born to a jobless, potentially homeless mom."

"She?" Caitie raised an eyebrow.

Harper shrugged. "Yeah, she." Okay so she didn't know the sex, but calling the baby *it* sounded so impersonal.

Caitie grinned. "So you're keeping...her?"

Harper pulled her lip between her teeth. "Yeah," she said slowly. "I guess I am." Even at nine weeks pregnant she felt different; protective. This little smaller-than-a-bean human growing inside her was Harper's responsibility. "Poor kid."

"Lucky kid," Caitie said, shaking her head. "Having a mom like you. Now let's talk plans. Have you located an obstetrician yet? Decided where to have the baby? Oh my god, I need to organize your baby shower. Where should we do it – here or Angel Sands?"

"Let's slow down. I'm nine weeks, not nine months." Harper couldn't help but grin. As soon as she'd seen those two lines form on the test she'd called Caitie and asked her to drive up to L.A. She didn't trust herself to drive to Angel Sands without causing an accident.

And talking to her best friend was already calming her. And as the reality was dawning, she somehow felt better about it all.

She was having a baby, and *somehow*, some way, they'd be okay.

"What about the father?" Caitie asked, her voice soft. "Have you told him?"

Harper grimaced. "I can't. I don't know his name, remember?"

"It was the guy at the resort?" Caitie's mouth dropped open. "Frank? Oh my god, you're having Frank Sinatra's baby. We should call up the Entertainment channel."

Harper burst out laughing. "Grace Kelly and Frank Sinatra's love child, born twenty years after their death. Imagine the headlines!"

"She'll be beautiful *and* talented. Lucky girl." Caitie leaned forward to squeeze Harper tight. "She really *is* lucky, you know." Her voice soft.

"So lucky I don't even know who her father is." Harper sighed. Along with the nausea, she was still getting used to the mood swings.

"You know who he is, just not his name. That's all; and we can work that out. I'll call Brooke, ask her for Aiden's help. We'll track down this guy. It's just a matter of time."

"And what if he doesn't want to know?" Harper swallowed hard. She knew what it was like, being rejected by the person who was supposed to love you.

"That's his choice," Caitie said. "But he deserves to know."

"You're right." Harper nodded. "That's one problem solved, I guess."

"What's the other problem?"

"A little matter of me having no steady income. I still haven't found a permanent job, and being pregnant isn't going to help. I've got no medical insurance, and I have no way of paying for all the bills this pregnancy is going to bring me. I can't even afford to pay the rent." Harper shook her head. "I'm going to be in debt for the rest of my life."

Caitie's expression was full of sympathy. "I can help. Breck can, too. Not just financially but we can give you support." Her brows knitted together as she stared down. "There has to be a way for you to do this." She tapped her finger against her lip a few times, before she looked up at Harper. "Maybe you should move to Angel Sands and stay with us. Just until the baby's here and you can get back on your feet. That way you won't need to worry about rent."

"I can't; my life is here. And I could never impose on you like that."

"You wouldn't be imposing," Caitie told her. "It'd save me driving up and down from Angel Sands to L.A. to check on you all the time. And I've missed you like crazy these past few months. Our spare bedroom is already set up for you, remember? You can design and make as many dresses as you like there."

Harper's eyes stung with tears. "I hate relying on other people. I'm turning into my mom."

"No, you're not." Caitie's voice was firm. "You're nothing like her. You're amazing, funny, and my best friend. Let me help you the way you've always helped me." She smiled. "I can't wait to be an Auntie to little Frank or Grace. It's going to be amazing."

Harper took in a deep breath. Caitie was right, she always was. There was no way Harper could do this alone. And unlike her mom, she wasn't planning on having this baby and abandoning it to whatever family member was a soft touch.

No, this baby would always feel wanted. Forever be loved. And she would never feel as though she'd ruined somebody's life. If that meant accepting the kindness of friends until Harper got back on her feet, then that's what she'd do.

"Thank you," she said, blowing out a mouthful of air. "I'll think about it. I promise."

"James!" His mom smiled as she opened the door and immediately pulled him into a bear hug. "How are you? Have you been eating? I swear, every time I see you there's nothing of you."

"I weigh two hundred pounds, Mom. I'm not exactly wasting away." He pulled back to look at her. "And I'm fine. I eat, I work out, I look after myself. You don't need to worry about me."

"I'll always worry about you," she said softly. "Now come in. Your dad's lighting the grill and you know how much he hates that. The Russells are here. I don't know if he warned you. Lucas and Ember are here, too. She's pregnant – did you know?" His mom twisted her fingers, her lips pressing together in a thin worried line.

The Russells were his parents' best friends from before he was even born. He'd grown up with them – they were almost family. Which made their son, Lucas, like a younger brother to him.

But like so many others, he'd lost touch with him over the past few years. "No, I didn't know," he said, shrugging. "How far along is she?"

"Six months, I think." His mom's expression softened. "Are you sure you're going to be okay, honey? I can make your excuses..."

"It's fine. People are allowed to have babies. Just because I lost mine, doesn't mean I get to hide away." He gave her a smile to let her know he meant it. It wasn't as if you could avoid babies or children in this world. Or pretty women, for that matter. It had been three years, after all. He should be okay by now.

Some days he actually believed that.

As soon as he walked into his parents' backyard, the four people sitting around the glass table turned to look at him. He recognized Deenie and Wallace, of course. Deenie didn't seemed to have changed a bit since he was fifteen and used to hang out in her bookshop. Her long silver hair was pulled back into a low bun, reflecting the rays of sun. Wallace may have put on some weight, but he, too, had the look of a man younger than his age. And both of them were smiling at him.

"Hello, James." Wallace was the first to stand. There was a

scrape of chairs as the others followed. Wallace reached for his hand and James shook it firmly before he gave Deenie a hug.

"You remember Lucas," she said softly. "And this is his wife, Ember."

"It's good to meet you," he said to Ember, shaking her hand before turning to Lucas. "And it's great to see you again."

"It's good to see you, too." Lucas gave him a tight hug that almost took James's breath away. It had been more than a while since he'd seen him. In that time he'd grown, got more muscles. Maybe that's what working at the fire department did to you. "How's work going?"

"Good. I just came from the hospital."

"Working on your day off again?" his mom said, sliding a non-alcoholic beer into his hands. "What have I told you about that?"

"Sickness doesn't wait for a weekday, Mom."

"That's what I always say about fire," Lucas said, grinning. "It doesn't follow a nine-to-five shift." James appreciated the understanding in his eyes. There were so few professions that understood being on call twenty-four-seven, and working whatever it took to make people better. Medical workers, police officers, firefighters... all of them did whatever it took to protect and serve.

"Sit down," Deenie said, patting the chair next to hers. "Tell me how you're doing."

He took the seat and smiled at her. "I'm fine. Just keeping on keeping on. I hear you're going to be a Grandma. Congratulations."

"It's wonderful," she agreed. "We're very happy." She licked her lips and looked him in the eye. "But there's a sadness, too. After what happened to Sara and Jacob..."

It was strange hearing their names. As the years passed

he'd noticed people didn't say them anymore. His beautiful wife and gorgeous baby had become 'them'. As in 'We miss them,' or 'how are you doing without them?' or even worse 'you should be over them by now...'

"You don't need to be sad," he replied, his voice thick. "You shouldn't be. Not with something like this. Sara would hate the thought of her death overshadowing your happiness. Having Jacob was the happiest day of her life." *His, too.*

Deenie's eyes were shining. "I think about him a lot. He'd be four by now, right? At pre-school. What happened to them was terrible." She shook her head. "Your parents are so proud of you, for how you're coping with it all. If it had been me I would have fallen apart."

There weren't many people who would talk to him like this. But Deenie had always been honest and open with everybody. From a young age he could remember her kind eyes and soft words.

"When's the baby due?" he asked.

"In three months. It's Ember's baby shower in a couple of weeks. Her mom's been driving us crazy with all the arrangements. It's the first grandbaby on both sides so we're all a little excited."

"Do you know what it is?"

She shook her head. "They want a surprise."

He glanced over at Ember. He'd never met her before but she had a glow only pregnant women seemed to get. She was smiling at Lucas, her hand resting on her bump, her eyes bright as they laughed about something with his mom and dad.

He could remember Sara looking exactly like that. He'd lie behind her, their bodies spooned together as his hand rested on her swollen belly. Sometimes he could swear he could still feel Jacob's tiny kicks against his hand as he drifted off to sleep.

He lifted his beer to his lips and took a deep mouthful. Weird how those thoughts came out of nowhere, washing over him like an ocean wave. He shook his head to dislodge them, not wanting to entertain the thoughts anymore.

Three years. That was a long time.

Too long to still be feeling like shit. He took another drink to chase the melancholy away.

"How's retirement treating you?" he asked, turning to Wallace. "Is your golf getting any better?"

"Better than your dad's," Wallace replied, not batting an eyelid at James's quick change of direction. "But that's not much of a stretch now, is it?"

"I take exception to that," James's dad shouted from the grill. "I beat you the other week."

James leaned back on his chair, listening to the two of them bicker. Deenie was leaning across the table to talk to Lucas, and Ember was smiling at them both. Only his own mom was still looking at him, her lips pressed together. He smiled at her and she smiled back, though it didn't reach her eyes.

He was still alive, still breathing. And some days he could laugh with the best of them. He wasn't sure what else he could do to prove to her he was doing okay.

Maybe nothing.

6

"So our next game is guess the size of the bump," Ember's mom, Laura, called out across the Beach Club ballroom. "Everybody write their guesses down and I'll measure her. The closest person wins a bottle of champagne."

"If you win, the champagne it's mine, okay?" Caitie whispered to Harper as they both wrote down a number. "I think I need it."

"I could do with a drink myself." Harper grinned. "It's hard being the designated driver for nine months."

Caitie lifted her own glass, filled with chardonnay. "It's okay, I'll drink enough for both of us." She took a sip and closed her eyes, sighing once the wine had gone down. "Cheers."

The party had been going for a couple of hours. They'd already played four games, and Ember had opened the gifts they'd all bought from the registry she and Lucas had created. The wine had been flowing all afternoon, making the guests a little giggly. The only two people who hadn't touched a drop were Harper and Ember, both for the same reason.

"It was nice of Ember to invite me," Harper said. "She didn't have to."

"Of course she did. You're a friend. And you live in Angel Sands now, so you're also a neighbor." Caitie shrugged. "Anyway, she sent you the invite when you were still living in L.A., because she likes you. Everybody does."

Harper couldn't help but feel warmed by that. She'd been overwhelmed by the kindness everybody had shown her since she'd moved to Angel Sands. Every time she walked into the coffee shop or the hardware store it was as though she was a minor celebrity. People were always so happy to see her.

"Okay, let's see your numbers," Ally said, leaning over the table to look at Caitie and Harper's guesses of the size of Ember's bump. "Twenty five inches?" she asked Caitie when she read her scrap of paper. "Really? I don't think her waist is that small even without a baby inside." She gave a little laugh. "Don't tell her I said that though."

Caitie shook her head, though the smile remained on her lips. "It's a good job you're her best friend. Anyway, I'm trying to be nice. Who wants to be told their stomach looks like it's forty inches wide? This is sisterhood. We build each other up, right?"

Ally wrinkled her nose. "That's true." She quickly scrubbed out her own guess and revised it down considerably. "I'm going to say thirty. Not too big, not too small."

"And no chance of winning the champagne," Brooke pointed out, her voice deadpan.

"What have you got, Harper?" Caitie asked her, leaning over the table to look at her paper.

"Thirty five and a half inches."

Caitie opened her mouth to reply when she was drowned out by the squeal of the microphone.

"Okay, has everybody guessed?" Ember's mom called out,

feedback scratching through her voice. "Okay, Ember, come here and let me measure you."

Ember groaned good-naturedly, but walked over anyway, letting her mom wrap a measuring tape around her waist. She caught Brooke and Ally's eyes and the two of them started to giggle. "She hates this," Brooke whispered. "Poor Ember."

"It's thirty five and a half inches," her mom called out. "Who's the closest? Do we have a winner?"

Ally turned to Caitie and then Harper, her mouth dropping open. "Oh my god, you were spot on," she said. "How did you know the size?"

"I can tell by looking," Harper admitted. "I'm a dressmaker. I measure people all the time. Is that cheating?"

"Hell no, it isn't cheating," Caitie told her. "You just used your expertise." Her eyes twinkled. "Now, go get me my champagne. I need to drink it for us both."

"Maybe they can give you a bottle of fruit juice instead," Brooke said, sympathetically.

"Harper got it on the dot!" Ally called out. "She's the winner."

"Congratulations, Harper." Ember's mom still hadn't figured out that she didn't need to shout into the microphone. The speakers screeched again, and everybody around the table winced. "Come on up and get your prize."

Grimacing, Harper stood and walked over to where Ember was standing with her mom, the tape still wrapped around her waist. Their eyes met and Harper gave her a commiserating smile. She also made a mental note; if she had a baby shower there was no way there would be games; she'd rather pull all her fingernails out.

Ember grinned sheepishly. "Congratulations on guessing how fat I am."

Harper couldn't help but laugh. "It's all baby in there," she said, looking down at Ember's bump. Funny to think her own stomach would be that big soon. "And anyway, you look amazing. I love your dress."

"Thank you." Ember glanced down at her grey-and-white flowered dress. "But I look like a whale. I keep thinking I can't get any bigger and then I do. How are you feeling?"

Harper wrinkled her nose. "Good days and bad. I was hoping you were going to tell me it all gets better after twelve weeks."

Ember laughed. "Honestly, it does. You won't feel so tired or so sick once you're in the second trimester. And you're a seamstress so clothes should be easy to find, right?"

"It's one good thing. And you know, if you want me to make you something I'd be glad to help. Just let me know what you're looking for."

"That's so kind of you." Ember's eyes softened. "I might take you up on that."

"Congratulations," her mom said. She still had the microphone on.

"Mom, you can turn that off now." Ember nodded at the mic.

"Can I?" she shouted into the mouthpiece. The sound echoed off the walls.

Ember sighed and took it from her mom, sliding the switch. "There," she said. "Isn't that better?" She turned to Harper. "Sorry about the champagne. I guess it's not much use to you right now. We could exchange it for something else?"

"It's fine," Harper told her. "Caitie says she'll drink it for both of us."

Ember burst out laughing. "That sounds like something she'd say." Ember stepped forward to grab the bottle, but the tape around her stomach loosened and tangled around her feet. The next moment, she was in the air, and Harper watched with horror as she landed on the ground in front of the stage with a loud thud, her head and behind slapping hard against the floor.

For a moment the room was filled with horrified silence, but then everybody was getting up and running over, shouting at each other that Ember was hurt.

Harper was the first to get to her, scrambling from the stage to scoot down beside her. "Oh my god, are you okay?" she asked Ember, reaching out to touch her arm. Ember opened her eyes, looking dazed as she glanced around. "Don't move. Just tell me if it hurts."

"My head..." Ember let out a mouthful of air and tried to sit up. She reached up to touch the back of her crown, and when she pulled her fingers back there was blood. "I think I caught it on the stage."

"And the baby? Do you have any pain?" Harper asked urgently.

Ember touched her bump. "I don't think so."

"We need to get you to the hospital," Ember's mom said, a sob in her voice. "Somebody should call an ambulance."

Ember was now sitting up right. The dazed look gone from her eyes. "I don't need an ambulance," she said, though her voice was wobbly. "And Lucas is on duty. I don't want him getting a call out to come here. I'll be fine. Just let me get my breath back and I'll stand up and we can get on with the shower."

"You've hit you're head. And you're pregnant," Brooke told her firmly. "You should go to the hospital just to be safe. They can take a look at your head and make sure the baby's fine. Let us call an ambulance."

"I'm not calling an ambulance for a bumped head," Ember said through gritted teeth. "I'm married to a firefighter. I know better than that."

"I'll take you," Harper blurted out, wanting to help her new friend. "My car's right outside."

"That's a great idea," Caitie said warmly, having joined them on the floor. "And I'll call Lucas and get him to meet us there. I know he'll panic, but he deserves to know."

"Okay. But I'm telling you, I'm all right." Ember's voice was thin. She turned to Harper. "Thank you. I appreciate it."

Harper smiled at her. "It's fine. I'm happy to help." And she really was. Strange how only a few months ago she was a big city woman without enough time in the day for friends. And yet now she was in the heart of a community, surrounded by people who helped each other without blinking an eye.

Maybe that's what having a baby did to a person.

"Ember's fine, and so's the baby," Lucas said, coming out to the waiting room where everybody was gathered. It was as though the baby shower had moved from the Beach Club to the hospital. The room was filled with the low hum of conversation. "It looked worse than it was. Her head has the tiniest bump. No stitches needed. I just need to keep an eye on her tonight."

"Thank god she's okay," Brooke whispered, and gave him a hug. "And how are you doing? You must have been terrified. You made it from the station to the hospital faster than a speeding bullet."

He smiled at her, and Harper could see the relief wash over his face. His love for his wife and unborn baby shone out of him.

"I'm fine," Lucas said. "Happy they're both okay. This definitely gave me a shock, though. I feel like I could sleep until next Tuesday."

Brooke laughed. "You probably need to get used to it. Nick hasn't stopped shocking me and he's almost eleven. That's the life of a parent."

Lucas smiled at her and Harper. "Thank you for keeping such a cool head," he said. "And for driving her here. I know she didn't want to make a fuss, but I'm glad you made her come and get checked out."

"It was a pleasure." Harper felt warmth wash over her again. Looking around this room, crammed with what felt like half the female population of Angel Sands, she was reminded again how caring everybody was. She'd done the right thing moving here.

It was the kind of place you could raise a child in and know they'd be taken care of. That was something she'd never had growing up, even though she'd wished she had so many times.

A group of older women in the corner – Ember's mom's friends, Harper guessed – broke out into raucous laughter.

"I'm telling you, the doctors here are hot," one of them said, fanning herself. "It's almost worth getting hurt to feel their hands on your body."

Lucas shifted his feet, and Harper bit down a grin. Even the strongest of men seemed to get uncomfortable when surrounded by a group of tipsy older women.

"That one's mine," another woman said, pointing toward the ER reception. "Tall, dark, and handsome, just the way I like 'em. If I faint do you think he'll rescue me?"

"I bet so. You fall and I'll scream out for help." They laughed again.

"That's my cue to leave," Lucas said, shaking his head. "I'm going back to help Ember get ready. We should be able to leave for home shortly. Thanks again, Harper." He leaned forward to kiss her on the cheek. "I'll speak to you later, sis," he said to Caitie.

"Sure," Caitie said. "I'm going to head back to the Beach Club with Brooke and Ally to tidy up. We'll bring your baby gifts over when we're done if that's okay?"

"I appreciate that. I want Ember to rest. She's a little worked up."

"And you should rest, too," Caitie said to Harper, as if she knew she was about to volunteer to help. "You can head back home and I'll meet you there later."

She thought about protesting, but she really was tired. The first trimester wasn't quite over yet. "Okay," she agreed.

"You need to be taking care of yourself, too." Caitie patted her shoulder.

A smile played on Harper's lips as she watched Lucas walk back to the double doors, leading to the examination rooms. In the corner, a doctor was talking to the receptionist, a few other physicians in white coats at the counter. He was wearing dark green scrubs, a stethoscope slung around his neck, his expression serious as he spoke.

She blinked.

No.

Surely it couldn't be?

Dark hair, high cheekbones, and eyes she still saw in her dreams. Frank was a doctor? Oh god. Her heart started hammering so fast she thought she was having a heart attack.

"Are you okay?" Caitie asked. "You've gone really pale."

Harper slowly peeled her fingers from her mouth and tried to breathe, because god knew this baby needed all the oxygen it could get.

"That's Frank over there," she said, her voice low.

"What?" Caitie followed her gaze to the reception desk, a frown pulling at her lips. "Frank? As in?" She did a double take. "*Your Frank?* The baby's father?"

"Yeah." Harper nodded, unable to take her eyes off him.

"Which one? The guy standing next to James Tanner?" Caitie rolled on her tiptoes, her head craning to look at the group.

"Who's James Tanner? I'm talking about the guy with the dark hair."

"James is the doctor in the green scrubs. His parents are friends with mine. I should go over and say hi. I haven't seen him in years."

It was too surreal. Harper shook her head to try and clear her thoughts, but it only made her feel dizzy. She reached out to steady herself on Caitie's arm.

She was trying really hard to get her thoughts straight. Ever since she'd seen the positive result on the pregnancy test, she'd given up hope of finding him. He was a needle in a haystack, a mythical creature, somebody who changed her life forever and disappeared.

But now he was back, standing right in front of her. If he turned he'd probably see her staring at him. *James Tanner*.

"Harper?" Caitie said, slowly turning to look at her. "Is James the father?"

"Yes," Harper breathed, her head still a little dizzy. "I'm sure of it."

Caitie's eyes widened as she looked from him to Harper. "James is your baby's dad?" she repeated. "This is so strange. I can't believe it." She turned back to her friend. "What the heck do we do now?"

James checked his watch as he waited for the registrar to bring up some details on her computer. It was more than two hours after his shift should have ended.

"Here you go," the woman said, looking up at him from behind the counter. "Her family doctor is based in Angel Sands." She pressed print on the computer. "Do you want me to call the office?"

"Yeah, please. Give them my contact details and ask them

to send over the history as soon as they can. I can't make any decisions until I've seen it."

"You work too hard," she pointed out kindly. "You should be resting at home."

"You sound like my mom."

She laughed. "Mothers know these things, I say the same thing to my kids. Maybe one day you'll listen to us moms."

"James?"

The voice came from behind him. His brows knitted together as he tried to place it – half recognizing the tone. He turned to look at the woman standing there. Mid-twenties, dark hair, and skin so pale she looked out of place in California.

"That's me," he said, still trying to figure out who she was. "Can I help you?"

"I'm Caitie Russell; Deenie and Wallace's daughter. I knew you back when I was a kid."

Of course it was. "Oh, hi," he said, smiling at her. "Is everything okay? Are you here for yourself?"

She blinked. "Oh no. I had to bring Lucas's wife in. She fell. She's..."

"Pregnant."

"Yeah. I didn't know if you knew."

"I met her at my parent's place. Ember, right? Is she okay?"

"Oh yeah, she's fine. Lucas is with her and they're getting ready to leave now."

He smiled. "That's good news. I'll try and catch them when they're on their way out. And how are you doing? It's been a while."

"About ten years, I think," Caitie said, her eyes darting to the left. "I've been living in New York for most of it. I only moved back recently."

"That's great. I bet your mom's pleased to have you home; it's a long way to New York."

Caitie smiled. "She is. And so am I." Her eyes dipped down and she pulled at a loose thread on her sleeve. "Um, this is a really weird thing to ask, but were you at the opening of the Silver Sands Resort a couple of months ago?"

James swallowed hard. He'd tried to not think about that night. Or about the beautiful blonde he'd spent the evening with.

He ran his thumb along his jaw, feeling the roughness. "Ah, yeah. I think I did. Why?"

Caitie shifted from one foot to the other. "Well the thing is, I um..." She took a deep breath. "I think you might have spent the night with my friend."

He could feel the blood in his cheeks heat up. "Your *friend*?" He blinked, trying to ignore the tug of unease in his stomach.

"Harper. Blonde hair with pink ends; looked amazing in a gold vintage dress."

Yeah she did. She looked beautiful. The tightness in his gut rose up, curling around his chest. "Um. Yeah, I know who you're talking about." He had no idea what else to say, *especially* to a family friend. *'Yeah, we had mind-blowing sex until the early hours and then I walked away'* didn't seem quite right.

"She's here," Caitie said softly.

"What?"

"Harper. She's here. Sitting over in the waiting area."

He tried not to show his shock, but from the expression on Caitie's face he failed miserably.

"She wants to talk to you. If that's okay."

He swallowed hard. "I have to get back to work. I have patients I need to see."

Caitie nodded. "Of course, but this is important. And it

won't take very long, I promise. We're leaving in a minute, but there's something she needs to tell you."

From the determined expression on Caitie's face, he wasn't going to be able to dodge this one. Slowly looking over his shoulder, his gaze fell on the bank of chairs at the far side of the entrance, filled with a group of women, all wearing dressy clothes and talking loudly. He scanned their faces, his mouth pressed together tightly, until finally he found the features he was looking for.

She was staring right at him. With her wide eyes and pale face she almost looked scared.

Dear god, was she going to tell him she had an STD?

"Okay." He nodded at Caitie. "I can spare ten minutes."

"Thank you," Caitie said, following his gaze to beckon her friend over. *Harper*. He watched as the girl stood up, taking in her long blonde waves as they cascaded over her shoulders, and the soft pink ends he could remember all too well.

She still had that certain something about her; it was in the way she stood tall, her shoulders back, her face calm. She strode across the room with the same confident gait she'd had in the bar, and the memory of their frantic night together hit him like a cannonball, reigniting all the feelings he'd tried to forget.

God, she was beautiful. He swallowed hard, trying to ignore the desire curling in the pit of his belly.

"Harper," Caitie said, when the girl came to a stop in front of them. "This is James. James, this is Harper." Her lips curled into a grimace. "I'm going to leave you guys... ah, yeah... to it."

He turned to the woman next to Caitie and felt a jolt of recognition. That smooth skin, those pretty eyes, the hair that no matter how many times he'd tried he couldn't quite forget about.

"Hi, Harper." She was smaller than he remembered, the

top of her head only reaching his shoulders. He had to drop his gaze to look at her.

"Hi." She licked her lips, pulling the bottom one between her teeth. "James. Or Frank. Whatever." She smiled, and it was the same as the first time. Full of sunshine and warmth.

He laughed in spite of himself, feeling his body relax as Caitie walked back to the waiting area. His blood felt warm at being alone with Harper. "James will do. Are you okay?"

Harper nodded. "Yeah, I'm good."

"No STDs?"

It was her turn to laugh, her lips pulling up and her eyes crinkling. "What? Is that what Caitie told you?"

He shook his head. "I just saw the nervous expression on your face and guessed."

"I don't have any STDs. But there's something I need to talk to you about. Is there somewhere private we could talk?"

"We have a break room. It should be empty about now."

"That sounds perfect." She nodded.

"I'm sorry I walked out that night," he said when he closed the break room door behind them. "I don't usually do that kind of thing."

"Walk out after a night of amazing sex?" She raised an eyebrow.

"I meant having the amazing sex in the first place. But yeah, I don't usually walk out without a word either." He shook his head. "It was an asshole thing to do. The least I could have done was taken you to breakfast."

"Don't worry. Breakfast was included with the room. And it isn't your midnight ghosting I wanted to talk about."

"It isn't?"

"Nope." She glanced at the door, as if to make extra sure it was closed. "Look, this is embarrassing and not at all how I imagined spending my day. I'd assumed I'd never see you again, and I was okay with that. Or as okay as you can be after waking up to an empty bed." She took a deep breath. "So anyway, the thing is, I didn't give you an STD that night, but you did give me something."

"You think I gave you an STD?" He shook his head. "I couldn't have." She was the first person he'd had sex with in three years. "You've got the wrong guy."

"I haven't." She pulled her lip between her teeth, her gaze meeting his. "It wasn't an STD you gave me, James. It was a few extra sperm; I'm pregnant."

7

"That's not possible," James said, her words echoed around in his ears as he tried to deny their truth. "You can't be pregnant. We used a condom."

"That's what I thought. But the tests don't lie. Nor does the morning sickness. Or the heartbeat I heard at my doctor's appointment. I'm definitely knocked up."

"Are you sure it's mine?" he asked.

She blinked and nodded her head. "I'm sure. You're the only guy I've slept with in months. It can't be anybody else's."

He blew out a mouthful of air. "So you're what, two and a half months along?"

"Eleven weeks. But they calculate it from your last period, so even though it hasn't been eleven weeks since we were together..." She'd rushed out before her voice cracked and her words fell short.

"Of course. I know that." He had to bite down his anger. It wasn't her fault, but... *damn*. "Are you planning on keeping it?"

She rubbed the back of her neck, and for the first time he

could see vulnerability creep in. "Yes I'm keeping it. *Her*. I'm keeping her."

"Her? How can you know it's a girl if you're only eleven weeks?"

She swallowed, her throat undulating. He could remember the way her skin felt against his lips. Soft, tender, and so damn smooth. She smiled, her gaze dipping down to her belly. "I don't actually know, but this baby feels like a her."

It was as though reality had run into the room and slapped him hard in the face. Almost three months pregnant. Jesus.

"You live in L.A., right?" he asked her, raking his hands through his hair. "What are you doing down here?"

"I moved here when I found out I was pregnant. I need the support of my friends who live here." She cleared her throat. "Look, I know it's a surprise. It was to me, too. But I thought you had the right to know; I don't expect any help, or for you to become father of the year." A short laugh. "I don't even know you. But whether you like it or not, this baby is coming, and it's going to be a part of you, too."

His pager buzzed in his pocket. Out of habit, he pulled it out and glanced down. A message to call the reception desk flashed up.

"Is that a pager?" Harper asked. "I didn't know anybody still used those; I thought they disappeared with rotary phones and conscription."

He smiled in spite of himself. "Most hospitals still use them, they're more reliable than cell phones." He slid it back into his pocket. "Sorry, force of habit."

"It's okay. You're working. It must be important if they paged."

"I'm waiting for some history to come through for a patient in the ER. Hopefully this is it."

"I should go anyway," Harper said, her eyes meeting his once more. "Caitie will be wondering where I am. It's been a hell of a day. Thanks for talking to me. I just thought you should know."

She turned to leave, her cascades of hair undulating with the movement. The pink and blonde caught the light from the overhead fluorescents, shining brightly.

"Wait!" he called out, reaching for her arm. His fingers slowly closed over her bicep. Her skin was so damn soft. The touch sent a shot of pleasure through his body. "Where can I find you? Where are you staying at?"

She turned, her eyes wide, her full lips parted. "I'm staying with Caitie and her boyfriend while I get settled. After that, I'm hoping to find a place of my own."

He swallowed hard. The mixture of emotions flowing through him were making him dizzy. Shock, regret... and a nagging deep down in his gut that he needed to see her again. And soon.

"Let me get your number." He reached for his phone right as his pager buzzed a second time. He grimaced, his eyes meeting hers. Without saying a word, she took the device from him and keyed her number in, passing it back so he could slide it into his pocket. "Maybe we can meet some time and talk?"

"Yeah, sure." Harper nodded.

"I've got some days off next week. Would that work?"

The door to the break room opened and a nurse walked in. "There you are," she said to James. "The charge nurse has been trying to get ahold of you. She has your patient's doctor on the line. They're waiting to speak to you."

"I'll go," Harper said softly. "I hope your patient is okay." She gave him the ghost of a smile. "Thanks again for talking with me."

This time she really left, and he watched her for a

moment, taking in her confident stride, her strong posture, and sexy-as-hell body.

A body that had his baby inside it.

His baby. Damn.

"Ow!" Harper pulled her finger away from the needle and slid it between her lips, tasting the bead of blood escaping from the tiny puncture wound. She was used to stabbing herself on needles and pins by now – it was an occupational hazard – but she still marveled at how much a tiny prick could hurt.

And of course the thought made her want to giggle.

She'd been home from the hospital for four hours, but instead of resting like Caitie had insisted, she'd managed to finish the last of that week's Etsy orders. Five custom-made fifties-style dresses, each of which she had charged over two hundred dollars for. Taking away the cost of the materials, that was a profit of seven hundred dollars that week. Not bad, but nowhere near what she needed to make to be able to afford her own place, or buy all the baby things she'd need.

Plus there was the small matter of sleep. Each dress took around ten hours to make, and where she could cope with the long days right now, she was sensible enough to realize that as she got closer to her due date, exhaustion would be sure to kick in. And after the baby arrived she'd be even worse.

She needed a job; preferably one with medical benefits. Because right now she was waiting for the other shoe to drop.

There was a rap at the door.

"Come in," she called out. A second later, Caitie pushed it open and stepped into what used to be her spare room and what now comprised Harper's bedroom and workroom combined. "Hey," Harper greeted her friend. "How's Ember?"

Caitie sat down on Harper's unmade bed, curling her legs

up beneath her and leaning her back on the wall. "She's fine. We managed to clear up the Beach Club and get all her gifts to her house, but she was already asleep when we got there." She picked up a remnant of fabric Harper hadn't yet thrown out, sliding the satin between her fingers. "How are you doing?" she asked. "I haven't had a chance to talk to you since the hospital."

"Since I spoke to James, you mean?" Harper said, a half-smile curling her lips.

"I can't believe it was James. I should have known from your description. Dark hair, blue eyes." Caitie shook her head. "All this time we thought he was just some stranger. Instead it's a guy I've known since I was a baby." She raised her eyebrows at Harper. "How did he take it?"

"About as well as you could expect. He looked shocked." Harper grimaced at the memory. "But that's understandable. I was pretty shocked myself when I found out." She leaned her head on her upturned palm, her elbow resting on her sewing desk. "He wanted to know how it happened, how far along I am, whether he was definitely the father." She shrugged. "The usual."

"There's a usual?" Caitie asked. "Who knew? So what happens next?"

"I don't know. He was paged and had to leave to see a patient. He said he would call later when he has a day off, but I'm not banking on it. I mean it's not like he wants this baby; he hadn't planned it or anything."

"Neither did you, but you want it."

A smile tugged at Harper's lips. "I do." If she could just work out how she could take care of both of them, her life would be complete. "Even if it came as a shock at the start."

"Maybe James will be the same," Caitie suggested. "He could come around like you have."

"Maybe. But if he doesn't, it's okay. He didn't look like he was overjoyed at the idea of being a daddy. Not that I can blame him. The poor guy didn't expect to see me again, and now here I am with the biggest shock of his life. That kind of thing takes some getting used to."

"James is a good guy. I can tell you that much. He'll want to talk to you about it. Support you. I know him and his family; he wouldn't walk away from something like this."

"I guess it's up to him whether he wants to be part of the baby's life." Harper touched her stomach, feeling the gentle swell. "I'd like him to be involved, of course. But if he's not into babies, I understand."

"Of course he's into babies. He had his own once."

Harper pulled her head up, her mouth turning dry. "What? He has children? He never mentioned them."

Caitie's face drained of blood, making her already-pale skin look almost ethereal. "You don't know about Sara and Jacob?" she asked, her bottom lip dropping open. She shook her head. "Of course you wouldn't. Why would you?"

"Who's Sara?"

"She's James's wife." Caitie bit her lip.

"He was married?" Harper's eyes widened. "Or is he *still* married? Ugh, please tell me he isn't? Because I'll hate myself."

"He isn't." Caitie looked down at the fabric she was twisting between her fingers. "Sara and Jacob died in a car crash about three years ago. Jacob was only a year old. Mom told me about it. It was horrific."

It was as though a cold downpour of water had washed all over her. His baby died? Harper's heart ached at the thought of it.

"I should have told you." Caitie shook her head. "But I didn't think it through. Didn't think that you really didn't know who he was or anything about his history. I'm so sorry."

"It's not your fault. You didn't know it was him until we were in the hospital today. And I didn't know either."

Harper tried to reconcile the sexy, confident, funny guy she'd slept with all those weeks ago with a man who'd lost his wife and child three years earlier.

Caitie inhaled deeply, offering her friend a rueful smile. "Poor you, and poor James. It feels like every time you solve one problem another pops up."

"I guess it's good preparation for parenthood. With the sleepless nights and constant anxiety I already feel like a mom."

Caitie stood and slid her arms around Harper, hugging her tightly. "It's going to be okay," she told her. "You've got me and Breck, and Ember and Lucas, not to mention Brooke and Ally and Nate and Aiden. Try not to worry so much. It's not good for the baby."

Harper hugged her back. "And now I'll worry about that, too," she joked.

"So let's take your mind off it. Let's go make some popcorn and watch a chick flick in the living room. That'll make everything okay."

Harper looked at the half-finished dress she'd narrowly avoided bleeding on. She really should finish it and get it sent out tomorrow, but the lure of sitting with her best friend and losing herself in a movie was too strong.

She could afford a couple of hours off. And when Caitie and Breck were asleep she'd quietly hand sew the dress to finish it up.

"Okay," she said, letting Caitie take her hand and pull her up to standing. "A chick flick sounds perfect. The cheesier the better."

Thanks to his years in medicine, James had developed a useful ability to compartmentalize his thoughts. It was almost essential for a doctor. If he thought too much about the body he was operating on, or the possibilities of what could go wrong, any sane surgeon would probably freeze. In the hours between painstakingly cutting into a patient's skin and sewing it up when surgery was over, his attention was narrowed into a pinpoint.

Life outside of the person in front of him didn't exist. Time didn't pass, stomachs didn't get hungry, people didn't call. Every emotion, thought, and fear were buried deep to enable him to do the job he was born to do.

But this evening his compartmentalization was sorely lacking. His hands were shaking, his chest felt tight, and no matter how much he tried to bury his thoughts they kept rising right up, refusing to be buried.

She was having his baby.

There was something he hadn't considered when he'd gotten out of bed this morning. Not even when Caitie Russell had mentioned her friend to him and pointed out who she was. Until the moment the words had escaped from Harper's lips he'd been oblivious.

It would be funny if he could find the will to laugh. The one time he'd let himself break all the rules, he'd ended up here. And now he had no idea what to do next.

He looked up from the patient chart he'd been staring at for the last ten minutes to see Rich leaning over him, a grin on his face.

"How long have you been there?" James asked, his brows knitting together. He hadn't even heard him walk up to the desk.

"Long enough." Rich shrugged. "You doing okay, man? I thought you were on days this week."

"I am."

Rich glanced at his watch. "But it's almost ten. You've been here for fourteen hours."

"Fifteen."

"And you're due back at eight?"

"Yep." But he'd get here earlier, he always did.

"You should go home, get some sleep. You look like you're almost there anyway." Rich shook his head. "You sure you're okay?"

James shrugged. "It's been a long day."

"All the more reason to get home. Eat some food, go to bed, and do it all over again tomorrow."

Home. It felt like somewhere he hadn't been for the longest of times. Three years, to be precise. "Yeah..."

"What's eating you?" Rich sat on the corner of the desk and folded his arms. "I'm on a break so you've got ten minutes to spill."

"I got a girl pregnant," James told him, the words spilling out of their own accord.

"What?" Rich started to laugh. "Who? How? What is it, the second virgin birth? You haven't slept with anybody since Sara. I should know, I've been trying to get you laid."

"It was one time," James said, rolling his eyes at himself because as a doctor he knew once was enough. He'd done a stint in obstetrics during his training. He'd heard all the stories. "It's a girl I met at the party we went to a few months back."

Rich tipped his head to the side. "So who is she? When did you find out? Shit man, I have a lot of questions here."

"Her name's Harper. She told me today, and she lives in Angel Sands."

"Have the two of you been dating?" Rich asked, leaning forward.

James shook his head. "I haven't seen her since that night. Until today."

Rich let out a low whistle. "So what are you going to do?"

"Don't you think I've done enough?" James asked, raising an eyebrow.

Rich laughed. "Well sure, but now the real fun begins, right? You've done the dad thing before. You know how it works."

Immediately James's thoughts went to Jacob. To his crumpled newborn face with those bright blue eyes. He'd come out with his fists curled up as though he was ready for a fight, and from the moment James had first seen him he'd fell in love.

And then he'd lost him and Sara, and everything went dark.

The thought of ever feeling that kind of pain again made him want to hide away. He'd spent the last three years bricking up the hole they'd left in his heart, unwilling to let it be breached again. He lived, he breathed, and he had a heart made of brick. That was the price he paid for surviving.

"I don't know what I'm going to do about the baby," he admitted, taking a long breath in. He didn't want to think about this any more. He wanted to work out how to lock it away with all the other dark thoughts. With a sigh he checked his watch. "I guess I should go home and get some sleep."

Rich patted his arm. "That sounds like a good idea. Maybe it will all look better in the morning."

8

One of the weirdest things about being pregnant were the vivid dreams Harper had every night. They were like a movie being screened for one person, lit in glorious Technicolor, except she was *in* the movie, not watching it. Last night's had been one to remember. It started with James Tanner screaming at her for getting pregnant, swiftly followed by Harper giving birth to a fully-formed two-year-old girl, complete with blonde hair with pink tips, and a Grace Kelly-style golden dress.

She'd woken up in a cold sweat and had run to the bathroom to splash water on her face. When she climbed back into bed a thought struck her. She grabbed her laptop and woke it up.

Matching mother and daughter dresses. Wouldn't that be a great marketing idea?

Typing in the search box was like opening up Pandora's box. Not only were there a demand for those kind of dresses, but women were willing to pay an extortionate price for them. Two matching mother-and-daughter dresses went for more than double what she'd been able to sell her handmade creations for. A quick mental calculation made her realize that making a second dress for a child would only cost a quarter of a full size dress.

Add that to the ease of stitching, and the fact that a child's dress didn't need darts or bodice rods or anything too intricate, and she would be able to make at least three times the profit off a single dress.

Later that morning, over breakfast, she explained the concept to Caitie. Breck was already at work – he was having to travel now that his construction company was working on a site up the coast – and Caitie was drinking her coffee before she had to drive up to L.A. for a meeting.

"People seriously want to dress their kids in the same clothes they're wearing?" Caitie asked, putting her mug down in front of her. "And they'll pay *that* much for it?"

"Yep. I know it's crazy, but it's a big market." Harper shoved a spoonful of frosted wheats into her mouth. Her appetite was finally back. Her second trimester was only a couple of days away and her body didn't seem to hate her quite as much as it had up to this point. In fact, she felt almost glowing. And growing, too, as the open button at the top of her jeans reminded her.

"Are you going to do it?" Caitie asked, her eyes lit up with interest. As a successful businesswoman herself, she loved to hear about ideas.

"Yep. I haven't really got anything to lose. I'm going to spend today making some designs and then I'll need to find some crazy person and their child to model them." Harper grabbed the carton of orange juice and poured herself a glass and swallowed it down in two mouthfuls. This baby sure was hungry. "If it works out the way I hope, I should be able to move out within a couple of months."

"You don't have to," Caitie said quickly. "I like having you here. With Breck having to travel so much it's almost like old times. And you'll need help when the baby comes."

"You're so sweet," Harper told her. "But you and Breck need your privacy, and I've been here for long enough. I'm also going to call around to some local boutiques and see if they'll stock my designs. That way I can get some local customers, too."

"I can ask around and see if we can find someone to model for you," Caitie suggested. "Ember knows almost everybody, and if she can't help I'm sure Brooke or Ally can. It's such a great idea. You're so clever."

Harper basked in the glow of Caitie's compliment. She wasn't as certain as her friend, but right now she was willing to try anything. With six months until she was due to give birth, she needed a viable business plan.

"Right," Caitie said, draining the last of her coffee from the bottom of her mug. "I need to go. I'll be really late tonight, and Breck is staying up near the site. Will you be okay on your own?"

"Sure." Harper nodded. "I'll be busy with my plans of world domination, one mom and baby dress at a time. Drive safely, okay?"

"I always do." Caitie went to pick up her empty mug, but Harper put her hand on it. "I'll load the dishwasher," she told her friend. "You go ahead and leave."

"I don't know what I'd do without you." Caitie blew her a kiss. "See you later, mashed potaytah."

Harper grinned. "Not if I see you first.

The doorbell buzzed right before lunchtime, making Harper jump as she put the finishing touches to her design. She'd spent the morning working, not even stopping for her usual mid-morning snack. As she went to go answer the door, she smiled at the sheets of paper laid out on the table, alongside fabrics she thought could work. With Caitie out all day and Breck away, she planned to have at least one design finished before the end of the day.

Her muscles groaned with relief as she walked into the hallway, reminding her she shouldn't be sitting in one position for too long. Maybe she'd look into a pre-natal yoga class. Being bent over a sewing machine for hours at a time wasn't great for her posture.

She opened the door to see Ember standing on the other side, a big bag in her hand. "Hi!" Harper said with a big grin, happy to see her looking so well. "How are you feeling?"

"I'm good." Ember leaned forward to kiss her cheek. "I've just come from the doctor and he's given me the all clear. Since I had some time on my hands I thought I'd stop by and thank you for taking me to the hospital on Saturday."

"It was no problem. Anybody would have done it, I just happened to be the only sober one." Harper stood to the side so Ember could pass her. "Come on in."

"Thank god you *were* sober. If my mom had her way there would have been three ambulances and George Clooney rushing into the Beach Club to operate on me." She shook her head. "I love her to bits, but she's not great in an emergency. I also brought you a few things I've grown out of." She lifted the laundry bag full of clothes up. "They might see you through the next few months until you have to wear full blown maternity clothes."

"Let me take that from you." Harper looped her fingers through the handle. "Would you like a drink or something?"

"Only if I'm not disturbing you."

Harper smiled. She really did like all of Caitie's friends. "You're not disturbing me at all, I was just working on some new designs."

"Is this the new idea Caitie was telling me about on the phone this morning?" Ember asked. "The mother and daughter dresses?"

Harper was still getting used to nothing being a secret around here. Not that she minded, she liked that people were interested in her work. It was so different to the dog-eat-dog environment of Hollywood, or even Broadway, where everybody was competition.

"Yeah, that's right. Want to come and see what I've been doing?"

Ember's face lit up. "I really do."

Leaving the bag in the hallway, Harper took Ember into the bedroom, the two of them huddling together to look at the designs and dresses she'd accrued inside. Ember listened carefully, asking questions about the marketing plan and Harper's next steps. With each word she said Harper could feel her confidence growing. This plan really could work, if she put her all into it. It could be compatible with having a baby, too. She could run the business from home, when the baby was sleeping, or even when the baby was in a swing watching. At the very worst it could see her through until she found a full-time job.

"These are so beautiful," Ember said, looking at the dresses Harper had ready to send out. "And worth so much more than you're charging."

Harper shrugged. "It's the market that decides the price. People aren't willing to pay more than a couple hundred dollars for a hand made dress."

"Unless they have a matching dress for their baby," Ember said, grinning.

"Exactly." Harper winked.

"I know someone who can help you with the modeling," Ember mused, staring down at Harper's designs. "There's a boy in my class, his mom used to be a model before having children. I've heard her talking about wanting to find some work again. She has a beautiful little girl, too, about three years old. I bet she'd be willing to help out if she could have some photos for her portfolio."

"Really?" Harper felt the excitement rise up inside her. "Do you think you could ask her? If she's willing I'd be happy to call her and explain the details."

"Of course. I'll send her an email; I'm almost certain she'll say yes."

"Thank you so much. That means a lot."

"It's no problem," Ember told her. "Really. We take care of each other here in Angel Sands."

"In that case, come to the kitchen and take a seat. I'll make us a sandwich and a drink."

"That sounds like my kind of treat." Ember followed her out of the bedroom and down the hallway. "And while we're eating you can tell me why Caitie was so evasive about what happened to you at the hospital last week. She started to say something about your baby's father but refused to elaborate."

Harper couldn't be annoyed at Caitie for letting things slip. She had a big mouth herself. And Ember felt like she was becoming a close friend – one who knew what it was like to go through pregnancy. Confiding in her felt like the right thing to do.

"Sit down," Harper said, pulling out a chair and helping Ember in it. "And maybe put your feet up, too. This is going to be a long story."

James sat on the deck of his cliffside house, looking out at the dark blue ocean. The sun was slipping down the sky, leaving orange kisses on the surface of the waves. He'd finished his last shift for the week a few hours earlier and finally had time to think; to open up the compartment he'd stuffed all of Harper's revelations into, and concentrate on the fact that in six months they were going to have a baby.

A breeze rose up and ruffled his hair, as he thought about everything Harper had told him. The shock on her face had been genuine enough. She was as surprised to bump into him at the hospital as he'd been to see her, and that fact alone told him there was no malice.

They were two people who should have known better than to have a surprise pregnancy. And yet this kind of thing happened every day. Even to doctors who knew exactly how the body worked, and how easy it was for contraception to fail.

One in a hundred. That's what he was. So what was he planning to do about it?

He hadn't confided in anyone but Rich about his situation. There was no way he was telling his parents – not until he'd decided what the next steps were. His mom had been devastated when Sara and Jacob had died, and he wasn't an asshole who'd dangle a new grandbaby in front of her only to tell her he didn't plan to be part of the baby's life.

He needed to think things through with a cool head. Tomorrow he'd call Harper and ask to meet her. And yeah, maybe the thought of seeing her again sent a shot of excitement through him, but that was merely muscle memory. She'd been his first sexual partner in three years. The first woman he'd been attracted to since he'd lost his wife and child. And the way that attraction had exploded into a night of passion still confused him. But it also made him feel alive.

And he liked that feeling more than he would admit.

Could he support Harper and the baby the way they needed it? Money wasn't a concern, he could provide that. He'd already spoken to the Human Resources department and arranged for Harper's medical expenses to be covered, along with the baby that would be arriving before the year was out. He could afford to buy Harper a house, to pay child support, and provide for all the baby's material needs.

But that was all he was sure of.

Pregnant women and new mothers needed strong, steady support; they deserved it. When Sara had been throwing up, or in the latter months of her pregnancy had suffered from sleepless nights and anxiety, James had been the one she had leaned on. He'd relished his role, delighting in being the strong one. And after birth, he'd loved cradling Jacob in his arms in the middle of the night to allow Sara to get one more hour of sleep. He'd raced home from work each night with a bag of takeout in one hand and a cupcake from the bakery in the other, so excited to see the beautiful family they'd created together.

And then it had been cruelly whipped away. More than most he understood the fickle whims of nature, how easily life could be given and taken away. It was part of his job, after all. But when it affected him personally he hadn't been prepared for the sheer and constant pain, nor for the blackness that seemed to follow him no matter where he went.

To provide the sort of care Harper and their baby needed, was to risk walking into the darkness again. To open the door to joy was to open the door to misery, too. He winced at the thought of it.

James let out a mouthful of air. What would Sara say if she knew what he'd gotten himself into? Would she be happy he was having another child, or devastated he would be replacing the perfect baby they'd made together?

Taking a sip of the whiskey he'd poured before he walked out to the deck, he closed his eyes, taking in the sound of the ocean as it lapped against the cliffs below. They'd talked about childproofing the house, the deck, and making sure there was no chance of Jacob being able to reach the cliff at the end of the yard, but in the end he'd died before they'd needed to do any of it. Would James have to do it now? Would he ask Harper for shared custody of their child? Have the little one every other weekend, or whatever kind of arrangements worked around her business and his shifts?

Another sip. He let the whiskey burn the back of his throat, warming him as it trickled down. Rich had said something about having so many questions, but they paled to insignificance compared to all the thoughts racing through James's head.

Putting his glass down on the wooden table next to his Adirondack chair, James picked up his phone and unlocked it, scrolling through his contacts until he found Harper's. He stared at it for a moment, picturing her warm eyes and pink-blonde hair. The hint of a smile curled at his lips.

If he wanted answers, she probably did, too, and there was only one way to get them.

It was time to face the music and arrange to meet her. They had a baby to talk about.

❧ 9 ❧

Week thirteen. Welcome to the second trimester! Most women will find their nausea begins to abate, unless they're one of the unlucky ones who suffer until the baby is born. Fingers crossed that's not you, my friend! But on the positive side, you will have more energy – and your partner will be happy to know your sex drive could increase, too. Make the most of it, we say. Maybe look at booking a babymoon to spend quality time with your partner. After the birth you may never want sex again. (Just kidding. Kinda.)

Harper stuffed the rest of the chocolate bar into her mouth and grabbed a glass of milk to wash it down, turning off her phone and the weekly countdown she'd stupidly clicked on. Babymoon? Ha! Though she really should go to that yoga class she'd looked into. Maybe she'd do that when she wasn't spending every hour awake at her sewing machine, making enough dresses for next week's photoshoot.

"Are you sure you don't want me to come with you today?" Caitie asked, walking into the kitchen, her hands fastening her earring. "I can cancel this meeting."

"No, I'll be fine," Harper said. "I'm meeting James in a public place. And Nate and Ally will be working at the coffee shop. If he tries to do anything, I'm sure one of them will vault over the counter and karate chop him."

Caitie chuckled, shaking her head. "I was more worried what you might do to him. Your bump won't look good in orange."

A smile played at the corner of Harper's lips. "I'll have you know I can rock orange. But anyway, we're just meeting to talk, that's all. He called last night and sounded very nice about it all."

"He's a nice guy," Caitie said. "But seriously, if you need anything, just call, okay? And I want to hear all the details later."

"Of course." Harper nodded, her expression mock-serious. "You'll get them along with all the grisly details. Unless I've been arrested that is." She poked her tongue out, and Caitie rolled her eyes.

An hour later Harper wasn't finding it quite so funny. Her stomach was churning as she walked toward the coffee shop overlooking the beach. Even outside, the aroma of coffee was strong, mixing with the sweet smell of pastries that made her mouth water.

James was already there. Sitting at a table right outside the open glass doors, his long denim-encased legs stretched out in front of him as he read one of the free newspapers you could pick up from the rack beside the counter. Harper stared at him for a moment. His dark hair looked like he'd recently had it cut, and his skin was warm and tan. Unlike when she'd seen him at the resort or the hospital he hadn't shaved, and the dark shadow around his jaw made her heart flip a little.

Maybe that weekly countdown was right about the sex drive thing. She decided to test it out, looking around the shop to see if there was another guy near her age that made her pulse start the hundred yard dash down her veins. But no, there was Frank Megassey in the corner, gossiping with Lorne Daniels, the owner of the surf shop, and apart from them the tables were mostly full of women.

Harper turned back to the deck, blowing out a mouthful of air as she looked at James once again. His dark shirt was smooth on his body, emphasizing his wide shoulders, defined biceps, and the rise and fall of his pectorals. If she'd been in Hollywood she would have assumed he was an actor. But here in Angel Sands he was just another good looking guy.

One who happened to be the father of her baby.

As if he could feel her scrutiny, James put the paper down on the table in front of him and slowly turned toward her. Their gazes caught, and his brows rose with recognition. He got to his feet, and she was shocked once again by how tall he was. Out of his tux – and his scrubs – he looked more relaxed, like any other guy sitting outside a coffee shop, watching the ocean lap against the shore. When he began to walk toward her Harper realized she hadn't moved an inch.

"Hi." He came to a stop in front of her. "I grabbed us a table outside. Thought we could probably both do with soaking up some vitamin D. Would you like a coffee?"

"A decaf latte would be great."

"Decaf. Of course." He smiled at her and it hit her right in her thighs. Was she blushing? She *never* blushed. She prided herself on being cool, calm, and confident. It had been instilled in her since birth, after all.

Damn you second trimester sex drive.

"Go and sit down," he said, indicating the table he'd just vacated. "I'll bring your coffee over."

Her cheeks still felt warm as she took the seat opposite his, pulling it around so she could face the ocean, too. It looked so beautiful today, the white-foam waves dancing as they rushed toward the shore, the bright sun reflecting off the water, coloring it an orange-gold. She closed her eyes and breathed in, tasting the salt of the air and the tang of ozone tickling the back of her throat. How was it that the ocean always made everything better? Maybe it was the way it was timeless. The waves didn't care what day it was. Heck, they didn't care what century it was. They just moved back and forth because that's what they did.

She could learn something from that.

"One decaf latte," James said. Harper opened her eyes to see him slide the cup in front of her. "I got you a blueberry muffin, too, in case you're hungry. Oh, and the couple behind the counter told me to tell you 'hi'."

Harper glanced over her shoulder and saw Ally waving at her. Next to her was Nate, raising an eyebrow as if to tell her he was here if she needed him.

Harper bit down a smile at his protectiveness and lifted her hand to wave back. "I had breakfast about an hour ago," she said as she turned back to James and reached for the muffin. "But I'd hate to see this go to waste." She ripped a piece off between her thumb and finger and slid it onto her tongue. "Oh god, this is delicious." She swallowed it down and let out a little sigh. "Why does everything taste so good?"

James looked torn between amusement and something else. It sparked his eyes and made him swallow in spite of not eating anything. "I guess you're over any nausea?" he said, his voice thick.

"Yeah. That was the worst," Harper said, taking another bite. "I swung between starvation and sickness for weeks. Now I'm swinging between eating and overeating."

He quirked an eyebrow. "You're eating for two now."

"And don't I know it. This baby is so demanding already.

Did you know she's only the size of a lemon? How can something that small want so much food?"

"Maybe it's my fault?" James asked, arching an eyebrow. "The baby could get that from me. I eat a lot."

"You're not eating now," Harper pointed out.

"Yeah, well I managed to finish two muffins before you arrived," he said with a grin.

Harper finished the pastry, using her thumb to scrape the case for the final crumbs, then licked them off. It was disgusting, she knew it, but damn, that muffin was amazing. Being pregnant was a great excuse to throw out all the rules.

"You want me to get you another?" James asked.

Yeah she did, but even in this state she needed to have some standards. "Maybe later," she said, meaning it.

She picked up her coffee cup and took a sip, letting the steamy drink envelop her tongue. "God this is good, too," she said. "If only it had caffeine my life would be complete."

"Only another six months. Or maybe more if you decide to breastfeed."

Harper looked up, surprised. She wasn't sure if it was because he'd mentioned her breasts, or whether the reality was sinking in. James, on the other hand, didn't blink at all.

"I don't know what I'm going to do yet in terms of feeding," she told him, her voice soft. "I'd like to breastfeed, at least at first, but I'm not going to beat myself up if it doesn't work out. I'll buy some bottles just in case and see what happens. I figure women have been doing this for thousands of years, it can't be that hard, can it?"

"It's amazing the help you can get nowadays, but it's your body and your decision. There's too much pressure put on new mothers as it is, you don't need any more."

She was aware their voices had dipped into serious conversation. And the anxiety she'd felt as she walked into the coffee shop reared its ugly head again. Along with the morning sickness and the jeans that didn't fit, anxiety was a new thing for her. She didn't like it one bit.

"Do you have any questions about the baby?" she asked him, running her finger around the rim of her cup. "I know it was a shock for you, and I'm sure you must have a million of them."

"Yeah, it was a shock. But I'm guessing it was for you, too." His gaze caught hers. "I'm sorry I didn't react well."

"You were no worse than I was when I found out." Harper shrugged. "But luckily for me I was alone when that second line appeared on the test." She widened her eyes. "Nobody to hear me scream."

He laughed. "You seem calm about it now. How far along were you when you took the test?"

"Well since we used a condom, I didn't even consider I was pregnant until I started to feel sick," Harper told him. "I was about eight weeks when I took the test, nine when I was able to get to the doctor and have it confirmed."

"So you only found out a month ago?"

"Yeah, that sounds right. Though it feels like longer. A lifetime even. A lot has happened since then. I've moved to Angel Sands, started to concentrate on my own business, and then I saw you again. So that kind of brings us up to date."

"Have you found an obstetrician yet?" he asked.

"I had one in L.A.. She was my OB/Gyno, so she was going to deliver the baby. But I need to sort it out now that I'm down here. Ember can probably help recommend someone."

"I know a couple of good ones at the hospital. I can set up an appointment for you." He leaned forward.

"Do you know if they take credit cards?" Harper asked. "Because I don't have medical insurance right now."

He frowned. "I've got it covered. I get a discount from

the hospital because I'm an employee. You don't need to worry about the cost."

She gave him a close-lipped smile. "It's okay. I'll cover it somehow." Even if she'd be paying it off for the rest of her life. From the time she'd left home at the age of eighteen she hadn't relied on anybody else's help. But now she seemed to be leaning on everybody.

She didn't like the way it made her feel so helpless.

"I have money, Harper. Maybe that's all I've got. I'm just as responsible for this baby as you are. I'd like to pay my portion, especially since you're doing all the heavy lifting."

"I just don't like being beholden to anybody. I'm not a gold digger."

He frowned. "I never said you were."

No, but she knew how people thought. Knew that gossip spread like wildfire, and that certain women saw rich men as their ticket to an easy life. She was never going to be that kind of person.

Not like her mom.

"Just think about it," he said, his voice low. "Babies are expensive. Having them, bringing them up, all of it adds up. I don't expect you to pay for all of it. This child is my responsibility, too."

"Okay," she said softly. "I'll think about it."

He nodded, but said nothing more. Silence hung in the air like a curtain, cutting the connection between the two of them. Harper tried to find her equilibrium, ignoring the nagging tug of her stomach.

"I'm sorry," she finally said. "I'm just not good at accepting help."

He raised an eyebrow. "I got that impression."

"I didn't tell you about the baby because I want your money. I don't expect it, not at all. I just thought you had the right to know."

"It's okay. I was a little insensitive. I'm sorry, too." He watched as she finished her coffee and put the cup down on the table. "Would you like to get out of here?" he asked her. "Maybe take a walk along the beach?"

She gave him the faintest of smiles. "Yeah, I would. A walk sounds really good."

❧ 10 ❧

"Tell me about yourself," James said as they made their way along the surf. To their left were a series of dunes. The golden sand dusted over blades of grass as they gave way to the flats and finally the houses overlooking the Pacific Ocean. It was prime real estate here; he and Sara had looked at a couple of houses along the beachfront before deciding they preferred the views from the cliffs. But he could see their appeal – the view from these houses were amazing, just golden sand and deep blue ocean stretching out for miles. It was peaceful and yet thrilling.

"You probably know everything worth knowing," Harper said. He liked the way she kicked through the water, not caring about the spray hitting her rolled up jeans. He was carrying both their shoes – his in one hand, hers in the other, but part of him wished he had an arm free to slide around her waist and hold her closer.

"Not really. Where were you born?"

"Connecticut."

"Is your family still there?"

Harper wrinkled her nose. "My dad died when I was little.

I was mostly brought up by my grandma – his mom. As for my mom, she's around somewhere. I guess wherever the latest boyfriend wants her to be."

Her voice was light but he could hear the hurt in it.

"So how did you end up in Hollywood?"

"It's a long story."

"We've got six months." He grinned at her, catching her gaze.

Harper smiled back. "I moved to California recently. I was in New York before that. I worked in a couple of costume departments on Broadway, but then wanted to try my hand at the movies."

"Have you always wanted to be a costume designer?"

"I wanted to be *some* kind of designer. I studied fashion and design at college, then specialized in theatrical costume design. When I graduated, I was offered a job in New York and Caitie was setting up her own business there, so it seemed like a good idea to move to the city."

"You and Caitie are close, huh?"

Harper shrugged. "We're like sisters. I don't have much family of my own, so she stepped in and became it for me." She licked the salt away from her lips. "So, when she moved back here it made sense for me to move, too. There was nothing keeping me in New York."

"You didn't have a boyfriend?" He could feel his stomach tighten. It aggravated him. What did he care about her dating history?

"Nobody special. I dated, but that was all."

"And in L.A.?"

She looked up at him, her eyes full of interest. "There was nobody there. I hadn't been there long before I lost my job and everything went to shit."

"When your department got shut down."

"You remember me telling you about that?" She raised an eyebrow.

"I remember a lot about that night," he told her. It wasn't an exaggeration. The way her hair felt between his fingers, the curve of her hip as it flared out to her thighs, the way her sighs caught in her throat as pleasure captured the rest of her.

Yeah, he could remember it all.

"Do you regret it?" she asked him.

Her question took him by surprise. A bird skimmed across the water, calling out with a loud squawk. As she turned to look at it – a cormorant from the shape of its black body and long bill – he pondered her question. Did he regret that he was here, walking along the shore with her and that the new life she was carrying was a part of him?

"I don't regret it, no." His voice was firm. How could he regret the creation of a new life?

She looked away from the bird and into his eyes. "Nor do I."

"You don't?" he asked, a smile playing at his lips. "Not even with everything you're going through?"

She stared into the distance, her chin tipped up, her neck long. Her lips were parted so he could see the white of her teeth and the pink tip of her tongue. He swallowed hard, feeling the flame of desire flicker inside him again.

With her eyes focused on a faraway point she shook her head. "If you'd have asked me about my plans for having babies a few months ago, I would have laughed in your face. I had no plans, no thoughts, nothing at all. Children were something I'd filed away as a distant concern for the future. Next to owning my home and getting in a monogamous relationship. But now that it's happened I can't regret it. This little thing." She rubbed her stomach. "It's a part of me. She's changed me in ways I can barely fathom and she's no bigger than the palm of my hand." Her lips curled into a smile. "I feel protective of her already. And I can't wait to meet her, to see what kind of personality she has, whether she giggles or guffaws.

"I can't wait to see her grow and become a little girl. I didn't have the easiest upbringing in the world, but I'm determined hers will be. She'll know she's wanted, that she's loved. I don't want her to have any doubt that she's the number one in my life. It's like all the things I've been through have been leading up to this."

Damn, she was beautiful. Her face glowed as she talked about their child, her skin blooming, her eyes lighting up. The urge to lean forward and kiss her was overwhelming.

Yeah, and also dangerous. They had enough to deal with. His libido could go take a hike.

"You can't always protect them," he said, his voice thick. "Maybe that's the hardest part about being a parent."

She turned to him, her eyes glistening as they caught his gaze. "I heard about your wife and child. I'm so sorry."

His gut clenched. In a way, he was glad he didn't have to tell her. As the mother of his child, she had every right to know about his loss. And yet it felt like his skin was being flayed open, revealing tender flesh beneath.

"What was your baby's name?" she asked softly, as though she could sense his turmoil.

"Jacob."

"That's a beautiful name."

"He was a beautiful kid." His voice was thick.

She lifted her hand to wipe away a tear. "Ignore me," she told him. "I'm constantly emotional. Yesterday I cried because I ran out of pink thread. I'm driving myself crazy."

"It's okay," he told her. She nodded at him, her eyes still watery.

"I can't imagine what it must have been like," she continued. "You must have been through hell."

"It was nearly three years ago. It's been a while."

"Three years isn't that long ago." The ocean breeze lifted the pink tips of her hair, fanning it over her shoulders. "I still hold grudges from twenty years ago."

He laughed. She was giving him an out from this difficult conversation. And he welcomed it. "Let's hope the baby takes after me then," he said lightly.

But deep inside, where the hold on his stomach was loosened a little, and he could feel something else, too. A wonder that he'd spent the last hour talking honestly to this woman – and that was longer than he'd been able to hold a conversation with anybody else in three years.

She said she was changing, thanks to this baby. For the first time he wondered if he could change, too.

"So it went better than you'd hoped?" Brooke asked as the five women sat on a large woolen blanket on the sand. It was Sunday morning – girl time, according to Ember and Ally – and they'd invited Caitie and Harper to join them. It was a tradition that Caitie's sister-in-law and her friends had followed for years. No matter how involved they got with life, work, or men, Sunday mornings were sacred.

Ally had brought them all coffees and pastries from Déjà Brew, a decaf latte and two blueberry muffins for Harper.

"You remembered," she said, her stomach gurgling at the sight of the cakes. "Thank you."

"How could I forget? It looked like some kind of smut film when you ate that muffin the other day." Ally's brows rose up and Ember and Brooke turned to grin at them. "Oooh, yes," she sighed loudly, doing a great impression of Harper. "That's so good."

"Stop it," Harper said, biting down a laugh. "I did not sound like that."

"You do it all the time." Caitie joined in. "Remember last night and that tub of Ben and Jerry's?" Caitie let out a low moan that sounded way too sexual. "That was you all evening. Even Breck started to get hot."

"What is this? Let's all pick on the pregnant woman day?"

"They're not picking on me," Ember pointed out. She rubbed her swollen stomach – already looking ready to pop in spite of her having two more months to go.

"Where's the sisterly support?" Harper asked her, grinning. "And back to your question, Brooke," she said, turning to the one person who *hadn't* teased her. "James seemed okay about it all. He wants to pay for the medical bills and seemed interested in how I was doing. That was more than I'd hoped for."

"That's positive," Brooke said, smiling. "I know how hard it is going through a pregnancy alone. I did it myself with Nick, though it seems like a long time ago now."

"It *was* a long time ago," Ally teased. "Nick's practically a teenager."

"Don't say that." Brooke gave a mock-shudder. "He's not even eleven yet. And he'll always be my baby."

Harper smiled at their gentle teasing. It was so lovely to be surrounded by friends, especially here on the beach. She couldn't imagine a better way of spending a Sunday morning. Lifting the first muffin, she took a deep inhale. The combination of fruit and sugar sent a shiver down her spine.

"See. Porn sigh," Ally said.

Harper opened her mouth to deny it, but her phone began to ring, James's name flashing across the screen. She rolled her eyes at Caitie as she accepted the call and lifted her phone to her ear.

"Hi." Her voice was soft.

"Hey. You okay?"

They'd spoken a couple of times since their meeting, but she knew James was back on shift. "I'm good. I'm at the beach, stuffing one of those amazing muffins down my throat."

"And making porn worthy noises," Ally shouted out.

"What was that?"

"Nothing. There are some strange people on the beach. Just ignore them." Harper shook her head, biting down a grin.

"Oh. Okay. Anyway, I was wondering if you're free next Friday. I spoke to a friend here at the hospital – an obstetrician – and she has a slot free if you'd like it. No pressure. If you don't like her then we can find somebody else. I know a few good ones."

"What's her name?"

"Eleanor O'Brien. Ellie. She's a very popular OB. But as I said, it's a personal choice." He paused for a second. "Should I not have picked a doctor for you?" he asked. "Would you rather find somebody yourself? We don't even need to go to a provider at my hospital if you'd prefer somewhere else."

"No," Harper said quickly. "You've done nothing wrong at all. I'm just surprised. I wasn't sure if you meant what you said about paying the medical bills."

"Of course I did. I don't say things unless I mean them."

She believed him. There was something authentic about the man.

"I'd like to take the appointment," she told him. "Thank you for setting it up. Will you be coming, too?"

"It's up to you. I don't want to make you uncomfortable."

Harper rolled her bottom lip between her teeth. She knew these first appointments involved the kinds of questions and examinations that might embarrass her in front of him. But he was the baby's father, and he wanted to be involved. She wouldn't take that from him. She remembered

Ember saying how important her OB appointments and ultrasounds were for Lucas to bond with the baby. Maybe James felt the same way.

"I'd like you to be there if you can make it," Harper said. Caitie caught her eye. She was smiling at her.

"Okay then. I don't have a shift that day, so can I pick you up? About eleven forty?"

"Works for me."

"See you then. Take it easy, Harper."

She smiled, liking the way he said her name. Maybe too much. "Thanks. You do the same."

He ended the call and she slid her phone back into her purse. It was only when she reached for her uneaten muffin that she realized they were all looking at her.

"What?" she asked them, tearing off a chunk.

"Nothing." Caitie winked. "Apart from you and James Tanner being pretty damn friendly."

"Is that bad?"

"No. I'd say it's very good," Ally teased. "What was that, him asking you out on a date?"

"Nope. He's arranged for me to meet an OB friend of his. Just doing his fatherly duty. That's all."

"Who's the OB?" Ember asked. "I might know them."

"Ellie O'Brien."

"That's my obstetrician," Ember said, grinning. "You'll love her. She's amazing. The best thing about her? She always warms her hands up before she puts her gloves on and touches you. There's nothing worse than freezing hands."

"That's sweet of him to organize that," Caitie said, smiling at Harper. "Do you think there's a possibility you and James might have something more going on?"

"Like what?"

"Like the kind of thing that led to this baby being made," Ally suggested, pointing at Harper's stomach.

"I don't think so." Harper gave a grim smile. "I don't think he sees it that way. Like you all told me, he's a good guy and he won't walk away from his responsibilities, but that's all this is."

"Is it all you want it to be?" Caitie asked, her voice gentle.

"Honestly? I don't know." Harper let out a sigh. "I mean, he's a handsome guy, and yeah, I'm attracted to him, but maybe that's just biology. My body probably wants me to be attracted to the baby's father, the same way it would have in caveman days."

Ally grinned. "So he's a caveman?"

Brooke laughed and Caitie let out a whistle. Ember shook her head.

"It wouldn't be a good idea even if I did want things to happen," Harper pointed out. "First of all, I'm a mess. I have no home, no job, and I'm three months pregnant. I'm not exactly a catch right now. And then there's his history. He was married to his soul mate. They had a baby together. He had everything he ever wanted. How could I ever compete with that?"

They were all silent for a moment, sympathy softening their gazes. Harper picked up her cup and took a sip of her decaf latte.

Yes, she liked him. More than she'd realized until this moment, but she was also certain nothing could come of it. And she wasn't planning on risking her relationship with her baby's father for the sake of caveman biology and her raging second trimester hormones.

Even if they were getting more difficult to ignore.

"Hi, I'm Doctor Ellie O'Brien. Please come on in." The obstetrician had one of the biggest smiles Harper had ever seen. With her blonde hair, athletic frame, and Australian accent she could have been Chris Hemsworth's younger sister.

"Take a seat," she said, pointing to the three chairs gathered around a low coffee table. "You, too, James." Ellie took the chair across from them, resting a cardboard file on her lap.

She looked at Harper. "Thanks for giving me the details of your doctor in L.A. He's sent your records through. Am I right in thinking you last saw him a little over four weeks ago?"

"Yes, I met with him prior to moving here to confirm pregnancy"

"Well, I've reviewed all your records and everything's looking great. Did the nurse take your vitals along with urine and blood samples before you came in?"

"Yep." Harper nodded.

Ellie picked up her electronic notebook from the coffee

table and swiped it open. "Yeah, there it is. And your blood pressure is fine, slightly high, but nothing to be concerned about. Just make sure you limit any caffeine intake and rest more as you continue in your pregnancy. The baby needs a lot of energy to grow."

"Sure." Harper nodded.

"Have you booked a tour of the facilities here?" Ellie asked. "There's the prenatal suite where you'll give birth, and of course the postnatal ward and nursery. You'll want to take a look at them all. I know how important these things are when you're making a decision about where you want to have your baby."

"I'll take her around after this," James suggested. "Save somebody the job."

"No problem." Ellie grinned at him. "Okay then, let's take a look at your baby. How about you hop up on the exam table?" she asked Harper.

"I can now. I'm not sure I'll be hopping anywhere in a few weeks."

Ellie laughed. "Touché. But hop while you can." She pulled the exam paper down onto the table and Harper climbed up. "Do you want to come and look, James?" Ellie asked, turning to him.

James looked at Harper. She nodded, and he stood to join them.

"I'm just going to examine your stomach first," Ellie told her, lifting Harper's top up to expose the bottom of her abdomen. She pressed firmly, moving her fingers around. "And now let's give you a measure," she said, taking her tape measure out and laying it on Harper's stomach. "Yep, fourteen weeks exactly," she said. "Perfect."

Harper looked up at James. He was watching Ellie's movement's carefully, his expression unreadable. Ellie touched

Harper's hands, "Any swelling on your hands or feet?" she asked her.

"No, nothing."

"Great. Well you're looking really good. Would you like to see your baby?"

"You're doing an ultrasound?" James asked her.

"I typically do the nuchal translucency test at this stage of pregnancy to check for any defects," Ellie said to him. "And then at twenty weeks we'll do the detailed scan. That's if it's okay with you guys? Even if you decide to go with another obstetrician, it'll be one thing less to worry about. And the test is best performed now, so I'd recommend it."

James looked at Harper and she nodded. "Sure, let's do it." She was almost certain she wanted to have Ellie as her OB. She liked her friendly, no-nonsense style. Ellie was the kind of person Harper could see herself being friends with in another life.

After smearing her stomach with cool gel, Ellie pulled the ultrasound equipment over and sat in a tall stool next to the table. She pressed the wand on Harper's stomach, and Harper swallowed hard, suddenly nervous about what she was going to see.

"You feeling okay?" Ellie asked, as though she could sense her unease. "There's no need to be worried, this is all normal." She moved the wand around again. "And your baby is growing beautifully. You want to see?"

Harper nodded. "Yeah." She felt a little breathless. Ellie moved the screen around so Harper could see it. It was mostly black, with a white grid around it and white shadows in the center.

"This is the head," Ellie murmured, pointing at the round shape, and suddenly the outline of the baby became clear. Harper could see her nose, lips, and rounded belly that dwarfed her stick-like legs. Her little arm moved, and Harper held her breath, emotion building up inside her like a tidal wave.

"Is she really okay?" Harper asked. Her chest felt so full it might burst.

"Everything's great. Can you see the heartbeat here?" Ellie asked, pointing at a tiny dark circle in the baby's chest.

Sure enough, the circle was rhythmically moving. A little tiny heart inside a little tiny baby. Harper's throat tightened.

When she turned her head, she saw James staring at the screen, his lips open, his eyes wide. He swallowed hard, making his Adam's apple bob.

"I'm going to take a few measurements," Ellie told them, pulling the screen back around so it was facing her. "And then I'll print you out a photo to keep. You want one or two?"

"Two," James said quickly. He looked at Harper with a strained smile. "If that's okay with you."

"It's fine," she said, nodding at him. Their eyes connected and it felt like a jolt of electricity shooting through her. He was staring at her the way he'd stared at the screen, and the intensity in his gaze took her breath away. Slowly, he smiled at her, and she felt herself smiling back.

She wondered if the baby could feel her racing heart.

"There you go," Ellie said, sliding the prints inside two cardboard envelopes. "Your baby's first portraits. One for mom and one for dad." She passed them over. "Have you thought about finding out the sex?"

Harper nodded. "I'd like to know." She caught James's eye. He shrugged. *It's your choice.*

"Well there's no rush. It's hospital policy not to look until the next ultrasound. It stops too many false gender reveals and you suing us." She grinned again, and wiped Harper's stomach with a paper towel, then pulled her top back down. "Let's go have a seat again, and you can shoot as many questions as you'd like at me."

James reached for Harper's hands and helped her down from the table, and her heart skipped a beat when she saw the big smile on his face.

Maybe this was going to work out after all. He hadn't said as much, but James seemed as excited about this baby as she was.

In six months' time they were going to be parents. For the first time, the thought didn't scare the hell out of her.

"Would you like to come inside?" Harper asked James as he walked her to the front door. "Caitie has a kick-ass coffee machine. And maybe we can fill in the medical history form Ellie gave us."

"Sure." James nodded. He was standing right behind her and she had this weird feeling of not wanting him to leave yet.

She slid her key in the lock and pushed the door open. As they walked in, James put his hand on the curve of her spine, the same way he had in the examination room.

"So this is my room," she said, as they passed the first door on the left of the hallway. "I'd show you but it's a mess."

"And there was me thinking you'd be a KonMari freak."

Harper laughed. "I don't have time. Anyway, it's not *that* bad, just stuffed with clothes." She pushed the handle down, opening it. "See?" she said. "You don't have to worry, I'm not a candidate for a hoarder show."

Her clothes rack was bursting with dresses. Every time she wanted to go to bed she had to brush past them; it was like walking through the wardrobe into Narnia.

"Wow." James raised an eyebrow. "You're not wrong. That's a lot of clothes."

"These are all samples. I'm planning on taking them to a

few boutiques, and see if they'll stock my designs." Harper shrugged.

"So you work in here, too?" James asked, his gaze landing on her sewing desk. It was clearer than the rest of the room – just her trusty machine and all her thread.

"Yep. There really isn't anywhere else."

"Have you thought about renting some workspace?" he asked her, his brows knitting together. "There has to be somewhere better than this."

"I have, but there's the small matter of cash flow." Harper shrugged. "Once I get a steady income that's first on my list. I can't keep working out of Caitie and Breck's home. They deserve their space."

"I have a room you could use." James blinked, as though surprised at his words. But then his expression softened, and he smiled at her. "There's a whole basement in my house that is empty. It's water tight, well lit, and I've never needed it. You could move all your work down there. You could make a hundred dresses and you'd still have space to move."

"That's a very sweet thought." It really was getting crazy in her room. And if she made a success of things then she'd definitely need more hanging space. She couldn't fit much more in, that was for sure.

But was it sensible? After the appointment today she was already finding it difficult to keep a distance from him. Lines were getting blurred everywhere and she owed it to this baby to be sensible. Not to be the type of woman who jumped at the first sign of a knight in shining armor.

She wasn't going to be *that* mom.

"I didn't say it to be sweet," he told her. "You should do it."

"I don't know..." her voice wavered then trailed off.

"It doesn't have to be forever. But of course you're welcome to use it as long as you'd like. It will probably be better for your sleep if this room's free of all your work, and you know how important rest is for the baby and you."

"I can't afford to pay any rent," she admitted, hating how that made her feel. "I'd just be mooching off you." *Again*. Ugh, she hated this.

James raised an eyebrow. "You're having my baby, I wouldn't ask you to pay rent. And as the father, it's in my interest to make your life as easy as possible, so don't think I'm doing this out of the goodness of my heart."

She smiled, because she knew he was doing exactly that. "I told you before I'm not good at accepting help."

He reached out and cupped her cheek. The warmth of his palm seared her, making her breath catch in her throat. Apart from the gentle pressure of his hand against her back, it was the first time he'd touched her since that night three months ago.

And it felt as good as she remembered.

"I'm not the kind of guy who sees taking care of the mother of his baby as 'help'," James said, his voice low. "It's my job. A father's duty to his kid is as equal to the mother's, and I take that seriously. I hate the kind of guy who says he's babysitting his kids. He's not babysitting, he's their damn father. He's doing what he's supposed to. And I know you're not used to asking for help, but that's not what I'm offering. What I'm offering is to help care for my child and its mother."

Her heart clenched. Just a little. "Are you sure?"

"Yes I'm sure. Whether you like it or not, we're going to be connected forever. This little baby growing inside you will see to that."

"Okay," she said, nodding. "In that case, I'd like to take you up on your offer." She held her breath for a moment, waiting for his response.

His mouth split into a grin. "Excellent. I'll arrange for a van to pick up all your work stuff."

An hour later, they were drinking coffee in the kitchen and filling out the family medical history form Ellie had given them. Harper was tapping the pen against her lips, frowning at the questions.

"Any history of heart disease in your family?" she asked.

"Not that I know of. How about yours?" He lifted the cup to his mouth, staring at her over the rim.

"None. My dad died in a car accident when I was a baby, and my grandfather died of colon cancer. My mom and my grandma are still alive."

He noticed her voice dipping with disdain when she mentioned her family. "Are they excited about the baby?" he asked.

She looked up, shaking her head. "I haven't told them."

"You haven't? Why not?"

She shrugged. "I don't speak to my mom very often. Maybe once a year or so. And I've been on bad terms with my grandma since I left home for college. She wasn't very happy with me about that."

James frowned. "Really? My parents were so excited when I got into college, and then into med school. I had to stop them from organizing a party every time I got an 'A' on an assignment."

Harper laughed. "Grandma wanted me to stay in Connecticut where she could keep an eye on me. She blamed college for my mom's flighty ways. Said her parents should never have let her leave home at that age."

"You said your grandma is your dad's mom, right?" James clarified.

"Yeah. She's the one who brought me up after dad died and mom left." Harper swallowed. "I guess I should tell her about the baby. She deserves to know."

"Not if telling her will hurt you."

"It'll confirm what she already thought about me. That I'm turning out to be just like my mom. Pregnant before marriage. Except I've one upped her and managed to get pregnant without even being in a relationship." She lifted a shaky hand to her brow.

He frowned. "Seriously? What kind of people think like that?" He tried to imagine his mom reacting like that to the news, but it was impossible. She never judged him or told him he was worthless. Her love was always unconditional. "Is your mom still in Connecticut?"

"No. She hasn't lived there since I was a baby. She moved to Boston with husband number two, and then when that went wrong she married number three in London." She shook her head.

James wasn't sure what to say to that.

"I can see your wide eyes." Harper grinned at him. "Why not widen them a bit more, because she's on marriage number eight. She's New England's Liz Taylor."

This time he laughed. "She sounds like a character."

"She likes being looked after, and she loves weddings. I think she probably went a bit crazy after my dad died and left her with a newborn baby and no money at all. His trust fund went back to my grandparents."

"He didn't leave any money to you?"

Harper shook her head. "No. My grandma controls everything. And when I left I told her I didn't want any of it." She shrugged. "She thought I'd be back within a year. Maybe two. But here I am, nearly ten years later, and I haven't asked for a dime." She rolled her shoulders back, her eyes glinting.

So that's why she hated accepting help. From the moment

she was born she was taught support always came with strings.

"How about you?" Harper asked, as though she was sick of talking about her life. "Have you told your parents?"

"Not yet, but I plan to. Now we know everything's looking good I guess I should let them know."

"Will they be upset with you?"

He laughed. "No. They'll be ecstatic. Mom loves kids. She absolutely adored Jacob. She'll be so excited, she'll probably go crazy." He looked down at his coffee cup. "They'll want to meet you."

"They will?"

"For sure." He nodded. "How do you feel about that?"

"Um, I don't know," she said. "I guess it would be okay. As long as you promise they won't call me a tramp, or even worse, 'just like your mother'." She rolled her eyes.

He laughed. "Since they don't know your mom, I'm pretty sure you're safe. And they won't think you're a tramp any more than they'll think I am. They're big supporters of women's rights."

She smiled at him. "I like the sound of them."

Yeah, well he was pretty sure they'd like her, too. That thought was strangely comforting. Weird how quickly he was getting used to this situation, to being a co-parent with a woman he barely knew.

You'd like to know her, though.

He took a sip of coffee, ignoring the voice in his head. As far as he was concerned it was talking crap anyway. The lines between the two of them were already so blurred they were almost non-existent. He didn't need his damn libido to kick in, too.

Co-parents. That's all they were and he was perfectly happy with that. Less emotional. Less messy. Less chance for him to get hurt again.

❧ 12 ❧

Harper looked around the basement, a smile playing at her lips. It had taken a few days to move all her dresses and equipment but everything was finally in the right place. James hadn't lied about his basement being perfect. It took up practically the whole footprint of the house, and the generous floor space had allowed her to set up separate zones. Her designs were in one part of the room, on a large table that was already down here, and her sewing table was in the other corner, along with a wall of shelves where she'd been able to put her rolls of fabrics and hundreds of threads.

Her three racks were placed in such a way they almost looked like a shop, next to an expansive mirror left over from the previous owner, who'd used this room as a yoga studio. Then there was the adjoining bathroom, which meant she wouldn't need to run up the stairs every time she needed to pee. Thanks to her pregnancy bladder, that felt like a major win.

James had been here for the first two days of moving in. In fact, he'd done half the work while she'd supervised the photoshoot she'd arranged with Ember's friend. The pictures had come out wonderfully – both mother and daughter had looked perfect in the clothes Harper had created – and she'd already had a slew of orders and interest from boutiques in the local area.

She had a feeling she was going to need every inch of this space.

Her stomach rumbled, reminding her lunchtime had come and gone. She rubbed her stomach – her bump perfectly rounded, as though somebody had stuffed a ball inside it.

Today she was wearing a pair of bleached rolled-up maternity jeans, along with a pretty laced tunic she'd made with some fabric remnants. Her hair was twisted and clipped up to keep it out of her face as she leaned over the sewing machine.

As she walked, barefoot, up to James's high-spec, gleaming kitchen, her stomach growled again, louder this time. She quickly grabbed the lunch bag she'd brought with her and pulled out an apple, biting down into it as she felt the juices spray her lips.

Mmm. That was good. With the apple in one hand, she grabbed the container of pasta and sauce with the other and put it into James's microwave, heating it on high for two minutes. As the turntable went around, she pulled out his drawers, searching for some cutlery.

The first one was full of knives. The second had chopping boards and baking trays. She chewed another chunk of her apple as she pulled the third one out, revealing only old papers and takeout menus.

What wouldn't she give for a hot chicken chow mein right now.

There was a key ring in the drawer. One of those photo ones you could get made at a drugstore. Curious, Harper pulled it out and lifted it into the light. A pretty brunette was grinning back at her, her long dark hair curled over one shoulder. She had a baby balanced on her hip – he looked to be about six months old. Harper recognized where the photo was taken – on the beach near the Déjà Brew coffee shop.

It had to be Sara and Jacob. Seeing them made tears sting at her eyes.

They were so happy, so carefree, and yet only a few months after this photograph was taken they were both in that terrible accident. Her heart ached as she traced her finger over the plastic holding the image.

James must have taken the photo. She could almost picture it. From the way Sara and Jacob were laughing, she imagined he was making faces at them, his eyes soft with love as he looked at his family.

How did somebody survive a loss like that?

And now here she was, bringing him a pile of trouble he hadn't asked for, and he wasn't complaining one bit. He'd done everything he could to make her life easier. From finding an obstetrician to letting her use his basement for no cost, James was making her feel things she hadn't felt for a long time.

Maybe ever.

The microwave pinged at the exact moment somebody rapped on the back door. Harper jumped, and her heart started to race in her chest.

Another rap. Blowing out a mouthful of air she walked around the corner to the glass doors. Standing on the deck was a woman of around sixty, her grey hair neatly styled into a bob that ended at her jaw.

"Hello?" Harper said as she made her way toward the door.

"Um, hi. Is James in?" the woman asked.

"No, he's at work. Can I help you?"

Harper stopped at the door. There was only a sheet of glass separating her from the woman. Figuring she looked nothing like a serial killer, Harper reached to unlatch the door, then pulled it open.

"Are you the new cleaner?" the woman asked. "I didn't know Maggie had left."

"No." Harper shook her head. "I'm not a cleaner. I'm a... friend. I've been borrowing James's basement."

The woman laughed. "How rude of me. I'm sorry." She reached out a hand. "I'm Louise Tanner, James's mom."

Oh boy. This wasn't how she imagined meeting his parents. In her mind they'd be primed, knowing exactly who she was and that she was pregnant with his baby. Not standing in the middle of the kitchen as this elegant older woman stared at her with interest.

The microwave pinged again to remind her it had finished. Harper flashed Louise a smile. "I was just warming my lunch," she told her. "Would you like to come in for coffee?"

"A glass of water would be lovely," Louise said, following Harper into the kitchen. "And you go ahead and eat. Don't let me interrupt you..." she trailed off. "I'm so sorry, I don't know your name."

"I'm Harper." She reached out a hand and Louise shook it.

"I didn't realize James was working today," Louise told Harper as she took her pasta out of the microwave. "I only popped by because he mentioned the hem on one of his curtains had come loose. He may be an amazing surgeon, but give him a needle and a thread and he's all thumbs and no fingers." She laughed. The way her eyes crinkled and her head tipped back reminded Harper of James.

Harper's stomach gurgled again, the sound echoing through the room.

"Oh my, you'd better eat something," Louise said. Then her eyes caught the swell of Harper's stomach and her brows knitted together. "Oh."

Without thinking, Harper cradled her bump with her hand, leaving James's mom with no room for doubt.

"You're pregnant," Louise said.

"Um, yeah."

"How far along?"

"Fifteen weeks tomorrow." Harper attempted a smile. "It feels like forever already."

"I bet. Now eat," Louise said, pointing at the pasta. "I can still remember what second trimester hunger is like. I used to drive my poor husband crazy with all my demands, but the way I saw it he'd contributed to the problem and he could help with the solution."

Harper laughed in spite of herself.

"How about your partner?" Louise asked. "Does he have to run out at midnight to grab you jars of pickles?"

"I don't have a partner," Harper told her. "I guess if I want pickles I'll go get them myself."

"Oh." Louise shifted in her seat. Harper was acutely aware how uncomfortable this situation was. In a few days, James would tell his mom about the baby, and presumably about Harper. Would she be angry Harper hadn't told her?

But it wasn't her place to say anything, was it? This was James's mom and it was his news to share. She'd already made enough mistakes, she didn't need any more.

"I should probably eat," Harper said. "I've got a ton of work to get done this afternoon."

"What is it you do?" Louise asked. She'd regained her calm demeanor.

"I'm a dress designer. That's what I'm doing down in James's basement."

"Well that's a relief. I was starting to worry you were some kind of serial killer. Or maybe you were running a BDSM club down there."

Harper coughed out a laugh, and a piece of pasta flew

from her mouth. "Oh god, I'm sorry. That's so disgusting." She covered her lips with her hand.

"It's my fault for making you laugh." Louise's eyes twinkled. "Sorry about that. I wasn't lying, though. I'm really curious about what you're doing down there."

"I'll tell you what, once I've finished my pasta I'll show you."

"If you promise not to tie me up to the wall, I might take you up on that offer." Louise grinned.

God, James's mom was nice. And so different from Harper's mom and grandma. Down to earth, funny, and kind.

More than a little bit like her son.

"So your mom popped in earlier," Harper told James when he'd arrived home that evening. She'd just finished her day's work and was ready to leave. Caitie had messaged to see if she wanted to meet at the diner. If it involved food and not having to make it, the answer was always yes.

"Yeah, I know. She called me." He kicked off his shoes.

"She did? What did she say?" Harper looked down at her bump. "She could tell I was pregnant but I didn't tell her about you being the father of the baby." Her face paled. "I hope I didn't cause you any problems."

"It's fine." He shrugged off his jacket and hung it on the back of the chair, his t-shirt rising up to reveal a thin sliver of his abdomen.

She wasn't going to look. No way, siree. But those damn hormones practically hijacked her gaze and forced her to glance at his smooth, tan skin, and the ridges of muscle there.

Was it getting hot in here?

"She was okay about it all?" Harper asked, leaning against the wall. A lock of hair fell across her eyes and she wiped it away, tucking it behind her ear. "She wasn't worried about some strange pregnant lady being in your house while you were gone? I was scared she was going to call the cops on me." She licked her dry lips. "Or that I'd blurt out the truth."

"I told her." He looked amused at her flustered response. "I explained who you are and she understood."

"What? Wait..." Harper shook her head. "You told her about the baby being yours?"

"Yeah."

"And she doesn't mind?"

He gave her a confused smile. "Why would she mind? It's not her life."

"But..." Harper blinked. She tried to imagine her grandmother's response if she'd been in the same position as James's mom. Her tight lips, judging eyes, and shaking head. "She must think I'm awful," she whispered. "For being here and being pregnant and everything."

"She said you were lovely. And she'd like you – or rather *us* – to go over for dinner one weekend." He took in her expression and his eyes softened. "Don't look so worried. It's me she's mad at for not warning her. In her words; *'that poor girl is probably panicking and it's all your fault, James.'*" He grinned.

Harper blinked. "She said that?"

"Yep. On the plus side, she cooks a mean pot pie and she's determined to feed you up. Especially after I told her how much you like eating."

"You're making it worse." She rose her eyebrows at him.

"Seriously, she can't wait to properly meet you now that she knows who you are. She'll probably drive you crazy asking a hundred questions about your pregnancy. And if you're really fortunate you'll get treated to photos of me as a baby."

"Naked?"

He winked. "If you're super lucky."

A smile curled at her lips. How she wished she had a mom

who thought like that. One who would invite her over and feed her. Someone who'd show interest in her baby or in her life. A mom she'd see more than once every few years when she was between husbands or boyfriends.

"Are you okay?" James asked her. "You don't have to meet them if you don't want to. I guess it's a bit weird, but I figure she's going to be around this baby once it's born, and you'll probably want to know her a bit better." He tipped his head to the side. "You don't have to decide right away. They leave for vacation in a few days and won't be back for a couple of weeks."

"I want to meet them both," Harper said quickly. She wasn't lying; she'd liked James's mom, and now that she knew Louise was excited about the baby the thought of sharing details with her warmed Harper. "I mean, it's not as though this baby is going to be surrounded by family. Not from my side at least. It's nice to know she'll have one doting grandmother."

He took a step closer, stopping only a couple of feet away from her. She swallowed, feeling the way she always did whenever he was close.

"Have you told your mom?"

Harper shook her head. "No. Not that she'll care."

"How about your grandma?"

"I'm dreading that phone call the most," she admitted. "So I've been putting it off."

"Why?"

"Because she'll be so disappointed in me. And I hate the way she looks and sounds when she's disappointed. She took me in when she didn't have to, and she dislikes the woman I've become. She spent a lot of money trying to craft me into becoming somebody she could be proud of, and I've dashed all her high hopes."

"But you're not a circus animal. You can't be somebody else just because they say so."

"Tell that to my grandma."

"I will if you'll let me." His voice was sure, strong. "If you want me to call her, I will."

She frowned. "But why? Why would you do that for me?"

He reached out, tracing the sharp line of her jaw with the tip of his finger. She felt a shiver wrack down her spine. "Because you're the mother of my baby. I don't like seeing you stressed." He tipped his head to the side, his eyes sweeping down as he slid his hand around her neck. It was warm and gentle and she couldn't help but lean into it. "I also think you're my friend." He smiled. "Friends look after friends."

His fingers brushed against the nape of her neck, and she shivered again. This time it hit her at the core, warming her, and making her want so much more than friendship.

Her eyes were still on his, wide and dilated. His jaw hardened, a dimple popping in and out on the side of his face. She wanted to touch it the way he was touching her. To run her finger along his cheekbones, down the predominant ridge of his nose to his soft lips below.

The memory of the night they'd slept together danced in her thoughts, making her heart bang against her chest. The way he'd kissed her jaw, her throat, his lips lingering in the dip of her neck. It made her want everything she knew she couldn't have.

"You should go home," he said, his hand still cupping her neck. "Get some dinner, and some rest."

"Yeah." She didn't move an inch.

"Harper?" His eyes dipped to her throat. He slid his fingers down to her chest, tracing the base of her neck, and her breath escaped with a loud sigh.

"Mmm?" She wasn't winning any awards for dialogue right now.

"Don't look at me like that."

"Like what?"

"Like I'm one of those blueberry muffins you get from Déjà Brew and you're the hungriest woman alive."

She laughed, she couldn't help it, and it cut through the electric atmosphere, dispersing the hiss and buzz that had been growing between them. "Hormones," she told him, wanting to hit herself for reacting that way. "To be honest, I'd probably jump the mail man if he knocked in the right way."

James pulled his hand away from her and shook his head, a ghost of a smile on his lips. "I'll walk you out," he said, taking a step back to increase the space between them.

She took a deep breath to regain her equilibrium. "It's okay. I can manage it by myself."

"You sure?"

She nodded quickly. She needed some distance between them before she did something stupid like rip his clothes off. "Goodbye, James. Have a good evening."

"You too."

As soon as she closed the front door behind her she let out a sigh. Her life was so damn messy already, and now her body was messing it up even more.

It was time to grow up and stop listening to her hormones. She had a baby to think of.

✣ 1 3 ✣

"Thank you for coming here with me," Ember said as she and Harper stood in front of a rack of baby clothes, rifling through the tiny onesies and dresses. Her bump was so big she had to stand back from the rack so she didn't hit it with a hanger every time she slid an outfit along the metal pole. "Lucas is so sick of shopping it hurts. And he's working all the hours he can to build up some leave for when the baby comes."

"Are you getting excited?" Harper asked.

"Kind of excited and kind of scared. It's all getting so real now. The baby's head is engaged and I can feel the damn thing every time I walk. I can't sleep at night and I'm constantly in the bathroom. I figure having a newborn baby can't be much worse than hitting this stage of pregnancy." Ember saw Harper's shocked expression and laughed. "Sorry, is that TMI?"

"No. I was just hoping the third trimester would be kind of like the second."

"It is for the most part," Ember reassured her. "It's just these last few weeks that have slowed me down. Trying to work full time and grow this little human has taken it out of me." She cupped the slope of her bump with her hands, smiling. "But I wouldn't have it any other way."

"How about the birth?" Harper leaned forward. "Have you written out a plan?"

"Yeah. I've had it written since I was six months." Ember smiled. "But older and wiser women have told me nothing ever happens as planned."

"Brooke?"

Ember grinned. "Yup."

"Have you decided if you'll have an epidural?" Harper asked her, running her finger down a soft onesie. They were all so tiny. Strange to think she'd be dressing her baby in miniature clothes like these.

"I initially wanted nothing, but decided to wait and see how I feel. I'm not keen on an epidural mainly because my mom couldn't walk for days after she had me. But if the pain is that bad..."

"Maybe I should take everything they'll give me," Harper said with a grin. "It has to be easier if you're high as a kite."

Ember laughed. "I'll tell you once I've experienced it."

Harper lifted a tiny pink tutu attached to a silver bodice from the rack, turning it around to inspect it. Her eyes widened as she caught sight of the price tag. "Jeez, have you seen the cost of this? And the fabric is so cheap. I could make it for a tenth of the price, and it would be far better quality."

"Are you making your baby's clothing?" Ember asked.

"I've made a couple of things," Harper told her, replacing the dress on the rack. "But I haven't really had much time. I had a big order from a boutique in Silver City come in, plus my direct orders have exploded. I've had to turn some work down."

"You have? That's amazing." Ember's eyes sparkled. "Your clothes are beautiful. Annabelle showed me the photos with her and her daughter in your dresses. I can't believe how lovely they are."

Harper felt her skin warm up. "Thank you. She did a great job modeling for them. I've got a lot of orders off those photos. I sent her some clothes to say thank you."

"She told me." Ember nodded. "She was delighted, too. But you didn't have to. She was just happy to have new photographs for her portfolio." They wandered over to the bedding shelves. They were an explosion of pastels, with soft yellows and pale greens, and the inevitable blues and pinks. "I hope you're getting some rest, too," Ember added. "Caitie told me you've been up late sewing most nights."

"I promised I'd take a break. That's why I turned down some work. And why I'm here right now," Harper told her. Everybody has been telling her the same thing. *Slow down, take it easy, this baby needs all the energy you need.* When it wasn't Caitie worrying about her, it was James asking if she'd taken too much on. "But I can't stop altogether. I've almost saved enough money for six months' rent. But I'll need to keep working until my due date if I want to take a couple of weeks off after the birth. Bills need to be paid."

Ember smiled sympathetically. "It must be tough doing all this on your own. I'm so impressed by how well you're handling it all."

"You think I'm handling it well?"

"Yeah. Look at you. You're building up a business, growing a baby, and you're looking so full of health and happiness it's making me want to bask in your glow. All the while I'm laying in bed worrying that I'll hate breastfeeding, or that I'll never want to have sex with Lucas again."

Harper laughed. "Well I don't need to worry about the sex part. I'm pretty sure being a single mom will put most guys off."

"Only the weak ones. The strong ones won't care. Look at

Brooke. She was a single mom for years but then Aiden came around and fell in love with both her and Nick. He's planning on adopting him." She squeezed Harper's hand. "There's a happy-ever-after out there for everybody."

"Hmm." Harper raised her brows.

"You don't believe me?"

"I just think most guys want a woman who hasn't had a baby with another guy. A fresh slate. In their eyes I'll be damaged goods. Or at least returned goods. Not that it matters, because I don't want to be the kind of mom who's more concerned about the guy she's dating than the child she gave birth to. I don't see myself dating for a long time."

"That's so sad." Ember sighed. "Because you're so funny, kind, and beautiful. Any guy would see you as a catch."

Harper blushed.

"Don't look at me like that." Ember laughed. "It's true. Every word."

"Well you're very sweet, and I'm so glad I have you as a friend." Harper slid her arm around Ember's waist and hugged her, careful not to press her bump. "But that's enough about my love life – or lack of it. We need to concentrate on buying things for this baby. You only have a month before he or she arrives."

"Do you want to go grab a drink?" Rich asked James as the two of them stood at their lockers. "Maybe get a bite to eat. It's been a while since we had a night out."

James reached into his locker and grabbed his bag, slinging it over his shoulder. His hair was glistening from the shower he'd just taken. He was more aware than ever of infection control now that Harper was working in his basement. Since they passed at least once a day the last thing he wanted was to bring any germs home and infect her and the baby. His skin felt raw from the scrubbing he'd given himself.

"I can't tonight. Maybe another time."

"This weekend? Ah, wait, I'm working on Saturday. How about Sunday?"

James shook his head. "Can't do. I'm on call. Let me check the schedule and get back to you."

"I guess it's just me, a bottle of red, and whatever lucky woman I swipe right on then." Rich grinned.

"Whatever floats your boat." James shook his head. "I need to head home. I'll catch you later."

"What's the hurry?" Rich asked. "You'd rather go home to an empty house than have a drink with me?"

James didn't tell him the house wasn't exactly empty. At least it wasn't when he arrived home. Harper was usually finishing up in the basement or waiting for him in the hallway when he finished a day shift, and he was beginning to get used to it. More than that, he was enjoying it.

When he pulled his car onto his blacktop driveway, he could see Harper's Toyota parked in front of the steps, and he felt his body warm from his toes to his head. For three years he'd hated coming home. Hated the reminders that hit him every time he stepped into the hallway and heard the empty echoes of his footfalls. But now he could hear the whirr of Harper's sewing machine, or the sound of her humming as she walked up the basement stairs. Even the house smelled different now that she was here. Sweet and full of life. He wanted to capture it in a bottle and keep it safe, in case she stopped coming.

He climbed out of his car, shaking his head at himself. Of course she'd stop coming here. She'd told him herself that she'd saved enough money for her own place, and was actively looking for somewhere that could fit her, the baby, and her business.

He was still frowning when he opened the front door and walked inside. There was no sign of Harper, no clicking and whirring coming from the basement. "Hello?" he called out.

Panic hit him like a sledgehammer, taking him straight back to the day when he'd walked into a quiet house to find the police and his father waiting for him.

There was no reply. He took a deep breath in to stave off the rising fear, then pushed the basement door open. "Harper?" he called louder this time.

"James?"

The relief that washed over him was as strong as the panic. He ran down the stairs, his feet slapping out a fast rhythm, then into the main room, searching her out.

She was sitting on the old sofa in the corner, a pair of headphones wrapped around her swollen stomach. She was blinking, her cheeks pink with sleep. "Hey," she said, smiling. "Is it that time already?"

He smiled back at her, still drunk with relief. "It's almost six." He glanced at her belly again. "What are you doing with those headphones?"

Harper laughed self-consciously. "I've been playing Mozart to the baby. I read somewhere that she can hear sounds now, and I figure it's never too early to shape her musical tastes."

"I took you for more of a rock chick."

"I am, but I don't want to burst those tiny eardrums. I like classical, too, and I'm hoping this kid is going to become a genius like her daddy."

A shot of warmth rushed through him. He walked over to where she was laying and scooted down beside her, gently pulling the earphones from her bump. "I'm hoping she'll turn out more like you."

"You're admitting she's a girl then?" she looked at him through her thick lashes. Her skin still creased with sleep.

"I'm just humoring you until the ultrasound. That's if you still want to find out."

"I do." She moved her hands down to her bump, caressing it softly. He was so close he could smell the sweet fragrance of her body lotion. He swallowed hard, trying to ignore the urge to touch her. He'd been doing so well, keeping a level of distance between them since that day his mom had visited her. Pushing down the need to be close to her, to touch her, to breathe her in.

"You can touch it, you know," Harper said softly, as though she could read his mind. He glanced over at her, and their gazes caught. "I don't mind you feeling the bump. Maybe she'll like it."

He swallowed hard as she pulled her top up to reveal the pale swell of her stomach. Desire pulsed in him, making his hot blood pool in his groin, as he reached out a hand and placed it gently on the side of her stomach.

God, she was warm. Her skin tender and smooth. He moved his fingers, tracing along her flesh, and he heard her breath catch.

"I'm getting stretch marks," she whispered. "They're ugly."

"No they're not. They're beautiful."

The urge to press his lips against her was like a drum in his head, beating out a rhythm he had to fight to ignore. He wanted to slide his hands up, to feel her waist, her breasts, then cup her face until it was angled perfectly to his.

"You should say something to her," Harper suggested. "Get her used to your voice."

It was as though he was in some kind of trance. He lowered his head until his lips were only a breath away from her skin, and she let out a long, deep sigh. He licked his lips, trying to think of what to say.

Then Harper's hand was on his head, her fingers weaving

into his hair, and it felt amazing. How he missed this, this feeling of skin on skin. Of a connection with another human being.

"Hey," he breathed out, his lips an inch from her skin. "Hello, little baby, this is your daddy."

Harper's stomach moved as she took in a lungful of air.

"You stay safe in there," he whispered. "Your mommy's taking good care of you right now. And when you're ready to come out, I'll be here to look after you, too."

He slid his hand up, his fingers caressing her skin, and Harper let out a sigh. It went straight to his groin, making him ache for her. Shit, this was so messed up.

He let out another breath, the warm air caressing her, and Harper sighed again. This time her stomach moved, until his lips were less than a half an inch from her stomach.

He closed the gap.

He slid his lips along her stomach, closing his eyes to breathe her in. Her back arched as he reached the peak of her, then kissed the dip below her breasts.

"James," she whispered, low and deep. When he looked at her, her eyes were on fire. Her lips were parted, her breath coming in short pants, and her back arching into his touch.

He slid his hand up until his fingers feathered against her breasts, cupping them. Feeling their weight, their swell.

"For god's sake, kiss me." She grabbed his free hand and placed his palm against her lips.

"You're beautiful," he whispered, running his thumb across her bottom lip. He loved the way her breath caught in her throat. Christ, he wanted her; wanted to feel every inch of her body against his. Wanted to devour her in the same way she was consuming him.

She curled her fingers around the back of his neck, urging him toward her. He gave in willingly, moving until his head was over hers. She was staring up at him, blinking like he was the sun.

Slowly he lowered his head until the tip of his nose skimmed hers. They were so close he could feel the heat radiating from her skin. He let his lips brush against hers and she gasped again, until he deepened the kiss and swallowed every moan.

It was as though somebody had lit the fuse. Electricity sparked between them as they kissed, their lips moving quickly, their tongues caressing, his hands holding her so close he could feel her against him everywhere.

She looped her arms around his neck, moving closer still. Her breasts pressed against his chest and her thighs fell open, as she tugged him closer.

He braced himself against the cushions, not wanting to put any weight on her, and kissed her again, loving the feel of her soft lips, her warm mouth, and her demanding fingers digging deep into his flesh.

With a moan that vibrated against his lips, she hooked her legs around his hips, her heels digging into the back of his upper thighs. An exquisite shiver racked down his spine as he felt his groin pressing against hers. Christ, he was turned on.

She was panting against his lips, her tiny moans warmed him down to his toes. "James," she whispered, rolling her hips until he was pressing against her again, moaning softly as her thighs tightened against his body. "I'm going crazy," she told him. "You're driving me... oh... you're..."

He dipped his head, sliding his lips along her jaw, then down her neck. She shivered beneath him, her hips still rolling, and it took every atom of restraint he had not to grind himself against her.

He kissed her again and she caught his bottom lip between her teeth, dragging them against his soft flesh. Her fingers dug into his back as she moved against him, her cries becoming higher, longer, as her muscles tightened all over.

He loved how close she was. How she responded to him. His focus was her pleasure, her need, and his desperate desire to sate it.

"James," she cried out.

"I'm here. I've got you."

"I can't stop, I can't... ah..." Her words dissolved into the air, replaced by a long, drawn out moan as her thighs clamped around him. He watched as her head fell back, her skin flushed with pleasure, and her eyes closed as her body convulsed beneath him.

Damn, she was beautiful when she came. Watching her let go was like looking at a piece of art – nature's masterpiece. He held her tightly as she rode the wave, his eyes drinking in her pleasure as she slowly came down.

It took a minute for her breath to regain its normal rhythm. Her back arched slowly as she sunk into the cushions, her body loose and warm beneath him. He swallowed hard. Her eyes opened, widening as she took him in.

"Oh god," she said. "I'm so sorry. I didn't mean to do this." Her brow dipped as she scrambled beneath him. He pulled back, releasing his hold on the cushions, as his feet slipped to the floor.

She stood and ran her hand through her hair, though it was a futile gesture. It was a tangled mess; in the end she twisted it over her shoulder.

"Are you okay?" he asked her, unsure what to say.

She could barely meet his gaze. "I should go," she said, pulling her top down to cover her stomach. "It's late and I need to feed this monster."

"Harper..."

"It's okay. You don't need to say anything. I'm sorry I took advantage of you." She grabbed her shoes next to the sofa, pulling them onto her feet. "Thank you for talking to the baby, and for... ah... yeah. I'll speak to you soon, okay?"

With that, she was hurrying up the stairs. He watched, bemused, as she disappeared from view. A moment later he heard the slam of the front door.

It was only as he went to leave the basement that he noticed something on the sewing table. Harper had forgotten her phone.

He shook his head with a grin. She was going to miss that thing pretty damn soon.

❧ 14 ❧

What the hell had she just done? Harper slid her key into the ignition and started up the engine, trying to ignore the way her heart was hammering against her chest. Regret and embarrassment mixed with the lingering pleasure she still felt from James's body against hers. As she pulled out of his driveway, the cocktail of emotions made her muscles ache and her skin heat up.

It took ten minutes to drive from James's house to the exclusive block of condos where Caitie and Breck lived, but it was nowhere near long enough to sort through the maelstrom of thoughts rushing through her mind.

Thankfully, Caitie and Breck were out when she let herself into the condo. She headed straight for her bedroom – now light and breezy thanks to the lack of clothes and rolls of fabric blocking the window. Dropping her bag onto the floor she slumped onto her bed, the mattress dipping beneath her.

"Well," she whispered, rubbing her stomach with her palm. "I've made another mess, little one. Once again with your daddy. You'd think I'd have learned better by now."

Their first encounter had led to being knocked up. Their second to her feeling and acting crazy.

"It's kind of your fault," she told her stomach. "If it wasn't for all these hormones I wouldn't have jumped him as soon as he walked through the door."

She'd been a woman possessed; desperate, needy, and so ready to feel a body against hers.

And boy had it felt good. More than good. Delicious. But then shame had washed over her as she came out of the delicious haze, and she'd realized exactly what she'd done.

Used him for her pleasure. She'd taken without giving, and he'd let her.

And then she'd run away. She covered her face with her hands and groaned. She could still picture him standing in that basement, watching her run away, a confused expression on his face.

How was she going to face him tomorrow? She could barely face herself.

"It's okay," she told her bump. "We can just run away to Paris. Change our names, pretend we're some kind of European royalty. Your daddy will never find us."

A tiny gas bubble popped in her belly. *Seriously?* Now she was dealing with gas, too? There it was again, a little harder this time.

But more of a nudge than a pop.

A nudge! She sat straight up and stared down at her stomach. "Baby?" she said, rubbing her stomach. "Is that you?" She waited for a moment. "If it was you, do it again." Laying back down, she crossed her fingers and waited. Sure enough, a minute later, there was another push on the inside of her.

She ran her hand down her abdomen, cupping her stomach. "Hey, little one," she crooned. "It's so amazing to meet you. Are you feeling happy in there?"

Another tiny movement. Pure happiness washed over her.

"You stay safe in there," she said. She swallowed hard, remembering that James said the same thing. Before she'd wrapped her legs around him and used him as a scratching post. "And if you could dial down on the hormones a little, that would be good, too," she continued. "Not all of them. Just the ones that make me crazy whenever I look at your dad. I'm trying to be a grown up here, but you're making it really hard."

Hard. That made her think of James, too.

"I figure we'll be better parents if we don't mess things up between us. Sex always confuses things, look at my mom. She trailed around after guys like a bitch in heat, forgetting I ever existed. I don't want that for you, baby. I want you to be number one in both our lives." She sighed. "You deserve everything, and I plan on giving it to you."

She closed her eyes and breathed in again, letting her body relax for the first time since she'd left James's house. She had to be stronger, that was all. There was no need to repeat history and all of her mom's mistakes. She was better than that.

"You're making me tired." Maybe she should get used to the baby being in control. It was going to be her life for the next twenty years. So she gave into the grogginess, letting her breaths even out until they were a slow, steady rhythm. Within minutes she was at the cusp of deep, lovely sleep.

"Harper?" A voice called out, reaching her through her slumber.

She sat up, her heart racing. Without thinking, she reached down to shield her bump.

"Are you here?" Caitie called out. The next minute she was pushing the bedroom door open. "Oh thank god." She put her hand to her chest, taking in a deep breath. "I tried to call you but it kept going to voicemail. I was panicking there was something wrong."

Harper frowned and opened her purse, but there was no phone in there. "Maybe I left it in the car," she said, trying to remember the last time she'd seen it. Everything after leaving James's house felt like a blur.

"But you're okay? I was only calling to let you know we're heading out for dinner. Breck's home early and so we thought we'd grab some sushi." She grimaced. "I'd ask you to come but..."

Harper lifted her hands up. "Hey, I'm all good here. No raw seafood and no public displays of affection to worry about."

Caitie grinned, knowing she was teasing. Harper never cared about PDAs. She'd walked in on them after the first time they'd made love, after all, and managed to carry on a long conversation with Breck without blinking an eye.

"Are you sure you're okay?" Caitie asked, sitting on the end of the bed. "It's not like you to nap in the evenings. You should slow down..."

"I know, I know." Harper nodded. "And yeah, everything's fine. More than fine." She grinned. "I felt the baby move for the first time."

"You did?" Caitie's mouth dropped open. "That's amazing. Can I feel it, too?"

"There's nothing to feel at the moment; hopefully in a couple more weeks." Harper warmed at her friend's excitement.

"It's getting so real." Caitie smiled at her. "Only a few more months and we'll get to meet him or her. Did you tell James about the kicks?"

"No. It happened once I was home, and I clearly have no idea where my phone is."

"Let me find it for you before I head back out. Where do you think you left it?"

"Probably in my car. But I can look." Harper swung her legs off the bed and stood up, stretching her arms out to release the kinks in her muscles. "You go back to Breck. I cause enough problems for the two of you, I don't want to make any more."

"You don't cause problems. We love you being here." The two of them walked into the hallway and Harper grabbed her car keys from the table. "Breck wants you to stay here after you give birth. He's worried about you being on your own with the baby."

"Scared I might drop her?" Harper teased.

"No. I think he's scared he might not get enough baby cuddles." Caitie shook her head and opened the door. "I swear he's getting broodier with every day that passes. Oh!"

Her exclamation got Harper's attention. She looked over at the front door to see the cause, her skin heating up as she met his gaze.

James. Standing in the doorway with her phone in his hand.

"Hey," Caitie said, her voice warm. "How are you doing?"

"I'm good." He grinned, then looked at Harper. "I brought your phone over. You left it at my place."

"I'll leave you to it." Caitie blew Harper a kiss then gave James a peck on the cheek, before heading out into the main hallway. "See you later, guys."

Her footsteps echoed down the hallway. Harper sucked some air through her lips as she waited for the main building door to bang. James was leaning against the doorjamb, his eyes on her, a smile playing at his lips. Why the heck was he looking so relaxed?

"Thanks for bringing it over," she finally said, ignoring the way her heart sped up as soon as he stepped inside. Did he *have* to look that good? As he passed her the phone, she could smell the low notes of his cologne, and her muscles tensed.

"I figured you might need it," he said, stopping next to her. "And I thought it might be good to have a talk. Clear the air."

Her stomach growled, as though it agreed with every word. She laughed and shook her head. "Sorry about that. I skipped dinner in favor of a nap."

"Let me make you something."

She tipped her head. "Can you cook?"

"Passably. I'm a guy living on my own. It's either that or starve."

She shrugged and led him into the kitchen. "I've no idea what's in the refrigerator," she warned him. "I went to the grocery store on Sunday but I got distracted by the chocolate. The rest is a haze."

He laughed and pulled the refrigerator door open, making the light flicker on. She could see the dimple in his jaw tick as he took in the contents. "You have eggs," he said, pulling the carton out. "And some herbs and cheese. I'll make us omelets."

"I'll grab the pan," she said, scooting down and pulling it out of the cupboard. He took it from her and placed it on the stove top.

"Take a seat," he suggested.

"You sure I can't help?"

"I'm pretty confident I can handle an omelet, Harper. But you can help by showing me where everything is."

A minute later, they were both silent as he broke the eggs into a large glass bowl and whipped them with a fork until they were creamy. He poured a spoonful of oil into the pan, then poured the eggs in, swishing them around until they were clinging to the bottom of the pan.

He pulled the grater out of the utensil drawer and slid the

cheese against it, tiny strings raining down into the bowl. Even after the craziness of today, Harper couldn't help but smile as she watched him work. He was so damn capable.

It was making her hot, again.

"I don't think a guy's ever cooked for me before," she told him. "Most of my exes only knew how to order takeout."

"Maybe that's the different between boys and men." He shrugged. "Nutrition is important. Takeout is okay once in a while, but if it's your main source of food then eventually you're going to get sick."

"Do you cook for yourself every night?" She placed her chin on her palm, her eyes still following his every move.

"Mostly. It's pretty easy when I'm on days. I have my groceries delivered so I have a choice of what to eat. When I'm on night shift I try to at least cook breakfast before I head for bed." He glanced at her. "Where are the plates?"

She pointed at the cupboard hanging over the counter and he reached up to take two out. His t-shirt lifted with the movement, and she swallowed hard.

It was impossible not to remember the delicious weight of him as he held himself over her on his sofa, their bodies pressed together. And those lips, those teasing lips. She wanted to feel them all over her again.

"Can you tuck your t-shirt in?" she asked him, pulling her eyes away, determined not to let the hormones win this time.

He grinned and tucked the fabric into his waistband, as though he knew exactly the effect he was having on her.

"And maybe next time you can wear some looser jeans," she suggested, on a roll now. "The kind that don't hug your butt and thighs like they want to be your best friend."

James laughed. "You want me to wear baggy clothes?"

"Only when you're around me." Harper traced a vein in the marble worktop. "It's for your own protection. From my crazy hormones. You don't want a repeat of today."

"Don't I?"

She looked up, her eyes catching his. He held her gaze as he sprinkled the cheese onto the omelet, expertly folding it before sliding it onto the plate. Grabbing a knife and fork from the drawer, he slid the plate over to her. "Eat," he said, nodding at the food.

She speared a forkful and slid it between her lips, tasting the seasoned eggs and oozing cheese as they lingered on her tongue. "Dear god, is there nothing you can't do?" she asked him between mouthfuls. "Saving lives, cooking. I bet next you'll tell me you can do your own laundry, too."

"What kind of guys have you been hanging out with?" he asked, a smile curling his lips as he cracked more eggs for himself.

"The wrong ones clearly," she mumbled after another mouthful. "Actors, mostly."

"Ones who can't cook?" He shook his head. "It's not rocket science. I'm thirty-four-years-old, Harper. If I couldn't cook or do laundry there'd be something wrong with me. Sounds like maybe you set your bars too low."

"Story of my life." She shrugged. "If you don't have expectations you don't get disappointed."

"But you also sell yourself short. Don't you think you deserve the good things in life?"

She swallowed the last mouthful of omelet and put her silverware on the plate with a clang. "That was delicious, thank you." She stood to grab herself a drink, but he was already in motion, grabbing her a glass.

"What can I get you?"

"How did you know I wanted a drink?"

"You've just eaten. It's kind of normal to want a drink."

That made sense. "Water, please. The tap will do."

He filled the glass and passed it to her, taking her empty plate and rinsing it before placing it in the dishwasher.

"You're kind of an enigma," he said, turning back to the pan. "You know that?"

"I am?" She blinked.

"Yeah. The first time I met you there was this innate confidence about you. You walked across the room like you owned it; everybody turned and stared at you, everybody wanted to be the one to buy you a drink. I've noticed it a few times. You have this presence." He slid the second omelet on his plate and carried it to where she was perched on the stool. "But then you have this other side to you. You're so uncertain about yourself. About other people. It's like a chink in your armor."

"It's a combination of an expensive education and a lonely childhood," she told him, shocked how accurate his description was. "When you're brought up with money there are expectations on you. You have to dress a certain way, talk a certain way, even your walk has to meet those expectations. I can remember my grandma shouting at me for slouching, telling me to stand up straight. I soon learned the way to avoid getting shouted at was to do exactly what was required of me."

His eyes were soft as he gazed at her. "Sounds tough."

She laughed but there was no humor in it. "Not really. It's the same old story, poor little rich girl. I wasn't any different than all the other students at school. We knew we'd grow up to become the kind of women our parents wanted us to be. Beautiful, compliant, and completely messed up."

"You don't seem that messed up to me." He speared a piece of omelet with his fork.

"Maybe I hide it well." She pulled her lip between her teeth. "Hey, I'm not giving you ammunition for a custody battle, am I?"

"I'd never take our baby away from you."

"You're a good man," she told him. "Maybe one of the

nicest guys I've met. If the condom had to fail with anybody, I'm glad it was you."

He coughed out a laugh. "Is that a compliment?"

She couldn't help but grin. As hard as it was to think back to her childhood, to the sheer loneliness of it all, she wasn't there anymore. She was here, in Angel Sands, talking to the father of her child.

A good man who just made her food; that alone made him a god.

"About what happened earlier," she said, taking a deep breath to steady herself. "It shouldn't have. I'm sorry. I was kind of kidding when I blamed it on my hormones, because I know I have more control than that. It was my fault for pulling you on top of me, for begging you to kiss me. And then to run out like a child, refusing to talk about it." She covered her face with her hands. "How embarrassing."

He put his silverware down and peeled her hands away from her face, leaning in close to her. "Don't be embarrassed. And it wasn't all one sided. Did you see me complaining?" He folded her hands in his. She loved how strong they were, how warm and big. As though he could do anything, solve anything.

"No."

"And did you feel how much I was... ah... *enjoying* it?"

There was no guile in his face. Just an honesty that cut her in two. "I felt it," she whispered.

"You're a beautiful woman, Harper. You look good, you smell good, and you have this way of entrancing everybody you meet. What man in his right mind would turn you down?" He ran the tips of his fingers along her cheekbone.

She closed her eyes, feeling the spark once more. She'd never felt a need this strong, never felt this attracted to somebody. And yeah, she could blame the hormones, but it was more than that.

It was him. She'd known it from the first moment they met. Before the baby, before the hormones. She wasn't attracted to him because of added chemicals flowing through her body, or because of the fact he'd cooked her dinner. It was more, so much more, and she had no idea what to do with that.

It wasn't compatible with becoming the kind of mother she wanted to be. This need for him threatened to engulf everything, and she couldn't let that happen.

"I like taking care of you," James said, his voice low. "Whether that means providing space for your business, cooking you dinner, or..." He picked up their plates and carried them over to the dishwasher. "Meeting your other needs, then I'm here for that."

She was silent as he cleaned up the kitchen, before he walked over to her, cupping her face in his palm. She felt dazed, her eyes widening as he leaned closer to brush his lips gently across hers. "I'm going to head home now," he whispered against her mouth. "You get some rest, okay? And I'll see you tomorrow after work."

She nodded, and he cupped her jaw in his palm, deepening the kiss until it left her breathless. Then he turned and walked away. "I'll see myself out," he called, leaving her staring breathlessly after him, wondering what the heck just happened. *Again.*

15

"Should we agree on a safe word?" James asked her as he lifted his hand to ring the bell.

"A safe word?" she asked him, a half-frown curling her lips. "Why would we need that?"

"In case my parents overwhelm you and you want me to get you out of here; you say the word and we're gone."

The frown dissolved away. "They can't be *that* bad. You said yourself you got along well with your parents."

"Yeah, well let's say they're excited to meet you. Again." He raised an eyebrow. "They've called five times this morning asking me whether you can eat rare steaks and if you prefer ice tea or soda. I'm just warning you things could get scary in there."

"That's sweet," Harper said, her eyes softening. "I like your mom already."

"On your own head be it." He pressed the bell.

She reached down to rub her stomach, smiling when she felt another kick. She was getting used to them now. At twenty weeks her belly was perfectly round, like somebody had stuffed a basketball up her dress and tied it around her waist.

"Is the baby moving?" James asked her.

"Yeah." She grabbed his hand and placed it on the left side of her stomach, the place the baby seemed to like to kick the most. She'd been doing this for three weeks now, trying to get him to feel the kicks the way she felt them, but every time he'd missed them.

"I can't—" He stopped talking and held his breath. "That was it, wasn't it?" A grin slowly broke out on his face. "Was that a kick?" His voice was low and breathless. Her heart skipped a beat as he leaned close enough that she could smell his cologne.

"Yep." She loved the way he looked. His eyes were alight, his face relaxed, and everything about him radiated warmth. She felt warm herself, the way she always did whenever he was near. Though she'd managed to stop herself from making any more stupid decisions over the past few weeks, there had been a few close calls.

And yeah, those hormones weren't going away.

"James, Harper, come on in." Louise Tanner opened the door and hugged them both. Harper tried not to look shocked at the intimate gesture. "It's so wonderful to meet you again," his mom told her. "I'm just sorry it's been so long."

"That was my bad. I was on call the last two weekends. Greg had to take some emergency leave." James shrugged. "But we're here now."

"Yes you are. And we're so happy to have you both here." His mom grabbed Harper's hand and led her down the hallway. "How are you feeling?" she asked her. "What are you now, twenty weeks?"

"That's right. I'm feeling good," Harper said as they walked into the oversized kitchen. It was filled with light that bounced off the whitewashed walls and the polished wooden floor. Everything looked new, from the granite counters to the gleaming appliances she could see herself reflected in.

It was hard not to get kitchen envy.

"Can I get you a drink?" his mom asked. "We have iced tea or soda?"

From the corner of her eye Harper could see James biting down a grin. She swallowed her own laugh and nodded. "I'd love an iced tea please, Mrs. Tanner."

"Call me Louise, please," his mom told her. "And here comes Dennis; Darling, Harper and James are here."

"They are? Why didn't you tell me?" James's dad walked in and gave his son a huge bear hug. He looked like an older version of James, with the same muscled frame and broad shoulders. But unlike James his hair was fair.

Then he turned to Harper and held out his hand. She shook it with relief, unsure if she could have withstood one of those bear hugs. "It's nice to meet you," he said. "James has told us a lot about you." He gestured at the kitchen stools to her left. "Take a seat, you need to conserve your energy."

"I'm only twenty weeks pregnant, there's plenty of time for that."

"While you're at our house, it's always time for you to relax," Louise told her, passing her a glass of iced tea. "That's the rule."

She was beginning to see where James got his kindness.

"So tell me about yourself, dear?" Louise said, taking the stool next to her. "How did you and James meet?"

Harper took a sip of tea and tried not to catch James's gaze, afraid she'd laugh. "Um, we met at the opening of the Silver Sands Resort."

"Oh, I heard that was a fabulous party. And you live in Angel Sands with Caitie Russell, is that right? Did you know her mom is one of my best friends?"

"Everybody in Angel Sands is one of your best friends, Mom," James teased. He leaned on the counter, his body close to Harper's. His hand rested on her shoulder as though he was protecting her. "We had an ultrasound on Wednesday," he said, changing the subject. "I've got a photo somewhere." He pulled his wallet from his pocket and took the black and white print out.

"Oh my goodness," Louise said, putting her hand on her chest as she stared at the printout. "What a beautiful baby." She blinked, lifting her hand to wipe a tear away. "Did everything go well?"

"It was fine, Mom," James said gently. "She's absolutely fine."

"*She?*" Louise asked, her brows knitting together.

"We're having a little girl." James grinned and winked at Harper. He'd lost their bet and had to buy her a blueberry muffin to make up for it.

Louise covered her mouth with her hand and squeezed her eyes shut. "I'm sorry," she said, shaking her head. Tears leaked from her tightly closed eyes. "I said I wouldn't get emotional. I promised your father."

Dennis wrapped her in his arms and pressed her face against his chest, running his hands through her hair. He whispered into her ear, though Harper couldn't make out what he was saying. She looked over at James who swallowed hard. Were those tears in his own eyes, too? He shook his head and gave her a wry smile.

"I'm okay," Louise said, wiping her eyes as she pulled away from her husband's embrace. "Harper, please forgive me. I didn't expect to react like that."

"It's fine," Harper told her. "And completely understandable. You've been through a lot, all of you. And this must all have come as a shock."

"A wonderful, happy shock," Louise said, picking the

picture up again. "What a beautiful little girl she is."

James grinned. "We almost didn't find out. She spent most of the time refusing to let us see."

"She's as stubborn as her father," Louise said, ruffling James's hair.

"Hey, Harper's stubborn, too."

"Don't be rude." Louise raised her eyebrows. "Harper's our guest." She passed the photo to her husband who stared at it with warm eyes. "Isn't she a beautiful baby, Dennis?"

"Yep. Must take after me." He winked at Harper.

James took the photo from his dad and slipped it back into his wallet. "Lets hope the baby takes after Harper," he said wryly. "Otherwise the poor kid is already out of luck."

Harper couldn't help but smile. The love his parents had for James was palpable. It was in the way they talked to him, smiled at him, teased him. It made her heart ache for what she didn't have.

But maybe this baby could have it; a family who loved her unconditionally. Wouldn't that be a blessing? She cupped her stomach protectively and watched as James laughed at something his father said.

If she had to choose a father for this child, she'd choose James every time. And wasn't that a blessing?

———

"James?" his mom called out as he and Harper were walking down the front steps toward his car. It was early evening, though you wouldn't know it from the warmth of the air surrounding them. The sweater Harper had brought with her was still on the backseat of his car where she'd left it when he'd picked her up.

"You go get in the car," he suggested to Harper, passing her the keys. "I'll see what she wants."

"She probably wants to talk about me."

He chuckled. "Probably."

Harper continued down the stairs, her blonde-and-pink waves bouncing on her shoulders. He watched as she walked over to his car, clicking the button to open it. From behind, you wouldn't know she was pregnant. She still had those curves that had captivated him the first time he'd seen her. Generous hips, luscious behind, and legs that went on forever.

She pulled open the door and turned her head to look at him. When she noticed he was staring right at her, her brows dipped into a question. She shook her head and climbed inside, and he turned back to his mom who was waiting at the top of the steps.

"She's lovely," she said, a big smile on her face. "You should bring her over again."

"Maybe. It depends on my shifts, and Harper has work, too."

"I'll send you some dates." She pulled her lip between her teeth, as though she was hesitating. "I wanted to ask you something else. I know it's none of my business but it's been bugging me all day."

He could feel the alarm bells warming up. "What?"

"Are you two a couple? I know you told me you weren't, but I saw the way you were looking at her." She smiled softly. "It reminded me of how you used to look at Sara."

The mention of Sara's name felt like a bucket of cold water being poured over him. He frowned, realizing he'd barely thought about her and Jacob all day. He could feel the familiar tightness in his chest as they seeped back into his consciousness.

"We're not a couple," he managed, trying to ignore the ache.

His mom nodded. "I guess I was just hoping." She ruffled

his hair, her eyes reflecting his pain. "But if you feel something for her, that's okay, too. Sara wouldn't have wanted you to mourn her forever. You deserve happiness, James, and to have somebody to take care of you. I've hated watching you be so lonely for all these years."

"None of us know what Sara would have wanted," he said, his voice low. "And she's not around to ask anymore."

"I didn't mean..."

"I know." He put up his hand. "But this stuff isn't helping. It's hard enough trying to figure out how we're going to co-parent this baby without people making assumptions and gossiping and pushing us toward each other. I like Harper. She's a friend and the mom of my child. But that's all we are."

"Okay," she said softly. "I'm sorry for asking. I guess I was just hoping for the happily-ever-after."

"I think we both know they don't exist." Not for him, at least. He tried to push down the anger his mom's line of questioning was stirring up. "I should go. Harper's waiting and she needs to get home."

"Of course." His mom leaned forward and hugged him. His body was stiff as she slowly stepped back and gave him a sad smile. "I love you, sweetheart."

"Love you, too."

As he ran down the steps he could feel the warmth of her scrutiny on his back. No doubt she'd spend the evening fretting about him, the way she had done for years. Even though it did none of them any good. He wished they'd all stop, and treat him like they used to. A man who had his life under control; one who knew where he was going and when he was going to get there.

But that man had disappeared the day he'd lost his wife and son. Right now he wasn't sure how to get him back.

James had been silent since they'd left his parents' house. Harper wasn't sure what his mom had said to him, but whatever it was clearly played on his mind as he drove her back to Caitie and Breck's apartment. His jaw was tight, his eyes fixed on the road ahead, and she found herself rubbing her stomach awkwardly.

"Your parents are lovely," she finally said. "It was so kind of them to invite me over."

"Yeah. They're good people." He cleared his throat, his eyes trained on the road ahead.

More silence. She pulled her lip between her teeth as the car turned left onto Main Street, past Megassey's Hardware Store and the bookshop. Everything was closed up on this Sunday evening, but there were still a few people walking back from a day at the beach, carrying towels and coolers, umbrellas and sleeping children.

"What kind of parents were they when you were growing up?" she asked him when he pulled to a stop light.

"Huh?" He turned to look at her, blinking as though he was surprised she was there. "Did you say something?"

"It's okay." She shook her head. "I was just making conversation."

He ran his hand through his hair, then placed it back on the wheel, accelerating as the light turned green. "I'm sorry, I'm a little distracted. Ask me again."

"I was only asking what kind of parents they were. Were they strict? Laid back? Did they used to ground you a lot?"

"It's hard to remember." The ghost of a smile played at his lips. "I guess they were somewhere in between. They let me do what I wanted unless I hurt myself or somebody else. And they were fanatical about me making good grades. I can remember being grounded homecoming weekend because I'd got a 'D' on an English paper." Furrows crisscrossed his brow. "But even when they punished me I knew it was coming from a place of love. Because they wanted the best for me." He glanced at her from the corner of his eye. "How about you?"

"Me?"

"You've said your grandma had a lot of expectations. Was she strict about those?"

Harper swallowed. "Um, yeah, pretty strict. I went to an all-girls prep school, and I wasn't allowed to have boyfriends or wear makeup. The only time I really talked to boys was when we were visiting her friends who had children or grand-children my age. So when I went to college I went pretty crazy."

His smile widened, and it warmed her. "I think a lot of people go crazy when they go to college."

"Oh yeah? Were you the med school stud?"

He laughed. "Not really. I had a few relationships and then I met Sara. After that we were a couple until she died."

"How long were you together?"

"Eleven years."

"Oh." Her heart ached for him. She wanted to reach out, comfort him, do something to make it all better.

Instead, here she was causing more complications than he ever knew possible.

"Did you tell your grandma or your mom about the baby yet?" he asked.

"Nope. I'm still waiting for the right time."

"When will that be?" They'd reached the condos. He pulled into a visitor's parking space and cut the engine.

"I'm thinking when this kid reaches twenty-one." She rubbed her stomach.

He turned to look at her, tipping his head to the side. "What's the worst that could happen?"

"When you put it like that, nothing. They can't do anything that's going to stop this baby from coming. And my grandma's long since given up trying to make me come home." She let out a sigh. "But it's not just physical things that can hurt people. Words can cut, criticism can bruise. I spent a lifetime cowering away from feeling the pain of her disapproval. I don't really want to go back to that feeling." She glanced down at her bump. "And I don't want this little one to ever feel that way."

"Then don't tell her."

"That doesn't seem right either. I'm not ashamed of this baby, or of myself. And if I try to hide things from her, that's how it feels."

"Have you thought about writing a letter?" he asked. "That way you've let her know but you don't have to worry about her response; you can just let it go."

"I hadn't thought about that, but it's a good idea. I could maybe send a copy of the ultrasound, too. If she wants to reply, she can, but at least I don't have to hear some cutting response through the phone." She smiled at him. "Thank you."

His eyes met hers. "You're welcome. Are you working at mine tomorrow?"

"Yeah. I've had another batch of orders come in. It's time to start looking at some apartments, too, when I get a chance to research." She reached for the door knob. "Are you working?"

"No. I have a rest day. I'll probably sleep for some of it, and then I need to head out to meet a few people, so I won't be in your hair."

"I wouldn't mind you getting in my hair." She grinned. "I guess I'll see you tomorrow," she said, leaning across to kiss his cheek. She could feel the scrape of his beard growth on her lips. And there it was again, that shot of electricity. Her toes curled with the pleasure of it.

"See you tomorrow," he replied, his voice gruff.

Yeah. She was looking forward to it.

❦ 16 ❧

J ames pulled his car into the parking lot and looked
through the windshield. A wide expanse of verdant grass
dotted with pearlescent white headstones lay beyond
the black iron railings in front of his car. Tall cedar and oak
trees provided shade, their leafy branches stooping over the
graves. He grabbed the flowers he'd bought from the florist
down the road and climbed out of the car, heading for the
large double gates at the entrance of the cemetery.

It had been a while since he'd visited. Too long, probably.
But something had called to him today; a need to be here, in
the quiet of their final resting place, to feel the calm air
around him as he tried to sort through his thoughts.

He didn't sleep well last night. For most of the night he'd
tossed and turned, his brain too alert to submit to the weari-
ness of his body, his thoughts zapping him awake like paddles
to his heart.

In the end, he'd got up right after daybreak and ran for
miles along the coast, pushing himself to run faster, harder.
Anything to get those damn thoughts out of his head. For a
while a cormorant had kept pace with him, dipping and rising

in flight above the crashing waves as it flew parallel to him. The bird had gotten bored in the end, turning left to head out to the sea, leaving him alone once again.

His feet knew the route to their graves by heart. A few hundred yards up the path, left at the second tree, right at the mausoleum that interred the bodies of the Paxton family, the original founders of Angel Sands. And then there were the two gravestones, one bigger than the other, signaling the final resting place of all he'd once held dear.

He separated the bouquet he'd bought, sliding flowers into each of their vases, then poured in water he'd brought along with him. Placing the water bottle on the grass, he leaned forward to touch the cool marble with his son's name engraved on it.

Jacob was going to have a little sister. He tried to imagine his tiny little boy growing up, taking pride in being a big brother, teaching the younger children things he'd only recently learned himself. James pressed his lips together, his lungs tight as he tried to push those thoughts away. One day the baby in Harper's stomach would be older than Jacob was when he died – please god. She would learn to walk, to talk, to read and write in a way Jacob never had. He was a frozen moment in time, and it hurt to know he'd never experience those things.

"Sleep tight," James whispered, lifting his hand off the cool stone. "Daddy loves you."

Ignoring the sting in his eyes, he turned to Sara's grave. *Beloved wife of James. Adored mother of Jacob. Heaven gained another star today. May she always shine on.*

He blew out some air, but it didn't ease the ache in his chest. Scooting down once more, he reached his hand out, running his fingers over the inscription.

"I'm going to be a dad again, Sara," he said, his voice cracking. "In a few months I'll have a new baby. And I don't know how to do it without feeling like I'm forgetting everything we had. It's like I'm moving on, and with every step I take, you and Jacob feel further and further behind. I even went for hours without thinking about you yesterday. I laughed and ate and drank and did everything you can't, and then I hated myself for it."

He took a deep breath. "And then there's Harper. She's the mom of the baby. I think you'd like her if you met her. She's kind and funny and I know she's gonna make a kick-ass mother." He swallowed hard. "And I think I might have feelings for her, too."

He closed his eyes, a single tear sliding down his cheek. "I haven't felt this way in a long time. Like I've come back to life again. But the more alive I feel, the more I realize you're gone and are never coming back. I don't want you to hate me for feeling like this. I don't want you to think I'm going to forget you and Jacob. You'll always be with me. *Always*. He'll always be this baby's older brother."

He shook his head, his eyes still shut. "I'm afraid," he admitted. "I have no idea what to do. Sometimes I wish I could talk to you. You always gave such good advice."

A warm breeze ruffled his hair. He opened his eyes and lifted his hand to straighten it. A leaf had caught in his mussed hair and he plucked it out.

No, not a leaf. A feather. A white one, with soft downy barbs. He stared at it, his brows pinching together. "Sara?" he said, his voice a whisper.

Then he shook his head at himself. How many times had he looked for a sign from her? There were birds everywhere in this cemetery, the trees full of nests. It wasn't a sign, it was just the wind.

And yet holding that feather made his heart ache a little less. He inhaled deeply, the tightness in his chest gone. Maybe it wasn't a sign he needed, but to actually listen to his own heart for a change. To stop beating himself up and allow himself to live again.

"I'll bring the baby to meet you both once she's here," he said, biting down a smile because he was as bad as Harper with saying 'she'. "And maybe Harper, too, if she'll come."

Another breeze. This time it lifted the feather from his hold, causing it to dance in the wind before it slowly floated to the ground. He lifted his head, staring beyond the grassy lawns and the gleaming headstones, to the cliffs towering over the Pacific coast.

Three years ago he'd buried his heart here, along with the family he'd lost. Maybe now it was time to claim it back.

"What are these for?" his mom asked when James handed her the second bouquet he'd bought from the florist.

"I saw them and thought of you." He shrugged. "I wanted to say thank you for yesterday." His voice lowered. "And sorry for leaving the way I did."

"Would you like to come in?" she asked him. "I've just put some coffee on."

"No thank you," he said, glancing at his watch. "There are a couple more things I need to do before I head home, and I want to catch Harper before she leaves."

His mom's eyes lit up at the mention of Harper. It was impossible not to notice. He knew she'd made an impression on her, that she was beginning to hope for things she hadn't in a long time.

Maybe they both were. He could hardly blame her for thinking about the same things he was.

"As long as we're apologizing, I have one to make, too," she told him, hugging the bouquet to her chest. "I was out of line bringing up Harper and Sara. It's none of my business. I'm sorry I mentioned it."

"You were only saying it because you care." His mind drifted back to the conversation he'd had about his parents with Harper in the car. The gap between her upbringing and his felt so stark. No, she hadn't suffered physical abuse, but it was clear her childhood had left other, less visible scars. He was grateful his parents had shown him nothing but love. "I know the past few years haven't been easy for any of us."

Her expression softened. "It's *you* I worry about," she whispered. "Losing your family so young was a terrible thing. I know it's not something you ever get over, but my heart aches to see you so alone. This baby is the best thing that's happened to any of us for a long while, and whatever happens between you and Harper doesn't change that." She reached for his hand, squeezing it tightly. "You're my son. I'll never stop worrying about you. Or loving you, either."

The corner of his lip quirked up. "I like her."

His mom blinked. "Harper?"

"Yeah." He nodded. "But right now I have no idea where to go with that thought."

Her voice was soft. "Sometimes we just have to see where life takes us. Maybe it will go somewhere, maybe it will go nowhere, but the important thing is you're opening yourself up to it."

"It doesn't mean I didn't love Sara and Jacob."

"Oh honey, of course it doesn't. I know how much you love them. They knew it, too. But you have more than enough love to go around." Her eyes filled with tears. "I don't know what it's like to lose a child, but I do know how it feels to watch a child you love more than life itself go through the worst thing any person can experience. My heart broke in a million pieces for you. If I could I'd take it all away. The pain, the hurt, everything. But I can't." Her voice cracked.

He leaned forward and hugged her, trying not to squash the bouquet of flowers she was still holding to her chest. "Thanks, Mom," he said, his voice gruff.

When he released her, she was smiling through her tears. "Are you sure you don't want to come in?" she asked him.

"Not this time. I still have a few things to do. But let's get together again soon. Maybe I'll even bring Harper with me." He hugged her again, and headed down the steps, lifting his hand in goodbye.

"Thank you for the flowers," she called after him.

"It was my pleasure."

Harper was finishing up a dress when James returned to the house. She threaded the needle through the fabric to attach the embellishments, edging the little-girl version of the dress with a braided ribbon. She was concentrating hard, her brows pulled together in a deep-v, as she made sure the stitches were even and invisible to the naked eye.

"Hey."

James was at the bottom of the stairs, wearing jeans and a navy Henley, the sleeves pushed up to his elbow.

"Hi." She felt that familiar warmth flood her veins. His top was tight, enough for her to see the outlines of his muscles beneath. But it wasn't his body that got her attention, it was his face. "Is everything okay?" she asked him.

"Yeah, all good. Why?"

"I don't know. You just look different."

"Different how?" A half-smile curled his lips as he walked over to the sewing table.

She looked at him, trying to figure it out. "I can't put my finger on it. Maybe it's your eyes. They look lighter. Are you wearing contacts?"

He laughed. "No. But they sometimes look a different color depending on what I'm wearing. My mom used to call them chameleon eyes. It's probably the shirt I've got on. The darker the clothes the lighter they look."

"I believe you, doctor." She grinned and glanced down at her bump. "I wonder what color eyes this little one will have."

"Blue."

"How can you be so sure?"

"Most Caucasian babies are born with blue eyes. They don't change color until they're around a year old."

"What?" Her mouth dropped open. "How could I not have known that? I don't remember reading about that on the baby sites." She frowned. "God, there's so much I don't know. Like how to hold the baby without hurting it's neck, or how to change a diaper. I'm going to be the worst mom in the world."

"Harper..."

"Seriously, this poor kid got the short straw. I know nothing about babies. What idiot decided to let me loose with a child?"

"Harper," he said again, his voice soft. "It's okay. Why would you know that if you didn't need to?"

"You knew it."

"I worked on a maternity ward during my medical training. It's my job to know that kind of thing."

She could feel tears filling her eyes. "I'm going to mess this all up," she whispered. "I know it."

Gently, he took her hands in his, and pulled her up from the chair. She looked at him, blinking back the tears. Even through the haze she could see his beauty. He pulled her into his arms, his hands pressing against her back. God, he was warm. She nestled her face against his ridged chest and breathed him in.

"Parenting isn't about knowing everything," he said,

pressing his lips against her head. "It's about listening to your instincts, but also being willing to take advice when you need to." He slid his thumb under her chin, tipping her face up until their gazes met. "It's about talking and listening, and more than anything, it's about love. And I know you, Harper. You've got more than enough love for this baby."

He wiped the dampness from her cheeks, his eyes not leaving hers. "Do you know how beautiful you look right now?" His voice was low. Full of need. It made the muscles in her legs clench.

"No." Her smile was watery.

He traced his finger along her jaw, her cheek, and the bridge of her nose. Then he reached her mouth, slightly open with the wonder of him. Her bottom lip trembled as he slid his finger along it.

"Tell me what you want," he whispered, thick eyelashes sweeping down as he stared intently at her.

"I want you to touch me."

"I *am* touching you." He ran his finger along her top lip to prove it.

"More," she said, her voice catching in her throat. "I want more."

"More what?"

God, this man knew how to set her on fire. With his words, his gaze, his touch. It was as though her body was hollow before he came along, her mind waiting for his thoughts, her skin waiting for his touch.

It couldn't just be hormones. Hormones didn't make your heart swell inside your chest. They didn't make your throat feel tight because it was hard to breathe every time you looked at him. He wasn't just a scratch to itch anymore, he was so much more.

She ached for him.

"Harper."

"Kiss me, James."

This time, when their mouths met there was a softness, a sweetness that hadn't been there before. His kiss was gentle, almost lazy, as he took his time to savor her. His hand cupped her jaw, tilting her head to the right angle. She could feel his hot fingers splayed against her cheek, branding her, as he slid his tongue along the seam of her lips to deepen the kiss.

Her legs shook, and she had to grasp onto his arms to steady herself. His biceps flexed beneath her hands, reminding her how strong he was. It was easy to forget when he was so gentle. With his hand still cupping her face, he tilted it back, sliding his lips to her neck, kissing and sucking her throat until every cell in her body began to sing.

"You taste sweet," he murmured. "Like a damn fruit bowl."

"I've been bingeing on candy." She laughed, but the sound died in her mouth as he moved his hand down her throat, along her chest, to the aching swell of her breasts. When he brushed his fingers against the aching peaks of her nipples, she gasped.

"I love that sound," he told her, lifting his head to kiss her lips again. He rolled her nipple between his thumb and finger, making her moan. Swallowing her cries, he lifted her onto the sewing table, pushing away the scraps of fabric and spools of cotton that littered the surface. She hooked her thighs around his waist as he pressed himself against her, his thick ridge hard and demanding against her core. "Can you feel it?" he whispered. "How much I want you."

She nodded and he kissed her again, sliding his hands inside her shirt, his fingers feather-soft against her skin. Then he was unfastening her shirt, his movements deft, until it fell open to reveal her creamy abdomen. His eyes darkened as he traced the center of her stomach, rising up and then falling again to her breasts.

"Can I take this off?" he asked her, his fingers toying at the bottom of her bra.

"Do what you want," she whispered. "I'm yours."

His jaw tightened at her words, his chest pressing out as he took in a deep inhale. With practiced fingers, he unfastened her bra, pulling the straps down her arms until she was free, her nipples hardening as the air caressed them. He ran his palms over their peaks, then slid them down to cup the weight of her breasts. "Beautiful," he whispered, leaning forward to capture her nipple between his lips. Oh the sucking, the delightful pull of him. It made her cry out.

"Take your shirt off," she told him, tugging at the hem. He lifted his arms, allowing her to expose the hard ridges of his stomach, the thick steel of his pectorals, the skin peppered with hair.

The next moment his chest was pressed against hers, warm and taut and everything she needed. His mouth devoured hers. His sighs matched her own as she ran her fingers down the muscles of his back.

God, he was hard. She couldn't help but squirm against him. Loving how the pleasure shot down her thighs, her calves, sparking in the curl of her toes. Sliding her hands to the front of his jeans, she tugged at his belt. But he pulled her hands away. His eyes narrowed with desire, his hands pulling at her own jeans.

"You first," he said gruffly. "Then me."

It wasn't a command. More a matter of fact. But she liked the way he took the lead, making her feel like she was a piece of fragile china in his hands. He tugged at her jeans as she lifted up her behind, allowing the denim to slide down her legs.

He was kissing her again, his hands fumbling at his belt, as though he couldn't bear to release her and concentrate on what he was doing. As he took his jeans off, she hooked her hands over his shoulders, marveling at the taut warmth of his skin as it stretched across his muscles. Then they were naked, apart from their underwear, their bodies pressed together.

"You okay?" he asked as he stroked her face, moving his hands down until he captured her breasts once more. She closed her eyes, feeling the pleasure of his touch on her tender skin, her back arching at the sensation.

He slid his fingers down her stomach, then to her core. Just a brush of his fingers against her was enough to make her gasp, her thighs tightening around his hips as he pressed harder against her.

"James," she whispered, the desire for him coiling inside her. "Please...I need..."

"What do you need?"

"You. I need you."

"You've got me." He pulled her panties off, smoothing his hands over her bump, his eyes soft as he watched the rise and fall of her chest. She watched as he removed his shorts, dropping them on the floor. Then he was pressed against her again, hot and hard. "Should I get something?" he asked her.

"I'm clean," she told him. "And I'm pregnant, so I don't think you have to worry there."

His eyes crinkled. "I get tested every month for work." A half-smile pulled at his lips. "And there hasn't been anyone but you for a long time."

He hooked his hands around her thighs, pulling her forward until she was perched on the edge of the table. His hips aligned perfectly with hers, the thickness of him pressing against her before he slowly slid himself inside.

Her breath caught in her throat. She hooked her arms around his neck, pulling him down to kiss her once more as he filled her. As he created a rhythm between them that neither of them wanted to stop, her thighs quivered, the pleasure already building.

The first time they were together it had been sex. Pure, simple, and mind-blowing. The second time? He'd scratched a need she couldn't control any more.

But this time was different; it was *more*. It wasn't just about their bodies, or their hormones, or the need that filled her every time she looked at him. It was about the way he made her feel when he smiled at her. The way he touched her like she was something precious. The way his eyes never left hers until they were both gasping for breath.

It was more, because *he* was more. And now that she had him, she wasn't sure she'd ever want to let him go.

❧ 17 ❧

"She didn't believe a word I just told her," Harper said as she walked into his living room from the deck. Her phone was still in her hand although she'd ended her call.

James grinned as she sat on the sofa next to him and picked up the plate of Chinese takeout he'd ordered for her. She was wearing the Henley sweater he'd shucked off earlier, the hem skimming the middle of her thighs. Her blonde hair spilled over her shoulders, the pink tips a contrast to the darkness of the top.

"What did you tell her?"

"That I was tired and spending the night in your spare room." Harper shook her head. "She said, 'if you're sleeping in his spare room then I'm the Queen of England.' Then she asked me if we'd done it only one time or two."

"Did you tell her it was three?"

"No." Harper grinned. "I figure that's our secret. And anyway, we may be able to get through a few more before the night is out. You're insatiable, Doctor Tanner."

"You were the one doing the begging." He winked.

"Yeah, well that's because you're a tease. I'm pregnant. If I want something, I want it now." She reached out to trace his bicep. He'd put his jeans back on, but with Harper stealing his shirt that was all he was wearing. "And I want you pretty much all the time."

"Is that right?" His voice was husky. God, she did things to him he didn't know were possible. "You should eat your dinner first," he told her, ignoring the heat rushing through his legs. "You're eating for two after all."

She grabbed a pair of chopsticks from the coffee table and scooped some rice and chicken between them, expertly lifting them to her lips. She swallowed it down, her eyes closing with pleasure, and he tried to ignore the desire building inside of him.

"Aren't you going to eat?" she asked after she'd swallowed her mouthful.

"In a minute. Right now I'm enjoying watching you." It was strange how easy it was to be with her. He loved the way she had a huge appetite for all things in life – including food and sex. She was like a whirlwind, transforming his life from sepia to glorious Technicolor.

"Come on. Eat something," she told him. "I'm starting to feel subconscious."

He grinned and picked up his plate. "You shouldn't. You're beautiful."

Her eyes softened. "And you're a sweet talker. You don't need to go all Mr. Seductive on me, you know? You've already got me exactly where you want me."

"Where's that?"

"Under you. Over you. Everywhere in between." Her eyes were hooded as she looked at him, and he felt his body responding to her. She was like a drug he never wanted to wean himself off of. His need for her kept on growing.

"Have you eaten enough?" he asked her.

She put her plate on the table. "What do you have in mind?"

"I thought I'd show you the spare room. Where you'll be sleeping." He grinned.

"Sleeping?"

"Okay, staying awake..." He held his hand out to her, helping her stand. "And then we'll head to my room where you'll really be sleeping and do it all over again."

"Sounds interesting," she said as he led her toward the hallway and up the stairs. "So far we've managed to dirty the basement, the kitchen, and the living room. I guess it's only fair we christen the top floor, too."

He opened the door to the spare room and beckoned her in with a flourish. "My thoughts exactly, Miss Hayes."

Harper cracked an eye open, her face screwed up as she tried to figure out if it was night time or morning. At some point they'd ended up in his bedroom, and though she'd felt as rung out as a dishcloth – a very sated, pleasured dishcloth – she'd insisted they christen it like he'd promised.

And then they'd crashed into sleep without taking another breath.

She sighed, stretching her arms out, and turned to look at the clock beside his bed.

Four a.m.

Her bladder began to throb, and she slid out of bed, grabbing James's sweater once again to pull over her naked body.

She padded into the bathroom, catching sight of herself in the mirror. Lord, she looked a mess. Her hair was like a bird's nest, all tangled and frizzy, and there were shadows beneath her eyes the size of Alaska. And yet she couldn't help but smile at her reflection. The happiness was spilling out of her.

When she'd washed her hands, she grabbed some tooth-paste and scrubbed it around her teeth with her finger. For good measure she sloshed some mouthwash around, then spat it into the sink before washing it away with some water.

James hadn't moved at all while she was in the bathroom. In the gloom of the night she could see the outline of his bare torso, the white sheet tangled around his waist. His arms were splayed out as though he'd fallen asleep mid-yawn, and she couldn't help but grin.

He was delicious.

As quietly as possible, she climbed back into bed, lifting the sheet around her as she snuggled against his chest. She felt his hand stroke her mussed up hair. "Hey," he said, his voice heavy with sleep. "Where have you been?"

"Bathroom," she whispered. "Sorry, did I wake you?"

He rolled closer, pressing his lips against her brow. "I've been skating on the edge of being awake all night. I don't sleep deeply. I blame it on all the medical training and constantly being woken up by my pager." He slid his lips to her cheek, making her skin tingle. "Do you need anything?" he asked her. "Water? Pickles dipped in chocolate?"

She laughed. "Do people actually crave those things? I can't think of anything worse."

"Cravings don't seem to follow any pattern. Every woman seems different. There's no conclusive reason for their exis-tence, or proof they fill any need." He slid his hand down her bare back. "As a guy, I'm inclined to believe they're a test to see if we'll make a good dad. If we run out as soon as you ask us for something, then you know you can rely on us."

The corner of her lip curled up. "Is that right?"

He shrugged. "Just a hypothesis." He kissed the skin at the side of her throat. She loved the way he couldn't keep his hands off her.

"Okay, then. So if I told you I needed a burger and fries

right now, would you drive to the all night diner and get me some?"

His eyes softened. "Yeah, but I'd make you come with me."

"But it's so cozy here," she said, snuggling into the crook of his arm. She breathed deeply, loving the warm smell of him. "I don't think I can move. Plus I can't think of anything I want less than a burger."

"Well that's a relief. Because I really didn't want to get up." He grinned at her, his nose sliding against hers. "But I'll take you out to breakfast if you want."

"It's a deal."

For a moment they were silent. She could hear his soft, rhythmic breathing and the beat of her heart. She snuggled closer to him, placing her hand on his chest, tracing his skin with her outstretched finger.

"Did Sara have cravings?" She glanced up at him.

James blinked. "Ah, yeah. She went crazy for eggs. Hard-boiled, scrambled, poached, whatever. She couldn't get enough of them."

Harper felt sadness wash over her. Another reminder of how vibrant Sara once was, how alive Jacob had been. How much James had loved them until he lost them so tragically. Her heart ached for him.

"Do you mind me asking about her?" she whispered. "I can stop if it's weird."

He licked his lips, his brow furrowing in thought. "No, I don't mind. I kind of like it. It's strange, trying to fit everything together in my thoughts. Being able to talk about them makes it easier somehow. Like I don't have to hide anything from you."

"I don't want you to hide anything," she said softly. "They were your life. They still are."

He traced his finger down her spine. "For the longest time

I didn't think I'd want to be with anybody else ever again. After Sara and Jacob died I assumed that was it for me. My chance at happiness was gone. I threw myself into work and spent time with my friends and my family, but I protected the space they'd once filled inside me. I didn't want to allow anyone in or forget about them, because that would mean I'd lost them forever." He swallowed hard. "And I couldn't do that."

"They're not gone," she whispered, splaying her hand out on his chest. "They're in here." She took his hand, and pressed it to her abdomen. "And here, too, because this little baby is Jacob's sister. And that connects us all."

"I went to the cemetery," he told her, his palm caressing her stomach.

"To visit their graves?"

"Yeah. I needed to think about things. Clear my head."

"Did it work?" she asked him.

He turned onto his side, placing his other palm on her stomach, too. She looked down, watching as he slowly cupped the swell of her bump. The gesture made her breath catch in her throat. When she looked at him, he was staring down at her, his brows knitted together, his lips parted.

He made her heart ache in the most delicious of ways. She wanted to lay here forever, the three of them, protected from all the pain the world could cause.

"Yeah," he finally said, his voice soft. "It worked." He was still gazing intently at her stomach. "I realized how much I want this. *Us.* This baby. And how fucking scared I am to lose it all again." He leaned down to press his lips tenderly against her stomach. She cupped his cheeks with her palms, feeling the roughness of his skin against her. It was hard to breathe, to think, to do anything except watch the rawness of his emotions.

"I was sitting by Sara's side in the hospital when they told me Jacob had died during surgery," he said, lips still pressed against her skin. "I've never felt a pain like it. I wanted to curl up and scream until I couldn't hear anything else. To block everything out until the world went dark." He let out a mouthful of air. "But instead I prayed. I prayed Sara would die, too; I never wanted her to know how bad it felt to lose our son. And I wanted her to be with him, wherever he was, because I couldn't cope with the thought of him being alone."

Harper's eyes filled with tears. When he looked up at her, his lids heavy, she could see the glisten of water in his, too. She pressed her lips together to stifle a sob, because this was his pain, not hers.

"Can you imagine wanting your spouse to die?" he whispered. "What kind of man does that make me?"

"A selfless one," she said, her voice cracking. "A man who'd do anything for the people he loves."

With her hands still cupping his cheeks, she dropped her head to press her lips against his. She could taste the salt of his tears mingling with her own. "I can't imagine what it was like to lose the two people you loved the most," she whispered. "To be the one left to carry all the pain and grief. The strength you showed... the strength you still show...it's almost incomprehensible."

Her body was filled with emotion for him. This strong, damaged man staring into her eyes. She wanted to take away his pain, to make everything better, and she ached knowing she couldn't.

And yet there was another thought, one that saddened her. The knowledge that if Sara and Jacob hadn't died this baby wouldn't be growing inside her. She wouldn't be here in his bed, laying in his arms, whispering to him that he was going to be all right.

She took a deep breath and kissed him again, feeling his lips move against hers as his arms slid around her waist. Life was complicated, sometimes confusing as hell, but the way she felt when he touched her was so simple it cut through everything else.

The past was gone, and though they could mourn it, they couldn't change a thing. The future was knocking on the door and they couldn't ignore it either.

And as they kissed, Harper was certain she wanted to fling it wide open and let the light of the new day flood the darkness away.

❧ 18 ❧

"It's official. I'm carrying around a week old baby in my stomach and I don't like it one bit." Ember sighed and looked down at her swollen stomach. "I've tried everything. Exercise, scary movies, spicy food." She lowered her voice and leaned across the table, her stomach pressing against the edge. "And sex. Lots of sex. Every position I can get myself into, and even that hasn't worked."

She and Harper were sitting at a window table inside Déjà Brew, overlooking the golden sand as it sprawled out to the ocean. The sky above them was full of wispy candy cotton clouds, the sun hazy as it tried to fight its way through them. The breeze lifting from the ocean was enough to cool Harper's skin, so they'd opted to stay inside instead of at their go-to table on the deck.

"Have you had any contractions at all?" she asked, looking down at her own stomach. At almost twenty-three weeks she felt huge, but compared to Ember's stomach her bump was tiny and compact. It was strange to think in a few months' time she would be that big. How would it even be possible to walk or keep her balance? Or more importantly, fit in any of her clothes?

"I don't know," Ember admitted. "Everything aches constantly. I can't sleep, I need to pee all the time, my pelvis feels like somebody is pulling it apart with the jaws of life." She grimaced. "I'm sorry, I shouldn't be telling you any of this. It really isn't that bad."

"Have you had any contractions while I've been making these?" Ally asked as she brought over their coffees, giving Harper a wink. "Should I go boil some water and fluff some towels?"

"Nothing. Nada. I'm never going to have this baby," Ember told her, gritting her teeth. "I'll be the only pregnant woman carrying around a teenager in her stomach. They'll put me on TV shows as a medical miracle."

"I should record this," Ally said, unable to bite down a grin. "Then next time you think about getting pregnant I'll bring it out and show you. It'll be better than any contraceptive."

"Don't worry, I'm never having another baby again. I've been pregnant for five years."

"Have you tried raspberry tea?" Ally asked.

"Yep. And spicy tacos, scary movies, and bouncing on a yoga ball chanting 'out, out, out.'" Ember took a sip of her coffee. "I want to drink caffeinated coffee, eat blue cheese, drink more than a mouthful of wine. Why won't this baby come out?"

"It'll come when it's ready," Harper said, trying to reassure her. "He or she is just comfortable in there for now."

"That's what I'm afraid of," Ember muttered. "I think it's painted the walls, set up a flat screen TV, and has decided to stay in there forev—"

Her mouth dropped open. "Oh." She touched her stomach and sighed. "I thought that might have been a contraction, but I think the baby was just changing channels."

Ally took their coffee cups, even though they were still half full. "You know what would do you good?" she said, though it sounded like a rhetorical question. "A long walk. I'll make you both a coffee to go, and then you can head up the beach and enjoy the view. There's no point sitting around here moping."

"I don't want to walk," Ember told her. "It hurts."

"It's probably a good idea." Harper smiled at her. "I'll come with you. I need the exercise. I've been cooped up in the basement for too long."

"Are you both trying to kill me? I'm carrying a teenager around in my belly," Ember chastised, though there was humor in her eyes. She slowly stood, then leaned on the table. "Okay, I'll try anything once. Don't expect me to walk very far, though."

"A marathon should do it." Ally grinned.

Ember laughed, then her eyes widened. "Stop making jokes," she whispered. "I just peed myself."

"It wasn't a joke..." Ally trailed off as Ember leaned against the back of the chair, her face filled with mortification. "Ember? Are you okay?"

"I'm so embarrassed," Ember whispered. "The pee won't stop. I need to go to the bathroom."

Sure enough, a puddle appeared around her feet. Harper glanced at it, then up at Ally. "Um, I don't think that's pee." She turned to Ember. "Your water's broke."

"What?" Ally's face paled. "Oh shit. What do we do?"

"Sit down," Harper said to Ember. "Let's call Lucas and see if he can take you to the hospital."

"He's at work," Ember said, her voice thin. "You should call the station."

"I'll go do that," Ally said, her voice trembling. "Harper,

you stay with Ember. If she starts to push, stop her." She ran over to the counter. "Nate! Ember's water has broken. We need a mop. And maybe some towels."

Nate came running out of the kitchen, his eyes wide. "You okay?" he asked Ember.

"No. Not really."

He wrapped his arm around her shoulder. "Don't be scared," he said softly. "It's going to be okay. You're about to experience the most amazing thing, seeing your baby come into the world."

"Yep," Ally said. "And that's great. But unless you mop up that puddle, we're all going to be in the hospital."

Nate winked at them, then walked back to the kitchen, as Ally frantically pressed numbers on her phone.

Harper couldn't help but laugh at the craziness of it all. But then she saw Ember's expression and the laughter dissolved into the air. She reached out for her hand. "It's okay," she told her. "Nate's right. It's exciting; you're going to see your baby soon."

"I'd better get a year of free coffee for this," Ember muttered. "Isn't that what happens when your water breaks in a store?"

"Don't you get free coffee anyway?" Harper asked her, glad of the distraction.

"Oh yeah, I do," Ember admitted.

"Maybe they'll give you a free muffin, too. They're pretty good."

Ally ran out of the kitchen and over to where they were sitting, being careful to avoid the puddle. "I spoke to Lucas, he's on his way. He sounded as panicked as you are."

"You told him to drive safely, right?" Ember asked.

"Of course." Ally grinned. "And this is Lucas we're talking about. Safety is his middle name." Behind her, Nate put a big yellow sign on the floor and began to mop up the mess.

Ember sucked in a mouthful of air. "Distract me," she pleaded. "Before I go crazy."

"Um, did I tell you Nate bought a new car?" Ally asked her.

"Yeah, you did. Tell me something else."

"Um..." Ally shook her head. "I've got nothing. I'm such a big mouth I always tell you everything when it happens." She looked over at Harper with a pleading expression. "How about you, Harper? You got anything good? Some juicy gossip that will take Ember's mind off things?"

Harper looked from Ally and back to Ember. They were both staring at her, their eyes wide with expectation. She frowned, wracking her brain for something about her work or the baby, but failed miserably.

She pulled her bottom lip between her teeth. "I've got nothing either. Unless..."

"Unless what?" Ember said, leaning forward with a groan. "Please, Harper, I'll take *anything*."

"I've been sleeping with James Tanner for the past three weeks," Harper blurted out. Her face heated up as she realized they were both staring at her with open mouths. Nate had stopped mopping, too. "Um... is that what you were looking for?"

For the first time since her water broke, Ember smiled. "Oh yeah, that'll do it. Now tell us more."

The following day Harper walked through the main entrance of the hospital carrying a gift bag in one hand and a bottle of champagne in the other. She couldn't stop grinning at the thought of seeing Ember and Lucas's baby boy. It was strange how little attention she used to pay to new babies. But now that she was carrying a child of her own she couldn't wait to see baby Arthur Russell.

When she reached the maternity ward she pressed on the buzzer, giving her name when the nurse answered. A second later, the door unlocked and she walked in, the nurse behind the desk directing her to the private room at the far end of the hallway.

"I guess we'll be seeing you here soon, too," the nurse said, smiling. "How long do you have to go?"

"Seventeen more weeks," Harper told her. "It feels like forever."

"You'll be surprised how quickly it flies by," the nurse said. "In no time at all you'll be walking through that door to have your own little one."

Harper tried to imagine how she would feel stepping inside the maternity ward knowing she was about to give birth. Afraid, of course, because she had no idea what she was getting herself into. Excited, too, because she was already imagining seeing this little baby, and holding her tightly. But it was so hard to picture what their baby was going to look like, and how it would really feel knowing she was responsible for such a tiny life. It was easy keeping her safe while she was curled up in the womb, but a whole other matter when it came to doing it in the outside world.

She swallowed, thinking of James and his loss. Automatically her hand went to her bump, caressing it. She felt the baby squirm and then a little jab to the side of her stomach, before a feeling of warmth washed over her.

It was going to be okay. She'd make sure it was.

A smile curled at her lips as she looked into the hospital room. Ember was laying in the bed, her dark hair pulled into a coil at the back of her neck, her face glowing as she looked at the chair next to her. Lucas was sitting there, their baby cradled in his muscled arms, his eyes warm with pride as he stared down at his son.

Harper stood in the doorway, watching their brand new family. It was almost magical, as though there was an invisible shield cocooning the three of them, protecting them with love. She put her hand to her chest, feeling her heart flutter against her ribcage. With Lucas's rugged good looks and Ember's glowing beauty the three of them looked as though they belonged in the pages of a catalogue, not the maternity ward.

"Harper! You made it," Ember said with a smile when she rapped on the door. "Come in."

"These are for you," Harper said, passing the gift bag and the champagne to Ember.

Ember pulled the bag open and lifted out the gift wrapped in tissue paper. "You didn't need to bring us anything. You already got us a gift at the shower."

"I know." Harper shrugged. "But this is more of a keepsake. I figure after pushing a baby out for hours on end you deserve something to commemorate it."

Ember carefully unwrapped it, putting the thin paper to one side. The large ivory blanket was hand-embroidered with Arthur's name and date of birth, along with his weight. Next to the details were intricately sewn animals. Elephants, giraffes, and monkeys hand stitched with precision.

"Did you make this?" Ember asked, looking at Harper with shining eyes. "Lucas, have you seen this?"

He looked up from the baby, his lips curling as Ember showed him the blanket. "That's beautiful," he said softly, his gaze moving to Harper. "Thank you."

"It's a pleasure."

"How the heck did you make this so fast?" Ember asked her. "I only gave birth yesterday; it must have taken forever."

"I had most of it done before you went into labor," Harper admitted. "I just added the name and details after Lucas called Caitie." She didn't tell them she was up half the night making it look perfect, wanting to give them something they could keep forever. "I don't think it will stand up to much laundering, though, so probably one for the keepsake box rather than playing with."

"I'm going to hang it on the nursery wall," Ember said, still staring at the blanket. "It's so beautiful everybody should see it. You're very talented." She leaned forward, wincing at the sudden movement. "Thank you," she whispered, hugging Harper tight. "I love it."

"Would you like to hold him?" Lucas asked. He stood with Arthur snug in his arms. Harper nodded and he gestured at the chair. "Sit down and I'll pass him to you."

Harper slid into the seat he'd just vacated. "I promise not to baby hog."

"Hog away. I'm hoping I can go grab a coffee while you're here." He grinned at her then leaned down, sliding Arthur into her waiting arms. The baby's tiny head nestled into the crook of her elbow and he smacked his lips together, staring up at her with an interested gaze.

"Hey baby," Harper said to him, a huge smile on her face. "You took your sweet time coming out. What do you think of this place? You enjoying the stay?"

He blinked, thick eyelashes sweeping down his cheeks. The scant hair that covered his scalp was as dark as Ember and Lucas's. And just as James had explained, the baby's eyes were bright blue. She wondered whether they'd change to Ember's brown as he grew older.

"He's beautiful," she whispered. Lucas grinned and nodded, a look of pride on his face. "You guys must be so happy."

"We are," Ember said softly, her eyes meeting Lucas's. Harper felt her heart melting all over again. They were such a striking couple. Then she felt a nudge right where Arthur was resting over her bump. It wasn't gentle, either.

"Oh my," she said, her eyes wide. "I think my baby just kicked your baby."

"Sounds like a chip off the old block."

Harper lifted her head to see who'd just spoken, spotting James in the doorway. He was dressed in green scrubs and black rubber shoes, his nametag clipped to his waist. "Hey," she said with a smile. "I didn't know you were coming. You didn't say anything this morning."

Just seeing him was enough to make her body heat up. In the three weeks since she'd first spent the night at his place her need for him hadn't abated at all. If anything it had increased, stoked by the knowledge of how tender and gentle he could be. Every time she saw him she wanted him.

"I haven't got long. Thought I'd say hi while you were here. I'm due in surgery in twenty minutes." He smiled at Ember and Lucas. "Congratulations, guys."

"Thanks." Lucas strolled over and shook James's hand. "I have a whole new appreciation for doctors after this. And pregnant women, too. They make firefighting look easy." He turned back to look at his wife and Harper. "They're pretty special, huh?"

"Yeah." James's voice was gruff. "They are."

"You want to hold him?" Ember asked. "That's if it's okay with Harper."

"Sure." Harper tipped her head to the side and looked at him. "You ready for this?"

There was a ghost of a smile on James's face as Harper slid baby Arthur into his arms. She watched as he cradled him, the baby's head fitting easily into his crook. There was no awkwardness to his hold, no self-consciousness. Just an easy confidence that made her skin tingle.

Like Lucas, James's body was huge next to Arthur's tiny form. His bicep muscles knotted as he gently rocked him. Harper blew out a mouthful of air and pulled her lip between her teeth.

James looked up, his eyes catching hers and for a moment everything else disappeared. It was just the three of them, and the sound of rushing blood past her ears.

"I need to go scrub in," he told her. "Can I just have a quick word first?"

"Sure."

He passed the baby back to Lucas. "He's beautiful, man. Congratulations again." Then he leaned down to kiss Ember's cheek. "You did a great job."

"Thank you."

He inclined his head to the door and Harper followed him out, wondering what was so urgent. As soon as he closed the door behind him, James slid his hand into hers and pulled her toward the end of the hallway. He looked around before pulling her toward him, cupping her jaw with his hand as he kissed her hard and fast.

"Christ you look hot," he whispered against her lips. "You want to give a guy a warning before you wear a dress like that?"

She looked down at the white lace dress she'd made to accommodate her growing bump. It had a sweetheart neck, fitted over her breasts before coming in to a pinch, and then flow out over her stomach. It stopped mid thigh, revealing her long, tan legs.

"It's just something I made yesterday since nothing fits anymore," she told him, smiling as he kissed her again. God she loved the way his mouth claimed hers, as though she was the oxygen he needed to live. As his warm hand cupped her neck, pulling her closer, her toes curled at the pleasure he gave her.

When their kiss ended, they were both breathless. The desire in his fiery eyes matched her own.

"Will you wait for me tonight?" he asked her, his voice low. "I should be back by seven."

She nodded with a smile. Staying over at his place was becoming a habit – one she wasn't willing to break. Yeah, she still went home sometimes to endure Caitie's smirk and Breck's raised eyebrow, but James's house was beginning to feel like home.

"I should go," he said, not moving an inch. "I need to scrub in."

"Then go."

"I don't want to." The corner of his lip quirked up. "I want to take you home right now."

"I'm not sure your patients would be impressed." She tucked a stray lock of hair behind her ear. "And I have work to do. I've got a custom order to finish and I need to deliver some samples to the Angel Sands Boutique."

He sighed. "Okay. Tonight then?"

She grinned, her heart still pounding. "Tonight."

"Hey, you want to come out for a drink?" James asked Rich as they were leaving the hospital a week later. "My friend Lucas is celebrating the birth of his baby."

"You're asking me to come for a drink?" Rich asked, feigning shock. "What's happened to the recluse we know and love?"

James pulled his keys from his pocket as they walked into the parking lot. "Do you want to come or not?"

"I want. I definitely want." Rich grinned. "As long as your friend doesn't mind."

"He won't mind at all. I'm going to drop my car off and meet you there. Lafterty's Bar on Main Street at eight."

"And you'll really be there?"

"Yep."

Rich didn't look as though he quite believed it. "Okay then, first drink is on you."

"Okay, let's all raise our bottles to Lucas," Griff called out, his rough voice cutting across the chatter of the bar. "Intrepid firefighter, champion surfer, and now husband and daddy. Is there nothing this guy can't do?"

"I can shut you up in one easy move," Lucas told him, raising an eyebrow. "But thanks for the effusive toast."

"To Lucas!" his friends called out. James grinned and lifted his bottle in salute, along with everybody else in the bar. It was hard to move with all the men standing in here – Lucas' fire station buddies, friends he grew up with, along with his family. In the corner, James could see his own dad talking to Wallace Russell, the two of them sat at a table as they looked out at the crowd of men.

"Your friends are nice," Rich said, inclining his head at the group surrounding Lucas. "Why haven't you introduced me before?"

"I don't know most of them that well," James told him. "I knew Lucas when we were kids, but I hadn't seen him for a few years. Then Ember got pregnant and we kind of reconnected."

"I guess you both have that dad thing going on." Rich took another mouthful of beer. "How's the baby doing?"

"Lucas's baby?"

"No, dumbass. Your baby. The one that's going to be here in a few months." Rich sighed. "Everything okay?"

"Yep. Had an ultrasound a few weeks ago and it's all looking good." James lifted his bottle to his lips.

"You told Sara's folks about the baby yet?"

His hand froze. "No, not yet." It was on his list of things to do, the same way it had been for weeks. But how the hell did you tell the parents of your dead wife you were having another baby? Even worse, how the hell could he explain what was happening between him and Harper?

On paper they knew he had his life in front of him, that his world wouldn't stop forever. And yet a feeling of intense guilt washed over him any time he thought about calling them; the same feeling he got whenever he avoided their calls.

He wasn't ready to face that yet. Not when he could be spending time with Harper, letting her light the darkness he'd been trapped in for so long.

"I'll tell them soon," he said as he put the beer on the tabletop.

"Hey, thanks for coming," Lucas said, wandering over and giving James a hug. You remember these guys, right? Griff, Jackson and Breck were all at school with me. And you know Nate who runs the coffee shop on the beach, and Aiden who runs the Silver Sands Resort."

James shook their hands. "This is Rich," he said, introducing his friend. "He works in the ER."

"Another doctor." Lucas shook his hand. "I've probably seen you in there a few times."

"Yeah, I know your face," Rich said nodding. "Congratulations on the baby."

"Thanks, man."

"I hear you're going to be a father, too," Griff said, shaking James's hand. "Congratulations."

James felt the slightest twinge at the words. He was already a father. But tonight wasn't the time to point that out.

"You're a lucky guy to land Harper," Jackson said, leaning on the counter. "She's a good one."

"They're not a couple," Lucas told him. "That's right, isn't it?"

"Well, yeah," James said. Another twinge. There were way too many of them tonight.

"They aren't?" Nate frowned, and his eyes met James's. There was something in there he couldn't quite work out.

"Well your loss is somebody else's gain." Griff shrugged. "I doubt she'll be single for long."

"That'll be weird," Jackson interjected. "Having another guy bringing up your baby."

"It's the modern world, man," Griff told him. "We're all adults here."

It was? James frowned, not liking the sound of that one bit. The baby was his, not somebody else's. And Harper? Well she belonged to nobody... but he wanted her all the same.

He took another mouthful of beer to wash away the bitter taste on his tongue. He liked her. A lot. Liked coming home to find her still there. Liked kissing the hell out of her when she least expected it. Liked the way she moaned softly when he was inside her, his hands cradling her like the precious cargo she was.

The thought of anybody else having that with her made him want to punch something.

"You okay?" Rich asked him. "Is it getting too much? I can drive you home."

That made him feel worse. Rich thought he was having memories of Sara and Jacob, when the two of them had barely crossed his mind. Guilt immediately washed over him, mixing in with the jealousy that was already there.

The cocktail of emotions made him want to crawl into a

corner and hide. This pregnancy – and this thing with Harper, whatever it was – was making him feel raw. For years he'd hidden from emotions, trying to avoid the pain they inevitably brought along for the ride.

And now? He wasn't sure where he was or what he was doing. And that was as confusing as hell.

🌿 19 🌿

"What do you think?" Harper asked James as they walked around the empty apartment. The realtor was in the kitchen, subtly allowing them to explore the other rooms. "I could use that room as a nursery," she said, pointing at the smallest room, next to the master. "And then this one would be mine. And I'm thinking the walk-in closet would make a good storage area for the business."

"Where would you put your own clothes?"

"I'm still figuring that out," she admitted. "I guess I'll need to buy some freestanding closets or put some shelves up."

"There won't be a lot of space once you've got everything in here. Maybe you should look for something bigger?" James suggested.

"Well beggars can't be choosers, and I need to move before the baby comes. Caitie and Breck are wonderful for letting me stay with them, but there's no way I'm imposing on them longer than I have to." She shrugged. "I can afford this place and it's in a good area; I'm going to take it."

"I could help you with the rent. We need to talk about

child support and other things anyway. I get paid enough for you to have more floor space." He looked around the apartment, trying to picture her and their baby here. For some reason it felt like a kick in the gut.

"I'm not taking money from you." Harper frowned.

"Are we doing this again?" He smiled, shaking his head. "The money wouldn't be for you. It's for the baby."

She turned to him, her hands on her hips. There was a no-nonsense expression on her face. "We've agreed to fifty-fifty custody," she told him. "That means we each pay our own expenses. I can afford this place by myself. It's small but it's perfect for what we need." She rubbed her stomach with her palm. "I've checked my budget and this is what fits."

"What if the baby needs things? Am I not allowed to buy them?"

Her eyes softened. "You can buy what you'd like for the baby. I want you to. But you're not paying any rent for me."

"You're insufferable."

She grinned. "That's why you like me so much." She rolled onto the balls of her feet and brushed her lips against his. "Don't look so grumpy. We'll be perfectly fine here. And you'll get your basement back. There's something to look forward to."

His stomach turned at the thought of the basement being empty again. Of coming home to a house filled with silence instead of the constant whirr of Harper's sewing machine. "You could still use my place for work," he suggested. "That way you'd have more space here."

"That's so sweet," she said, her eyes catching his. "But that was only a temporary arrangement." She smiled. "This will work for us just fine."

He still didn't like it. They'd only been sleeping with each other for a few weeks, but it was confusing the hell out of him. In four months time they'd be parents and everything would change. No more nights curled up in each other's arms. No more sex in the basement when he came home and saw her leaning over her sewing table.

Instead she and the baby would be here. And yeah, he'd have custody, too. But that wasn't what he wanted.

He wanted her. He wanted it all.

This was so messed up and he had no idea how to untangle it.

"You know, I think I might finally be growing up," Harper said, running her finger over the windowsill. "I've got my own business, my own apartment. When I finally call my grandma I'll be able to say I'm finally an adult."

"You haven't called her yet?"

"I sent her the letter like we talked about but she didn't reply. I figure I should call and make sure it arrived." She wrinkled her nose. "As much as I hate to do it."

"I love how brave you are," he said, kissing the tip of her nose.

"This little thing makes me brave," she told him, caressing her stomach. "I'm not going to hide away any more. I'm going to stand up and be proud of who I am; that way she can be proud of herself, too."

His chest tightened. She was fantastic. He'd been avoiding his own demons. Hadn't made the phone call to Sara's parents to tell them about his new baby. Yeah, he could blame it on how busy he was, that between work and Harper and the baby he had no time to do anything, but the truth was, he didn't want to talk to them.

It was so much easier to be happy when he didn't have to think about the bad times.

"So what do you think?" the realtor asked, walking into the hallway. "Is it a contender?"

"It is." Harper nodded.

"We'll need to move fast if you want it," the realtor told

her. "There are another two couples already booked to look at it later, but if we want to make an offer I can call right now."

Harper looked at James, and despite his misgivings, he nodded. It was what she wanted, he was sure of it. And if it meant he had to be alone again, then so be it. He'd endured the loneliness before, he was sure he could do it again.

"I don't want you to go." Caitie pouted as Harper showed her photos of the apartment on her phone. "I want you to stay here."

"No you don't." Harper smiled at her. "I'm messy, I eat too much, and I hog the television. You'll be pleased to see the back of me."

"I really won't." Caitie scrolled through the photos. "Did James like the apartment?"

"Not really. He wanted me to look for someplace bigger. Started talking about helping me with the rent."

Caitie raised her eyebrows. "I bet that went over well."

"Like a lead balloon." Harper shook her head. "I told him thanks but no thanks."

"I thought he might ask you to move in with him," Caitie said, her eyes meeting Harper's.

Her chest tightened. "I'm glad he didn't. It's too soon. Things are messed up enough without us confusing things more. When the baby's born I'll be even more hormonal than I am now, as well as sleep deprived. I have no idea how we'll feel about each other then. The way I see it, it's best if we have separate places." If she said it enough times, maybe she'd even believe it.

"So when do you move in?" Caitie asked.

"I get the keys next week."

"On the plus side, that means you'll be settled before your

baby shower. I sent the invitations out yesterday, by the way."
Caitie grinned. "I'm so excited."

"I don't know how you managed to talk me into it,"
Harper told her, though there was a smile in her voice. "If you
make people guess the circumference of my stomach you're
dead meat."

"Hey. Everybody loved that game at Ember's party." Caitie
laughed at Harper's expression. "Don't look at me like that. I
already promised you there would be no games. Just music
and fun. You'll enjoy it."

"Thank you." Harper hugged her friend.

"There was one thing I wanted to ask you," Caitie said. "I
haven't sent an invitation to your mom or grandmother. I
thought I should check with you first." She knew more than
anybody about Harper's fractured relationship with her
family. She'd witnessed a lot of the angst first hand.

"They wouldn't come anyway," Harper told her. "And I
wouldn't want them to."

"You don't know that." Caitie's voice was soft. "Maybe you
should ask."

"I think Mom's out of the country."

"And your grandmother?"

Harper swallowed, her mouth dry. "I'll call her," she said.
"I need to speak to her anyway. But she won't come."

Caitie squeezed her hand. "Try not to look so scared. She
can't hurt you. Not anymore. And if she tried she'd have me
to deal with. And James. And pretty much everybody in
Angel Sands. We all love you."

"Well I guess there's no time like the present," Harper
said, standing and grabbing her phone. "I'll call her from my
room. Shield you from the screaming."

"Your grandmother would never scream."

"True story," Harper said, nodding. "But I might."

Five minutes later she held her phone to her ear and

listened to the ring tones as her call to New England connected.

"Hello?" her grandmother's butler answered with a deep voice. Harper's stomach clenched at the sound. He'd been working for her grandmother for the past five years, and though she'd never met him, he'd always been very polite when she called.

Which wasn't very often.

"Um, hi. Is my grandmother home? It's Harper."

"Hello, Miss Hayes," he replied. "Let me see if she's home."

A minute later the phone was taken off mute.

"I was wondering when you would call." Strange how a voice could make your body shiver like crazy. Even thousands of miles away, Martha Hayes had that affect on her.

"Hello, Grandmother. How are you?"

"As well as can be expected." Her voice was terse. "I received your letter. I expect you want me to congratulate you."

Harper licked her dry lips. "I don't have any expectations."

"Well that's good. I've learned over the years they're rarely met. Especially when it comes to family." Her grandmother clicked her tongue. "What is it you want, Harper? Money?"

"No. I don't need money. I just thought you should know. This baby's your great grandchild, after all. Your flesh and blood."

"From the way she was conceived I'd say she takes more after your mother's side."

Yeah, Harper had been expecting that. Even still, it stung.

"Are you planning on getting married?" her grandmother asked.

"No. The father and I are just friends."

A long sigh. "I thought nobody could top your mother,

but you've managed to. At least she married my son before you were born, even if it was a close run thing."

"Have you heard from Mom?" Harper asked, ignoring the tightness in her chest. "I've tried contacting her but I think she's out of the country."

"I spoke to her last week. She asked for money, of course. And I told her about the baby."

"You did?"

"Yes. But then she started telling me about her latest boyfriend and we got off track." Another sigh. "I need to go now. My bridge club starts at three. Was there anything else you wanted?"

Harper pulled her lip between her teeth, wincing as they dug into the soft flesh. She wasn't going to invite her to the shower. She wasn't sure she could endure another rejection. "Um, no."

"Very well then. Thank you for calling." It was a dismissal. Harper'd had enough of those over her life to recognize it.

"Shall I call you when the baby's born?" Harper asked her. "So you know?"

"If you want. It's completely up to you. Goodbye, Harper. And good luck. I have a feeling you might need it."

Harper put her phone down and took a deep breath, but it did nothing to stem the flow of tears.

She shouldn't have called. It only hurt her when she did. There were some things that could never be mended, no matter how hard you tried.

At least she had the baby. That was something. And she had Caitie and Ember and all their friends, too.

And then there was James. She wasn't sure what was going to happen with him, but she knew he'd always be in their baby's life, supporting her the way Harper had never been supported.

For that she was truly thankful.

20

"Can you believe it?" Caitie asked, squeezing Harper's hand. "It feels like only yesterday we were at Ember's baby shower, and now we're doing it all over again for you." They walked into the elegant lobby of the Silver Sands Resort Hotel, where they'd hired an event room for the party. It had been a toss up between the hotel and the Beach Club, but in the end Harper had chosen the hotel. It seemed right, since that was where this baby had begun.

Harper grinned when she saw the sign on the front desk. Baby Hayes-Tanner's Shower – Main Ballroom. "I can't believe it's only ten weeks until this little lady arrives," she admitted. "The past couple of months have flown by. I've been so busy trying to get everything done I don't feel like I've had time to breathe."

She'd moved most of her things into the new apartment, though her sewing machines and dresses were still in James's basement. She'd agreed to keep working there until the baby arrived. That way she could decorate the apartment without worrying about ruining her work. And then there was James.

When she wasn't working or decorating, she was spending time with him.

She smiled as she remembered how he'd come straight to Caitie's apartment after she'd spoken to her grandmother. He'd gathered Harper in his arms and held her tightly, wiping her tears away with soft fingers. His tender kisses and sweet words had almost made up for the hurt that telephone call had inflicted.

Shaking her head, she pushed all thoughts of her family from her mind. They didn't matter. What mattered were the people here. The ones who loved her and wanted to celebrate her impending birth with her. Caitie had worked hard on this shower, Harper was determined to enjoy it.

A loud cheer erupted as they walked into the room. The tables were full of familiar faces. There was Ember with baby Arthur on her lap, and next to her were Ally and Brooke. Then there were the tables filled with her friends from L.A., and a few who'd flown in from New York. In the center of the room she could see Louise Tanner, sitting with Caitlin's mom, Deenie, and a group of their friends. Everyone was smiling as though they were delighted to see her, and it brought tears to her eyes.

"You're not supposed to cry at a baby shower," Caitie whispered in her ear.

"Did you do all this?" She turned to her friend. "Thank you," she said, her voice cracking. "I wasn't expecting to see so many people here."

"We could have had more but I didn't want to overwhelm you," Caitie told her as she led her inside. It took a while for them to reach the table at the front of the hall, as everybody wanted to hug Harper and tell her how beautiful she looked. "You've made a lot of friends since you arrived in Angel Sands."

As they reached the table where Louise was sitting, she

stood and hugged Harper tightly. "Thank you for inviting me," she said, a huge smile on her face. "I'm so excited to be here."

"Thank you for coming. It means a lot to me."

"Is your mom planning on joining us?" she asked.

Harper shook her head. "She couldn't make it." It was only a little lie.

"Maybe we'll meet her after the baby is born," James's mom said, shrugging. "And in the meantime, I'm happy to fill any grandmotherly duties you might need." She hugged Harper again. "Maybe we can go for coffee next week?"

Harper nodded. "I'd really like that."

"It's a date. Now go and enjoy your shower." His mom sat down. "I'll catch up with you later."

"So we're not doing any games, just like you requested." Caitie slid her arm through Harper's and led her over to her table. "We're going to have some music and dancing, and of course lots of food. Just a lovely few hours where you can talk to everybody you know and have a good time."

"And get lots of gifts," Ally said, grinning as they reached the table. "And I made you a blueberry muffin cake. It's awesome if I do say so myself."

"Where is it?" Harper asked, looking around. "Gimme."

Caitie laughed. "You have to wait. First let me introduce you to a couple of people. This is Ember's sister, Chelsea. She's visiting the new baby and we invited her along. I hope that's okay."

"Of course it is." Harper leaned forward to hug the girl who looked uncannily like a younger version of Ember. "Congratulations on becoming an aunt."

"Thanks." Chelsea winked. "It's been a lot of work."

"It will be." Ember laughed. "When I get you to babysit. You're going to love changing his diaper."

Caitie shook her head. "And this is Aria. She's not here for the shower, but she heard you were coming and I promised to introduce you. She runs the resort boutique."

"Hi." Aria walked over to where Harper was standing, a huge smile on her face. "I'm so excited to meet you. When Brooke told me you were the one responsible for those gorgeous dresses I keep seeing I asked for an introduction. I'm hoping you'll take my business card and call me tomorrow. I'm interested in stocking your designs." She passed Harper a thick embossed card.

"For the boutique here?"

"For all of our boutiques across the country. Silver Sands Resort is part of a larger chain, run by Carter Leisure. We like to work with designers to create exclusive ranges that our customers will love. I've sent details of your work to our lead buyer, and she's really excited about them. We have a big fashion show coming up next month, and she wants to talk to you about exhibiting your work there."

"Really?" Harper looked at the business card. "That sounds great."

Aria smiled. "Let's talk more tomorrow. In the meantime, have a wonderful shower. It looks like your friends have done an amazing job."

"I will. Thank you again." Harper turned to Caitie with wide eyes as Aria walked across the ballroom. "Did you hear that?" she asked, a slow smile breaking out on her face.

"Every word," Caitie said, her eyes just as wide. "That's so amazing, I can't believe it." She hugged her tightly.

"Nor can I. After everything that's happened this year, it feels like my life is finally turning around." Was it possible to have it all? The baby, the man, and the career she'd always hoped for?

For the first time in forever, she was beginning to think it was.

James was pulling his car into the Silver Sands Resort parking lot when his phone began to ring. The sun was slowly slipping down the sky in a riot of pinks and oranges, the silhouetted palm trees casting long shadows across the concrete as the daylight sang its last goodbye. He parked in a space next to the entrance and picked the phone up, frowning as he saw who was calling.

Alice Murray. Sara's sister.

"Hello?"

"James. How are you? We haven't heard from you for a while;. Mom and Dad were starting to worry." Just hearing Alice's voice made his breath catch in his throat. It was so similar to Sara's.

"I'm fine," he told her. "There's no need to worry about me. I'll try to call them this weekend."

"They'd love that. We talk about you a lot. And about Sara and Jacob, of course." Her voice lowered. "I still find it hard to accept they're gone sometimes. I guess it must be the same for you, too."

"Yeah."

"I'm sorry. I didn't mean to offload on you. I worry about you. I think about you roaming around in that big house with all of its memories and it makes me want to cry. I don't know how you do it sometimes."

He swallowed, even though his mouth was dry. "It has been hard," he said. It wasn't a lie. Just because his life felt easier – lighter – now, didn't mean he hadn't gone through the darkness to get here.

"So I was just calling about next month. We were planning on flying to Angel Sands next month for the anniversary. Mom and Dad want to visit their graves, and to see you, too.

I wanted to check your schedule to see if you'd be working on Saturday the twelfth."

Anniversary. James blinked, and let out a mouthful of air. How the hell had he forgotten about that? Three years since he'd sat by Sara's side and watched her die. Three years since he'd watched two coffins lowered into the ground.

What kind of man was he?

"The anniversary's three weeks away."

"I know." She was always so gentle, the way Sara had been. "I'm sorry for the late notice. Mom was planning to discuss it with you when you called. I can't believe it's been three years."

"The twelfth is fine," he told her. "I'll be around. Are you planning on staying the night?"

"I don't think so. We'll probably fly back that evening. Dad doesn't like sleeping in any bed that's not his, and I'm concerned it may all be too much for Mom. Maybe we can have dinner before we leave. I hear the new resort is up and running. Or we could go to Delmonico's on the pier. Sara always loved that place."

James looked up at the resort in front of him. The front door opened and a group of young women walked out, smiling and laughing as they made their way down the stairs. His stomach contracted when he realized they could be from the baby shower. With Alice on the phone it was like his past and future were trying to collide.

"We'll go to Delmonico's," he said firmly. "I'll call and make a reservation. Send me your flight details and I'll pick you up from the airport."

"Are you sure? We can rent a car."

"I'm sure. I'll be there."

"Thanks, James. It'll be good to see you again. And maybe we can find some happiness in talking about the old times."

"I'll see you on the twelfth," he said, wanting to end the

call as soon as possible. He didn't like the way his old and new life were colliding. "Don't forget to send me those flight details."

"I won't. In a weird way I'm looking forward to it."

Yeah, he thought as he ended the call and slid his phone into his pocket. *Well that made one of them.*

As he headed up the steps to the main hotel and walked through the door, he tried to put the thought of Sara's family out of his mind. Maybe it had been a mistake to offer to pick up Harper and bring home all the gifts from the party, but it felt wrong to expect her to do it by herself. She was six months pregnant and there was no way he wanted her lifting things. That was *his* job. But as he pushed the door to the ballroom open he didn't like the way people turned to look at him, either. Even though the shower had finished, there were still a lot of people mingling around. He pressed his lips together and tried to ignore their interested gazes.

There was only one person in this room he was concerned with, anyway. Or two if you counted their baby.

His eyes were drawn to her. She was standing with Caitie and Ember, one hand on her bump, the other reaching out to tickle baby Arthur under his chin. He swallowed as he watched her lips curl into a smile. Christ, she was beautiful. A beacon of light that refused to be dulled, no matter how many arrows life slung at her.

"James?" his mother said, touching his arm. "I didn't know you were coming. I was just leaving and I saw you walk in."

"Hey, Mom." He smiled at her. "I offered to bring all the gifts home."

"To Harper's place?" she asked. "I heard she's just moved into a new apartment. Is she going to store everything there?"

He shook his head. "We're going to store everything in my spare room for now. Harper's still unpacking."

"Oh." His mom paused for a moment, then smiled. "She's a very lovely girl, isn't she?"

"Ah, yeah."

"Have you thought about having her live with you after the baby is born?"

The bluntness of her question shocked him. "Ah..."

"I mean in the spare room," she said quickly. "I wasn't implying anything more than that. I know you miss Sara and Jacob very much." She rubbed the top of his arm. "I'm sorry. It's none of my business."

Yeah, it was none of her business, but he wasn't planning on telling her that. Fact was, he had no idea what they were going to do about the future. That was his fault – he still couldn't bring himself to tell Harper how he felt. Maybe he was too afraid of being rejected. Better to keep his thoughts to himself than open himself up to that pain.

"I should go over and say hi to Harper. I'll talk to you later, okay?" Giving his mom a soft smile, he leaned forward and kissed her cheek.

She squeezed his arm. "Okay, honey. Take care."

He took a deep breath, trying to center himself. Why was life so much easier when it was just him and Harper curled up in his bed? When her body was pressed against his. With her soft hair caressing his skin, it felt like he could take on the world. And he would, just to protect her from it. Her and their baby.

Ember said something, and Harper nodded. Slowly, she turned her head, a smile breaking out on her face as she noticed James standing across the room. She lifted her hand in a wave, and he smiled at her, walking over to where she was standing.

"Hi." His voice was husky. He had to curl his hands not to touch her. "Did you have a good time?"

"Hey." She lifted her head until her eyes met his. "It was wonderful. Thanks for coming. There are a lot more gifts than I was expecting." She pointed over at the table, filled with gift bags and large boxes. She leaned forward to whisper in his ear, "Does a baby really need *all* this stuff?"

"Yeah," he said, deadpan. "That's why they had baby showers in prehistoric days."

"My apartment isn't that big. With all these things in there I'm going to end up sleeping in the bathtub. Do you think the baby will mind sleeping in the sink?"

He laughed.

"Harper, we're heading out. Thank you so much for inviting us, and remember to send us all the deets when the baby is born." A woman of around thirty leaned forward to hug her. "I can't believe you're gonna be a mom."

"Thank you for coming all this way. It means a lot," Harper said, hugging her friend back. "Um, this is James, by the way. The baby's father. James, this is Monica. We met when I was working on Broadway."

James blinked. For some reason being described like that rankled him. He wasn't *just* the baby's father. He was Harper's lover, her friend. Why the heck wasn't there a socially accept-able description of what they had going on?

Monica turned to look at him, her glossy black hair catching the light from the chandeliers. "Hi, James," she said smiling. "It's a pleasure to meet you."

"You, too." He shook her hand. Harper was looking at him with the strangest of expressions. Was he still frowning? "I'll start loading the car," he told Harper. "Then we can head home."

"To *your* home."

"That's what I meant." Damn, he was terrible at this. Maybe he shouldn't have come. Harper's friends could have easily delivered the gifts themselves, or he could have picked them up in the morning.

"Okay. Thanks." She was still gazing at him with concern. "Let's get this thing done."

21

"You okay?" James asked, turning over to look at Harper. She was turning from side to side in his bed, groaning as she slid her knees up to her bump and then back down again.

"No, I'm not. I can't get comfortable. I swear this baby is practicing Tai Kwon Do in here."

He smiled at her frustrated expression. "What can I do to help?" he asked softly.

"You can't do anything; you've done enough already. It's all your fault for putting her in there in the first place."

He tried to bite down a laugh, but it was futile. She was so damn cute when she got riled up. "You want me to give you a back rub?"

"Can you rub my calves? They keep cramping up and every time I try to rub them this damn belly gets in the way."

"Sure." He slid down the bed, rising to his knees as he gently took her leg between his hands. Her skin was soft and smooth, still clinging on to a light tan. He ran his fingers over her calf, pressing his thumbs down to ease the muscles.

"You've got a couple of knots in there," he told her, circling the pads against the tight muscles.

"I know. Ahhh... Jeez, I think you got it." She let out a sigh. "Does it get better? Tell me it gets better. I'm sick of every part of my body aching."

"You need to slow down. This is your body telling you it's time to take care of yourself. You can't keep working from seven in the morning until eight at night without rest." He took her other leg and placed it on his knee, sliding his thumbs along it until he found another knotted muscle.

"You can talk all you want. You work longer hours than me."

"But I'm not thirty-two weeks pregnant," he said lightly.

"Why is that?" she asked him, lifting her head from the pillow. "How come guys get all the good stuff?"

It was really hard not to smile at her. "Some people think pregnancy is the good stuff."

"Yeah. People who aren't pregnant." She huffed. "Can you rub my feet now?" she asked him. "I know it's gross, but every time I stretch them they hurt."

"Sure, baby."

She was firmly in the third trimester now, less than two months away from giving birth, and she'd never looked more glorious. Sometimes he came home from work and stared at her as she leaned over her sewing table, watching the way her brows pinched together as she concentrated on a design.

He was becoming addicted to the way she made him feel. Warm and strong and alive. His favorite part of the day was lying behind her as she slept, cupping her abdomen with his hand and feeling their baby kick against it. During those moments – when only he and the baby were awake – he felt like their protector. It was his job to make them safe and comfortable, and he was determined to do it right.

"I can't slow down, anyway," she told him as he rolled his thumb along her instep. "I've got too much to do. I have a fashion show in a month's time and a huge order to fill for Carter Leisure. I've had to turn down ten Etsy orders this week."

"Maybe you should think about getting some help."

She sighed. "I've thought about it, but I'm not established enough yet. The clothes placed in the boutiques on a sale or return basis, which means I don't get paid until a customer buys them. I need regular cash flow to employ staff, and I won't have that for at least six months. And in the meantime, I have rent to pay and a baby to provide for. There's no way I can slow down until I give birth."

"You should move in here." The words came out so casually. Although, they didn't feel casual. They felt like he was taking a can opener to his heart. But he'd been thinking about it ever since she'd moved into her apartment. Trying to work out a way to ask her.

She lifted herself up on her elbows, her brow furrowed. "What do you mean?"

He ran the tip of his tongue along his bottom lip. "I mean you could give up your apartment and live here with me. I have more space than I know what to do with, and you're already set up and running in the basement. It would make it easier for both of us if you lived here."

She stared at him for a moment. "That's probably the least romantic thing I've ever heard."

Shit. "I didn't mean it to come out like that. It was just a suggestion."

She sighed. "Everything that's happened between us has been backward. We slept together without dating. We got pregnant without being in a relationship. And now you're talking about me moving in like it's some kind of business deal." She pressed her lips together. "I don't want that. I want the fairytale. The happily-ever-after. I'm not moving in with you because it's easier on my finances."

He felt like a statue, frozen to the ground. Desperate to find the right words. "I want to give you that," he said, his voice cracking. "I do." His chest throbbed, as though that can opener had stabbed right through it.

"But you can't." She finished his words for him. "I get it." She pulled her foot from his grasp and turned onto her side, pulling her legs up in a fetal position. "I'm going to try and get some sleep. You should do the same."

James stared at her for a moment, trying to work out how his suggestion had gone so catastrophically wrong. Even before he'd lain back down beside her, her breaths had begun to even out, as she slipped into a deep slumber.

He squeezed his eyes shut and shook his head. Just like always, he was messing everything up. And he had no idea how to make things right.

"Hey," James said as he walked across the main hospital vestibule, heading for the reception desk. "You here on official business?"

Lucas glanced down at his standard firefighter's uniform of utility pants and dark t-shirt emblazoned with ASFD across his chest. "Nah, I just clocked off, but we brought a kid in earlier and I wanted to find out how he was doing." He shrugged. "According to the doctor his breathing is improving. They're hoping to get him off the oxygen tomorrow."

"Smoke inhalation?" James asked.

"Yeah. No burns, thankfully."

James glanced at his watch. He should have finished half an hour ago, but that was life as a doctor. "Actually, do you have a minute? Maybe we could go grab a coffee."

"Sure. Ember's at her mom's with the baby, I said I'd meet them there in an hour. A coffee first would be good."

They took the elevator to the café on the fifth floor, ordering two Americanos with room before taking a seat by the window. James took a sip of his coffee, letting the bitter liquid warm his throat, as he tried to let his body relax.

It was tough. When he left the house this morning Harper was still asleep, so he'd written her a note and promised to call her at lunchtime. When he'd dialed her number right after twelve she hadn't picked up so he'd left a voicemail. As of five minutes ago, she still hadn't returned his call.

He'd messed up. Hurt her. And he hated it. But every time he tried to think of a way to make things better his body tensed up. Could he give her what she wanted? What she and the baby needed? Right now, he had no idea.

"How are Ember and the baby doing?" he asked Lucas, putting his coffee cup on the table in front of him.

"They're good." Lucas smiled. "Ember's completely exhausted, of course, and it seems like Arthur's going through a growth spurt every other week. But there's nothing like going home after a hard day's work and seeing your family. I love it."

"I bet."

"And how are you doing?" Lucas asked. "Are Harper and the baby okay?"

"Yeah." James nodded. "They're doing good."

"She must be in the third trimester by now, right?"

"Thirty-two weeks. Almost thirty-three."

Lucas took a sip of coffee. "Can I ask you something?"

"Sure."

"Are you guys together? Or are you planning on co-parenting?" He rubbed his jaw with the pad of his thumb. "You don't have to answer if it's too personal."

"It's okay." James traced his finger over the cracks in the table. "The reality is, I don't know what we are. Originally we were going to co-parent, but now things are a little... messy." He grimaced. "Mostly my fault, by the way."

"What did you do?"

"I asked her to move in with me."

Lucas chuckled. "Doesn't sound messy. It sounds like you're wanting a commitment."

"Yeah, well that's not the way it sounded to Harper. She thought I was asking her for convenience's sake."

"Whoa." Lucas let out a low whistle. "How did you manage to mess that up?"

"I don't know," James admitted. "One minute I'm asking her to move in with me, the next she's telling me it's the most unromantic proposition she's ever had."

"Did you tell her how you feel about her?" Lucas asked him.

James frowned. "What do you mean?"

"I guess I'm asking how you asked her. It's a pretty big thing moving in with someone. Now that people are getting married less, it's kind of replaced a proposal as a declaration of your relationship."

James drained his cup, the frown still furrowing his brow. "I screwed it up," he told Lucas. "She was saying how hard it was going to be to fit everything in her apartment, and I told her I have plenty of space and she's welcome to move in."

"Jeez." Lucas spluttered out some coffee. "Yeah, that sounds like a major screw up. Did you even tell her you want her there? Or were you just offering to rent her some rooms?"

"It wasn't like that." Or at least he hadn't meant it to be. He blew out a mouthful of air, remembering the expression on Harper's face when he'd made the offer. There was hurt in her eyes and it cut him to the core to know he was the one who'd put it there.

"Do you want her to move in?" Lucas asked, the corner of his lip turned down.

"Yeah." James nodded. He wanted it all. He wanted what Lucas had – a family to go home to. He'd had it once and then lost it forever.

But Harper had given him a second chance.

"Yeah, I want it," he said again, his voice clearer.

"Why?"

"Because she's the best thing that's happened to me in a long time." He pictured her warm smile, her eyes that seemed to dance with amusement. "She's beautiful, she's funny, and she's having my baby. I want her close where I can take care of her."

"So why can't you tell her that?"

James swallowed hard, even though his coffee was long gone. "Because..." He trailed off, trying to work through the confusion in his brain. With so many thoughts whirling around, it was almost impossible to see his way through. "Because I'm scared," he finally admitted.

He was fucking terrified. For three years he'd lived a ghost of a life. Work, home, the occasional dinner with his parents or a friend. It was as though he'd tied an invisible barrier around himself, one that protected him from the intense, unbearable pain of losing everything he loved.

To remove that protection meant being vulnerable once more. And if he was honest, he wasn't sure his heart could take it.

Sometimes the only way to protect yourself was to be isolated. To be an island.

"Is it about Sara and Jacob?" Lucas asked, his voice full of sympathy. "Because what happened to you... man... I can't imagine how it must have felt. You've been through hell for the past three years. Lost everything you loved. It's okay to be scared." His voice dipped. "Do you feel guilty about moving on?"

James's throat felt thick, as though it was closing up. "I do," he admitted, his voice low. "And I should. They don't get to move on, they don't get to have another family. And here I am, asking another woman to move in with me."

"That's survivor's guilt. It's natural." Lucas nodded. "I see it all the time in my line of work. But at some point you have to either work through it or let it go."

"It's the anniversary of their deaths on Saturday," James told him. "Sara's parents and sister are coming in for the day. They want us all to visit her grave."

"Shit. I'm sorry." Lucas's eyes softened. "There are always reminders, huh?"

"Yeah." James took a deep breath. "They have no idea about Harper or the baby."

"You gonna tell them?"

"Not on Saturday." James shook his head. "That would be cruel. They're coming because of Sara. I'd break their hearts if I told them about the baby then."

"But you need to tell them soon."

"Yeah. And I will. I'll speak to Sara's sister when they're back in Phoenix." He rubbed his jaw with the heel of his hand.

"Maybe they'll be happy for you," Lucas suggested. "They can't want you to be on your own forever. They know you're a young guy with his whole life to live."

"I guess."

"And so is Harper." Lucas huffed out a laugh. "Not that she's a guy, but she does have her life to live. And it's partly up to you whether she does that with somebody else or with you."

The thought of her being with somebody else was like a punch to the gut. Of her smiling at another guy the way she smiled at him. At their baby reaching for another guy, maybe even calling him Dad.

She was his. Even if she didn't know it.

"I don't want that," he said, pressing his lips together.

"Well you may not have a choice." Lucas shrugged. "You know what you don't want, but what is it you *do* want? Once you work that out, the rest will follow."

"Maybe." James nodded. But the twist in his gut remained. Because even if he knew what he wanted, he had no idea how to make it happen.

❧ 2 2 ❧

"I don't get it," Caitie said, a frown pulling at her lips. "I thought you really liked him."

"I do," Harper agreed. "But we've never talked about making it official. Or about me moving in with him until now."

They were walking down the beach on Saturday morning, carrying their coffees from Déjà Brew in their hands. Caitie was gripping Harper's empty hand, anxiety pressing her fingers into Harper's soft skin. What was a simple walk along the beach for most people was an ordeal for Harper's best friend. Caitie had been afraid of the ocean for most of her life, but for the past year she'd been in therapy to try and control her phobia. This walk was recommended by her therapist — a half hour every week, as close to the water's edge as she could manage without feeling uncomfortable.

Though it was off-season, the beach was still filling up with locals, and the azure of the ocean was dotted with surfers trying to catch the waves. Breck was one of them out there. Far enough away for Caitie not to use him as someone to lean on, close enough to be here if she started to panic.

When he'd spotted them on the shore he'd waved and gestured he was here if they needed him in the next half hour. That gave them long enough to walk to Paxton's Pier and back, and maybe head back into Déjà Brew to grab one of those blueberry muffins.

"But you said no when he asked you to move in?" Caitie asked, taking a sip through the hole in the lid of her cup. She seemed grateful for the distraction of Harper's messed up love life. "Don't you want to be in a relationship with him?"

"I did. I mean, I do." Harper shook her head. "You see how messed up I already am? Between growing a baby and growing a business I'm finding it hard to think straight."

Caitie squeezed her hand. "Well let's concentrate on one thing at a time. Why did you say no?"

"Because..." Harper sighed. "He made it sound like a business proposition. You need something, I have something, let's make a deal."

"Hoo boy." Caitie whistled.

"Right? It's not that I was expecting a declaration of undying love or anything. But a little emotion would have helped."

A little boy ran in front of them, chasing a rolling ball. Caitie froze as he continued to the water's edge. Harper automatically looked to the left to see if an adult was following him, relieved when she saw his mom running down the beach.

"Are you okay?" she asked Caitie.

"Yeah. Let's just keep on walking. And talking. Did you tell him you wanted some emotion?"

They continued along the sand, their sandaled feet sinking as they walked. Caitie's grasp on her hand didn't loosen. "I said I wanted the fairytale."

A laugh escaped from Caitie's lips in spite of her anxiety. "What did he say?"

"He pretty much told me he couldn't give me that." Harper shrugged. "And then we went to sleep."

"But that was two days ago. Have you talked since?"

Harper shook her head. "We haven't had a chance. He had to work a double on Thursday, and then last night I had a late night meeting at the resort to run through the fashion show." She sighed. "Not that I think it matters. I have no idea what to say to him."

"Maybe that you're in love with him?"

Harper stopped walking. "What?"

"Well aren't you?"

"I..." Her mouth dropped open, her bottom lip trembling. "You think I'm in love with him?"

"Yeah, I do." Caitie took a sip of her coffee. "There's no need to look so scared about it. I've seen the way you smile whenever he's around. The way you glow when his name is mentioned. And I've heard about the hot sex, so..." She shrugged. "I think this is it for you."

Harper's chest tightened. "But what if he doesn't feel the same way?" she asked. "What if he doesn't love me?"

All those childhood fears gripped hold of her. Those reminders that she wasn't good enough for her mom to stay around, or for her grandma to give her praise. She was Harper Hayes, the girl who nobody wanted to keep around.

And it hurt so damn bad. She wasn't sure she could take it again.

She took a deep breath. She wasn't that girl anymore. She was a strong woman. One who had her own business, a child on the way, and a life to look forward to, no matter who was in it. And those memories? They needed to stay where they belonged, deep inside her.

In the past.

They'd almost reached Paxton's Pier. Delmonico's was already busting with customers eating brunch on the deck.

The air was filled with the sound of their chatter. On her right, she heard the crashing of a wave against the shore, and she looked up to see Breck's surfboard carry him in. Behind him, Harper could see Jackson and Griff sitting on their boards and waving. She lifted her hand to wave back.

"Hey," Caitie called out, as Breck waded through the shallows. "That was good timing."

"I aim to please." He grinned, lifting his board out of the water. "How are you holding up."

"Harper's distracting me, so it's all good." Caitie glanced at her watch. "It's been almost twenty minutes. That's some kind of record, right?"

His eyes softened. "Baby, you're doing great." He looked at Harper. "You doing okay?"

She nodded. "I'm good."

"No, she isn't. She has guy problems." Caitie pressed her lips together. "Hey, maybe you can give us a male perspective on this."

"If it's okay with Harper." He planted the end of his board in the sand, and leaned against it, the breeze ruffling his damp hair.

"Yeah, it's okay with me." She welcomed it. Maybe he could make sense of what the heck was going on in James's life.

"Okay, then," Caitie said, her eyes catching Breck's. "Why did you ask me to move in with you?"

"Because I couldn't live without you." He shrugged. "Is this a trick question?"

In spite of the location, Caitie melted. "You're the sweetest talker, you know that?"

"You guys want me to leave?" Harper grinned.

"Nope. Sorry, I just got distracted for a moment. So, back to this problem." Caitie shot her an apologetic glance. "How easy did you find it to tell me how you felt?"

"Before we moved in together? Or before we got together at all."

"The last one."

He shook his head, a smile playing at his lips. "She knows the answer to this already," he told Harper. "I was terrified. Didn't even want to admit it to myself. I kept kidding myself that I was being brotherly toward her. After all, she's Lucas's sister and he's one of my best friends. There's a code for that, you know?"

"The bro code," Harper agreed. "Yeah, I've heard of it."

"How long did it take you to tell me how you really feel?" Caitie continued, the smile still lifting her lips.

Harper knew some of the answer to this. Caitie had been her roommate for years, after all, giving Harper a ringside view to the push and pull of her friend's relationship with Brecken Miller. She'd had to watch silently – okay, maybe not so silently – as Caitie had pushed away her feelings for him, denying the attraction between them that was so obvious to everyone else.

But she'd never heard Breck's side of the story. Intrigued, she turned her gaze on him.

"It took me months to pull my head out of my ass," he admitted. "It wasn't so much I was hiding my feeling as denying them. I didn't want to admit to myself I'd fallen for you until I realized there was no other way."

"Why didn't you want to admit it?" Harper asked, her brows knitting together.

"Because I was scared." He blinked away a droplet of water that had fallen from his hair into his eyes. "Is this about James? What's happened?"

"He asked me to move in with him."

"Okay..." Confusion fogged his eyes.

"But he made her feel as if it was for convenience's sake," Caitie added. "He didn't tell her how he felt about her at all."

Breck sighed. "Sounds like a guy. You want me to go beat him up for you?"

Harper smiled. "Nah. I like him the way he is. Without bruises."

"Well the offer's open." He winked. "But seriously, from what I know of James, he's had a lot to go through. I lost my mom years ago and it still affects me. I have no idea how awful it must be to lose your wife and child. Those scars don't ever heal completely. They change your emotions, your outlook on life, your openness to other people. The kind of hurt he's experienced is unimaginable. And his first thought is probably to do whatever it takes to never feel that way again." He brought his soft gaze on Harper. "Including facing his feelings for you."

Her chest tightened at his words. At the thought of James being in so much pain. She hated it. Wanted to smooth it away with her fingers, to curl herself around him and protect him from all of it.

But she couldn't. Not if she wanted to protect herself, too. And now there was somebody else to think about. This baby growing inside of her. One day their daughter would want her father's love. For him to be honest and open with his emotions. She curled her hand protectively against her bump, knowing she'd do whatever it took to make sure her baby never felt the rejection she'd had from a parent.

"So how do we get him to face these feelings?" Caitie asked.

Breck shrugged. "You can't. It's up to him to fight his demons. I only fought mine when I thought I was going to lose you. That's when I pulled my head out of my ass and finally realized the way I'd been living wasn't going to work any more. Yeah, you can push those feelings down and pretend they're not there for a while, but eventually that's gonna rise up and bite you with teeth more painful than the original hurt. It's the old fight or flight response. You have to learn to fight."

Caitie released Harper's hand and slid her arms around Breck's waist, hugging him. "I'm so glad you fought," she whispered against his chest.

"Me, too. More than you know." He kissed the top of her head. "Now why don't you guys go and grab another coffee and I'll meet you at the café in a bit?" He slid his finger beneath Caitie's chin, tipping her head up to kiss her lips. "You did it, baby. You walked along the beach without panicking. I'm proud of you."

Caitie's smile shone from her face. "I'm proud of you, too."

Harper's heart clenched. This was what she wanted. A relationship full of honesty and vulnerability. And it hurt to know she might not be able to have that with James.

"Come on," Caitie said, releasing Breck and taking Harper's hand again. "I think that's enough therapy for both of us. Let's go grab a couple blueberry muffins."

The arrivals terminal was full of people when James walked into the airport, his car keys shoved in his jeans pocket, his phone curled in his hand. His stomach felt tight, as though he'd done too many sit-ups in the gym.

He really didn't want to be here. It wasn't that he disliked Sara's family. He'd always gotten along well with them whenever they'd visited. But after losing his wife and son, the relationship was another painful reminder, one that made him want to turn on his heels and walk out of the airport as fast as his legs would move.

But of course he didn't. Instead, he stood at the barrier waiting for an airplane-load of people to spill out into the main terminal. He knew from the monitors that hung above the doors that the flight from Phoenix had arrived twenty minutes earlier. Since they were only here for the day, her family wouldn't be bringing luggage with them. They should be out any minute, and the thought of it turned his stomach once again.

Any other Saturday and he'd be either checking in with his patients at the hospital, or helping Harper with her work. He'd taken to delivering her dresses to local boutiques to save her the trouble, and the carrying. Right now she was trying to get her apartment ready, and he could be helping her to paint the nursery, or building the crib that her friends had bought her off the registry she and James had spent a night agonizing over.

He let out a mouthful of air, thinking of their last conversation. His middle-of-the-night offer for her to move in. The confused expression on her face when he'd made it.

He still hadn't figured out how to make it better. But he knew he wanted to. After talking to Lucas he knew for certain that he wanted Harper and their baby in his life. Wanted to take care of them, protect them, and show them how much he cared.

But there was still a gap between them, and he had no idea how to cross it.

The doors opened and a group of people walked out, their voices loud as they chatted together. James swallowed. If he could just get through today, then he'd figure out what to do about his relationship with Harper tomorrow.

It had to be redeemable. Didn't it?

"James?" a voice called out. Then he saw Alice pushing her mom in a wheelchair, her father shuffling along beside her. She lifted a hand in greeting and he waved back, his teeth pressing together so hard it made the corner of his jaw twitch. Her lips lifted in a half-smile, the same way Sara's used to whenever he told her a lame joke. It was like a warm up for the full thing, and he found himself wanting to look away.

"Hey," he said when they reached him. He kissed Alice's cheek and shook her dad's hand, then leaned down to hug her mom. "How was your flight?"

"It was good. They gave us priority boarding which was a good help with Mom. And extra legroom for Dad." Alice smiled. "Thank you so much for meeting us."

Up close he could see how much Sara's parents had aged, even in the year since he'd seen them last. He knew from Alice that her mom's weak hips meant she had to spend most of her time in a wheelchair, and that her dad had a heart scare a few months ago.

But he wasn't prepared to see how it had affected them. A few years ago they'd been active, their faces lit with joy as they'd held Jacob in their arms for the first time. In the three years since his death, they seemed to have aged two decades, and it cut him to the core.

"I thought we could grab some coffee and head over to the cemetery," James said, taking the wheelchair from Alice and steering it toward the exit. "Then maybe head back to my place before our reservation at Delmonico's. Give you all a chance to rest."

From the looks of Alice's parents, they were going to need it.

"That sounds perfect." Alice smiled at him. "We need to be back here at eight for our flight home."

"That's fine. I can bring you back right from the restaurant."

"We appreciate that so much." Alice put her hand over his as he pushed the wheelchair. "Thank you for all you've done."

He nodded, coming to a stop in front of the oversized glass doors, waiting for them to swing open. When they did, he pushed the wheelchair through, his eyes blinking as they adjusted to the bright California light.

One day. That was all this was. And if he had to spend it with his chest hurting and his teeth grinding together then he'd do that for Sara and Jacob.

And tomorrow he'd sort out the rest of his life.

❦ 23 ❦

"Lift your head up for me, sweetie," Harper said softly. The little girl tipped her head back, and Harper took the pins out from between her lips, sliding them into the straps that needed tightening. "That's it," she told her, standing back to check the fit. "You look amazing."

"Can I see in the mirror?" Lola asked, so excited she was practically jumping up and down.

"Sure. Come with me. You need to walk carefully because there are pins everywhere. I don't want them to jab you." Harper took the little girl's hand and led her to the floor length mirror. She stood behind her, hands on her shoulders and watched her reflection as her face lit up.

"I look like a princess," Lola whispered.

"Yes you do. And on the day of the fashion show you'll feel like one, too. You'll be wearing a little silver crown with flowers in your hair. I can't wait to see what you look like."

They were in a small room in the Silver Sands Resort, fitting all the models for the fashion show in three weeks' time. Lola's mom was standing next to them, taking photographs of her daughter as she stared at herself in the mirror. "She's a natural," Harper whispered. "So grown up for a five-year-old."

"She's always been like this," Lola's mom agreed. "From the moment she was born she seemed like a mini-adult. We've been so lucky with her, being able to take her places without worrying she'll throw a tantrum or start screaming." She nodded at Harper's stomach. "How long until your little one arrives?"

"Seven weeks." Harper took a deep breath. When she said it like that, it didn't sound long at all. She was counting down the days until the fashion show. After that, she promised herself she'd slow down. She'd already paid the first three months' rent on her apartment, and had more saved in the bank to see her through the first few months after the baby was born. And she knew from the orders she'd received for her next season's collection that she had more than enough work to keep her cash flowing.

"Not long then. I had Lola at thirty-five weeks. She stopped growing so they took me in for an emergency C-section." She smiled. "It was so scary at the time, but now look at her. You wouldn't know she was premature at all."

"Thirty-five weeks?" Harper repeated. "That's early."

"Not any more. There were babies in the NICU much smaller than her. One was born at twenty-eight weeks. He was tiny, no bigger than my hand, and yet he survived." She smiled. "Lola looked like a giant compared to him."

Harper rubbed her stomach. "Well this baby isn't going anywhere," she said firmly. "I have too much to do before then."

Lola's mom laughed. "I'll keep my fingers crossed for you."

"Thank you. I'll take all the luck I can get."

She was still thinking about their conversation later as she pulled out of the parking lot and onto the main beach road leading to Angel Sands. The dresses she'd fitted were in the back of her car, ready to be adjusted prior to the fashion show. She glanced at the clock on her dash – she had no plans this afternoon. Maybe she'd get started on them now, then she could spend the next week concentrating on other orders.

Her sewing machine and supplies were still in James's basement. There was no way she wanted to risk them getting dusty, or even worse, splashed with paint, while she was decorating her apartment. When she pulled into his driveway she saw his car wasn't there. That wasn't unusual. He often spent Saturdays checking on his patients, even if he wasn't on shift.

Grabbing the key from her purse, she let herself in, carefully carrying the dresses down the stairs into the basement. Each one was covered in a protective bag and she hung them on the rack next to her sewing table, before she walked into the bathroom to make sure her hands were thoroughly clean.

These designs were too precious to leave a smudge or stain on them now. Each one perfectly fit to the model's body, ready to be worn on the night of the show. She tied her hair up and pulled on a pair of soft white gloves, then unzipped the first bag, carefully removing the dress from its hanger.

The rest of her life might be a mess, but at least her business was thriving. It gave her one less thing to worry about.

They drove in silence back from the cemetery. It had been tough, watching Sara's parents cry at her grave. Her mother had tried to swallow her sobs, but that almost made it worse. He understood the strangled cry of a parent who'd lost their child, after all.

Alice had left a tiny teddy bear next to Jacob's grave, nestling it among the other toys that had been left over the years. He'd watched, dry-eyed, as Alice had kissed his son's headstone, then wiped her own tears away from her cheeks.

It was only the third time they'd visited since his wife and child passed. They'd been here for the funeral, of course, but that was all a blur to James. He could barely remember the day at all. All that was left in his mind were blurred images of people surrounding the dug graves as their caskets were lowered into the ground. He knew he'd thrown in the first handful of earth, but couldn't conjure up that memory at all.

Most of that first year had been fuzzy. He'd gone back to work after two months, despite the protests of his parents and his boss. But it had been the best thing for him, burying himself in cases and the needs of his patients rather than wallowing in his pain alone at home.

Seeing the rawness of Sara's family's pain reminded him of those days. Like a magnet, they pulled him back to the man he used to be. Widower, grieving father, the man who could barely look at himself in the mirror.

"Whose car is that?" Alice asked as he pulled into the driveway. He looked at the red Toyota, his throat dry as he realized Harper must be here.

"It's a friend's," he said, his voice rough. "She's been using the basement for her business. I'm guessing she's down there now."

"She has a key?" Alice asked. He couldn't tell from her tone whether it was idle conversation or something more.

"It's easier. I work a lot."

"Of course."

The pulse in his temple was edging on painful. He rubbed it as he climbed out and pulled the wheelchair from the trunk, setting it up and helping Sara's mom out of the car. He pulled his keys out of his pocket and pushed her to the front door.

As soon as they were inside he felt the pull. The need to go downstairs and see her. Hear her voice. To know life was still going on, in the form of Harper and their baby, and to be sure they were both okay.

"I need the bathroom," Alice's mom said. "Can you take me, honey?"

Alice nodded. "Sure."

"You remember where it is? James asked, and Alice nodded. "Okay, I'll just go tell Harper we're here so we don't surprise her. Then I'll put some coffee on, before we head to Delmonico's."

His heart was pounding as he opened the basement door and walked down the stairs. He could hear the whirr of Harper's sewing machine and the soft music coming from the stereo in the corner. Then he saw her, her hair pulled back in a ponytail, bent over the machine as she fed the fabric beneath the needle.

"Harper?"

The machine stopped as she lifted her foot from the pedal. Slowly she turned around, her eyes blinking as she saw him standing there. "Hey," she said. "I wasn't expecting to see you. I assumed you were at the hospital."

"Not today. I... ah... had something else to do."

She stood, then groaned and slid her hand beneath her bump. "I swear this little monkey is on some kind of sugar high," she told him. "She hasn't stopped moving all day."

The need to touch her pulled at him. "Can I feel?"

"Yeah, of course." She walked toward him, though it was becoming more of a waddle now. On her small frame her stomach looked absurdly swollen. As though she was closer to full term than only thirty-three weeks. She stopped in front of him, her expression unreadable, as he slid his hands down her abdomen, swallowing hard at the feel of her body against his palms.

"Here," she said softly, moving his palm beneath her bump. "Can you feel her?"

Through the barrier of her skin he felt a thump against his hand. "Yeah," he said. "Is that a foot?"

"She's head down now. So I'm thinking it's a hand." Her lips curled. "She's high fiving you."

"Or punching me."

Harper laughed and the sound of it warmed him. "She had the hiccups last night. Every thirty seconds it was like an earthquake in my stomach. I couldn't sleep."

"I wish I'd felt it."

"I do, too."

"James, you're out of soap. Where do you keep it?" Alice's voice echoed from the top of the basement stairs.

He snatched his hands away from Harper's stomach. She blinked at the abruptness of his movement. How the hell hadn't he heard the basement door open? Had he left it open?

A second later he heard her footsteps on the stairs. "James?" she called again.

Harper's eyes met his. Her brow dipped. "Who's that?"

But then Alice had reached the bottom of the stairs and was standing five feet away from them. Her expression was as confused as Harper's. She opened her mouth and closed it again, biting down on her lip.

But it was Harper who grabbed his attention. She let out a cry and stepped backward, clutching her hand to her chest. "Sara?" she whispered, her voice cracking. "I thought you were dead."

❧ 24 ❧

L
ong dark hair, pulled into a low ponytail. Eyes so blue they looked almost unreal. But it was the expression on Sara's face that made Harper's heart start to hammer against her chest. The shock at seeing another woman in her basement, a pregnant woman at that.

Harper took another ragged breath and stepped back again, this time her hands cradling her stomach. Her first thought was to protect her unborn child, so vulnerable in her womb. Her heart was hammering like crazy against her chest.

"Who is she?" Sara asked, her eyes sweeping over Harper. "Why were you touching her, James?"

Harper's legs started to tremble, her muscles weakening with fear. She reached out for the chair to steady herself.

And James. Strong, sturdy James. He looked from one to the other as though he had no idea who either of them were. And for a moment all Harper could think about was an old movie she'd seen. Jane Eyre meeting the first Mrs. Rochester who'd been locked in the attic.

The urge to laugh came over her. This was so melodramatic. Things like this didn't happen to her. It was as though she was an observer, watching the scene play out on a flat screen. She wanted to scream at herself to leave before something bad happened.

"I need to go," she said, willing her legs to move herself forward. But as she passed James he grabbed her wrist.

"Sit down," he urged. "You look way too pale."

"Of course I'm pale. Your dead wife just walked into the basement."

"I'm not Sara." The woman with Sara's face shook her head. "I'm Alice. Her twin."

"Sara has a twin sister?" Harper looked at James. "Why didn't you tell me?"

"I... I never thought." It's his turn to frown. "Alice and her parents live in Phoenix."

"And who are you?" Alice asked again, confusion marring her face.

"I'm Harper." She still felt disoriented. The same kind of sick feeling she used to get when she stepped off a roller-coaster. "Harper Hayes."

"Okay." Alice nodded.

Harper breathed heavily. The shock of thinking she was Sara still hadn't quite worn off.

"Harper's the friend I was telling you about," James said. "She's been using the basement for her business."

Alice licked her lips, her brows pulled down as though she was trying to work something out. "You didn't say she was pregnant." She looked down at Harper's stomach. "I'm completely confused here. What's going on?"

Harper waited for James to explain. To tell Sara's sister about their baby, their relationship. Her chest ached as he looked from her and then back to Alice, his lips pressed together.

"It's complicated," he finally said. "I'll explain later." He barely glanced at Harper. "The new soap is in the bathroom cupboard. I'll come up and show you."

He was leaving? Harper couldn't quite believe it. She watched as he walked over to where Sara stood at the bottom of the stairs. Waited for him to turn back, hold his hand out for her, and introduce her properly to the sister of his dead wife.

But instead he gave Harper a nod. "I'll talk to you later."

Blood rushed through her ears, dulling the sound of his footsteps as he led Alice back up the stairs. Harper stood there, alone, her hand cradling the baby, feeling the press of a hand against her own. Her cheeks burned with the rejection, her throat so tight she was finding it hard to breathe.

Had he really just walked out and left her? She felt like the little girl she'd once been, watching at the window as her mom stepped into the car of yet another boyfriend. Harper had pressed her nose against the glass and prayed her mom would turn around, come back and tell her she wasn't really leaving.

But she always left. And Harper was always the forgotten child. The memory of it was like a knife to her chest. When she'd left home at the age of eighteen she'd sworn she'd never feel like this again. Unwanted, ignored, neglected.

Yet here she was, letting the man she'd fallen for make her feel worse than she'd ever felt in her life. The worst part was she'd let him. Let him pretend she was nobody, dismiss her like she was just some friend he'd met along the way. Maybe she wasn't the strong woman she'd thought she was.

She'd let herself down. And that was the worse betrayal of all.

James glanced at the basement door, pressing his lips together to stop himself from swearing. Because, *shit,* he'd been an idiot. He wanted to punch himself for putting Harper in that position. And Alice, too. He should have known something like this would happen. Just when it felt like his life was back on an even footing something came along to sabotage it.

No, not something. Someone. In this case, himself. Why the hell hadn't he spoken to Alice or her parents about Harper and the baby before now?

Because you didn't want to upset them. Or for them to think you were moving on too quickly.

Yeah, well that ship had well and truly sailed. There was nothing for it. He needed to speak to Alice and her parents *now.* And then somehow make it up to Harper. He shook his head at the memory of her face when she realized Alice didn't even know who she was.

What kind of man did that make him?

"I need to explain something to you," James said to Alice in a low voice as they walked along the hallway. "And then I need you to help me tell your parents without upsetting them any more."

"Explain what?" Alice asked him. "Is it about your friend?"

"Harper? Yeah." He nodded. His stomach still felt twisted, as though a pair of invisible hands were wringing it tightly. "But she's not just my friend. She's more than that."

"You're in a relationship?"

"We are." God, he wished he could define it more than that. But that's what not wanting to open yourself up got you. A mess of a life that you couldn't figure out how to fix.

"And the baby?"

"It's mine."

"Oh god, James." Alice let out a ragged sigh. "I didn't expect..."

"Of course you didn't. And I'm sorry I have to tell you like this. I should have warned you if nothing more."

"How far along is she?"

"Seven months."

"And you didn't think to tell us? To warn us? Were you going to have the baby and keep it a secret?" He watched as her expression changed, her eyes blinking too fast, her bottom lip trembling. "I don't understand."

"I was planning on telling you. Just not today when everything was so heightened. I know you wanted today to be about Sara and Jacob."

"When then?" She shook her head. "When were you going to tell us? It's not as if it's a new thing. She's seven months pregnant. In two months you're going to have a child, James, and you've hidden it from us. What did you think we were going to do?"

"I don't know. I don't..." He rubbed his jaw with the heel of his hand. "I didn't want you to find out like this. I know it must be a shock, with everything that happened with Sara and Jacob."

"It's a shock because you lied to us. Didn't you think we might bump into her while we were here? Or that I might see something on social media? When were you planning to tell us? When the baby started Kindergarten?" Her eyes flashed. "Or were you not going to say anything at all?"

"Alice? Do you have the soap, sweetheart?" her mom called out from the bathroom, her voice as thin as paper.

"I'm coming, Mom." Alice met James's gaze, her eyes full of anger. "I think we should leave," she told him. "I can't go out to eat and pretend everything's okay. I'll see if we can catch an earlier flight home."

"You don't need to do that."

"Actually, I think we do."

Behind him, he heard a click. He frowned, whipping around to see the blurred image of Harper through the glass front door. Where was she going? He looked at Alice. "I need to go speak to her."

"Alice?" her mom called again. "What's happening?"

"Nothing, Mom." Alice glared at him again. "I'll be right in." She lowered her voice as she spoke to James. "You go do what you need to do, and then you can come back and explain."

He was already halfway down the hall. His pulse sped as he reached for the front door, yanking it open and running onto the porch. Harper was climbing into her car, and he called out to her. "Wait up!"

It was as though he hadn't said anything. She climbed into the car and pulled the door shut behind her. He reached the bottom of the stairs and ran across the blacktop. "Harper, stop."

But she was already starting her car, the engine sparking to life. He pulled at the door knob, but she'd already locked it.

"Are you okay?" he shouted above the rumble of the engine, even though he knew she wasn't. "Let me talk to you, explain things. This can't be good for the baby."

Her hands trembled as she shifted the car into reverse, her knuckles bleaching as she grasped onto the wheel. He rapped on the window. "Harper," he called. "Please."

Her eyes slowly met his. And what he saw in them almost killed him; hurt, anger, and worse than anything, betrayal. He'd done this to her. He'd hurt her.

He stood as still as a statue as she pulled away from him, maneuvering the car out of the driveway and onto the road. As the last traces of fumes dissipated into the afternoon air, he could feel his body ache with the knowledge that this was all his fault.

Hurt people hurt people, wasn't that what they said? But

he was beyond hurt. He was broken. And now he'd broken the one thing he cared about the most.

"I feel so stupid," Harper muttered, her hands curled around her coffee cup, the warm china hot against her palms. "I'd built this thing up into my mind until it was real. I really believed he wanted what I did."

"What did you want?" Ember asked softly. They were sitting in her cottage, which Harper had driven right to upon leaving James's house. Caitie and Breck were away, and she couldn't think of anybody else to talk to. And she didn't want to be alone.

Not again.

"What everybody else wants," Harper said, her voice small. "A family."

Ember's face crumpled as she cradled Arthur tightly. "Oh sweetie."

Harper took a deep breath, but it did nothing to calm her nerves. The tears that had spilled as soon as she'd driven away from James had dried on her cheeks, making her skin feel salty and sticky. Her eyes filled again as she remembered the way he'd hidden her. Like she was some guilty secret he didn't want Sara's family to discover.

"I wanted it so bad, I ignored all the signs," Harper said, lifting her hand to wipe a tear from her cheek. "I really thought I could give this baby everything I never had. Two parents who wanted her. Who loved her. Who'd never make her feel like this."

"She *has* two parents who love her," Ember said, her voice gentle. "She does."

"But what good is that when she goes to Kindergarten and finds out she's the only one whose parents don't live together? I don't want her to be the kid who has to sit alone while everybody else's father comes to the classroom for *donuts with dad's* day. I don't want her to cry because she feels so left out. I want her to have everything I didn't have." She took a deep breath. "And I've failed her."

"No you haven't," Ember said firmly. "You haven't failed her at all. You've done nothing but think of her for the past seven months. I'm a first grade teacher, want to know how many of my kids don't have parents who are together any more? At least half of them. So don't start beating yourself up over that." She leaned forward, moving Arthur until he was resting in the crook of her left arm, taking Harper's hand in her right. "You of all people should know it's not where you've come from that matters, but where you're going."

Harper took a ragged breath. "I just thought I'd worked it out this time. I really believed in the fairytale, you know?"

"The fairytale?"

"The one where you meet your Prince Charming, get knocked up by him, and then somehow you both fall in love." Harper sighed. "I sound like such an idiot. You don't need to tell me."

"You're not an idiot. And for the record, fairytales suck. You ever read a real one? Not the Disney version, but as they were originally written? In Cinderella, the ugly stepsisters chop off their feet and have their eyes pecked out. The Little Mermaid gets left by the prince and pines for him forever in the ocean." Ember grimaced. "Seriously, don't ever aim for the fairytale."

Harper smiled through her tears. "Why doesn't that make me feel any better?"

"Because you're hurt and you're scared, and you've forgotten you're a strong woman who's going to become an amazing mother to your baby. Maybe you got so entranced by the fairytale you forgot who you are."

Harper blinked away a stray tear.

"Seriously," Ember continued. "Look at you. In the past seven months you've lost your job and built an empire. You've gotten knocked up and somehow managed to not only track down the father but build a friendship with him. And you've moved to this beautiful town where you know everybody has your back. You're winning at life, even if you don't know it."

Harper wanted to believe every word. But the voice in her head was too loud. Telling her she was exactly what her grandmother had told her she'd become. What her mother showed her she was by walking out on her time and time again.

Unwanted. Forgotten. A little girl lost.

Her phone buzzed on the arm of her chair. Harper glanced at it to see James's name lighting up the screen.

"Do you want to get that?" Ember asked her.

Harper shook her head. "I'm not ready to talk to him yet."

"He probably just wants to explain." Ember smiled. "Maybe you should let him."

"I will. Just not right now." Harper slid her thumb across the screen to reject the call. "I think I'm going to head home and get some sleep. The baby and I have had enough excitement for one day. I'm exhausted." She slid her phone into her pocket and leaned over to hug her friend, being careful not to squash Arthur. "Thank you," she whispered. "For being here and letting me talk."

"You're welcome to stay as long as you'd like. There's no rush for you to leave."

"You're very sweet." Harper nodded. "But I should go home. It's been a hell of a long day." She thought of those half-finished dresses still hanging in James's basement. Another reason she'd need to talk to him, if there weren't a million more important ones.

"Okay. Sleep should help. And hopefully things will look

better in the morning." Ember squeezed her hand. "If you need anything call me. Day or night. The likelihood is I'll be awake anyway."

Harper smiled. "Something else for me to look forward to."

"Being a mom is worth every minute of the sleepless nights." Ember kissed the top of Arthur's head. "You'll find that out, too. Soon enough."

Yeah, she would, and the thought of it didn't scare her. Instead it made her feel warm inside. Whatever happened, this baby growing inside her was more important than anything else. Harper was damned sure her child was going to know that.

"Thank you," she said again, pulling her keys from her purse. "And there's no need to get up and see me out. Arthur looks way too comfortable right there."

Ember snuggled him in closer. "If you're sure you're okay..."

"I am." She hugged her one last time. "I've got this. Or at least I will after some sleep. I'll call you tomorrow."

"Be sure you do." Ember winked. "Sweet dreams."

25

For the first time in days, sleep came easy for Harper. Maybe it was sheer exhaustion, or more likely her mind just didn't want to think any more. It was like an engine that had been over used and had finally burnt out.

When she woke the next morning, her eyes were stuck together with sleep. She slowly opened them and licked her dry lips, wrinkling her nose at the taste of her own morning breath.

Slowly the memories of yesterday returned. Sara's sister, James's denials, her own shocked response. Groaning, she sat up and checked her phone for the first time, pressing her lips together when she saw she had ten missed calls.

Her stomach jumped as the baby kicked her. She rubbed the spot at the top of her belly where a foot was still poking out. "You have big feet," she whispered, feeling the outline of a heel. "You must take after your daddy with that."

As if she could hear her, the baby shifted, making the skin on Harper's abdomen ripple. She was so used to it now, that it was going to be strange after the baby was born and she was no longer sharing space with her tiny body.

That's when the fun would really begin.

The baby jabbed her again, as if to get her attention, but at the exact same moment her phone began to vibrate. It was James, again. With a deep breath she picked it up and accepted his call.

"Hello."

"Harper? Are you okay? I've been worried about you."

"I know. I'm sorry I didn't answer your calls. I've been asleep since five last night. I was going to call you as soon as I got up."

"I'm going into an emergency surgery in half an hour. I just wanted to talk to you. Hear your voice."

She wasn't sure what to say to that. It was weird how calming his voice was in her ear. And yet it made her edgy, too. As though she didn't trust her own responses.

It was crazy how alluring that fairytale could be.

"Good luck with the surgery," she finally said.

"Are you working in the basement today? Maybe we can talk when I get home."

"I'm moving my things to my apartment today. I'll probably be gone by the time you get home. It's time I gave you your space back and started working from my home."

"But you haven't finished decorating."

"No, but it'll be fine."

"What about the space? Won't you be cramped with everything there? You know you're welcome to work at my place for as long as you want."

It felt as though somebody was squeezing her heart so tightly it hurt. He was being kind, she knew he was. But she didn't want kindness. She wanted love. She wanted him to beg her to stay because he missed her and wanted her with him. Not because she might run out of space.

"It's fine," she said firmly, ignoring the ache in her chest. "I've got it covered."

"Okay."

There. The voice in her head said. *Do you believe me now? He's not even going to fight for you.*

She shook her head to dislodge the thought. She was better than that. "Maybe we can talk on Friday," she suggested. "If you still want to come for my ultrasound."

"Yeah, of course. I'll be there."

That gave her five days to get over herself. To start acting like the mature mother she was supposed to be. "I should get up," she said. Not knowing how to end the conversation. "Good luck with your surgery."

"Thanks. Take it easy moving your things. No heavy lifting. I'm happy to help when I get home."

"Thank you," she said softly, already knowing she wouldn't take him up on his offer.

He wanted to be her knight in shining armor. She wanted him to be her Prince Charming. But neither of those things were good for her. Right now all she needed from James Tanner was for him to be the best dad he could ever be to their baby.

She knew from experience he had that handled.

James stared down at his hands as he scrubbed the antiseptic soap into his skin, being careful to cover every inch. Ten strokes to each side of the thumb, then to each of his fingers with the sterile sponge, before moving up to the base of his hands and his forearms. With a disposable pick he cleaned under his nails, throwing the blue stick into the trash can beside him.

One of the first things they'd taught at medical school was how to wash your hands properly. Now it was second nature, but he still paid attention. His patients' lives depended on it.

Each scrub lasted five minutes – and every member of the surgical team did the same thing. Infection control was key when it came to the operating room.

Next to him, one of the nurses was chatting with the anesthesiologist about a series they were both watching on Netflix, their voices muffled by the masks fixed across their mouths. Normally he'd join in, or at least listen, but today he was too busy trying to calm the thoughts in his head.

Five minutes. That's how long he had until he needed to concentrate on the body in front of him. A fourteen-year-old girl with a spinal injury pressing on her main nerve.

"How about you, James?" the nurse asked.

He turned to her. "Sorry?"

"What are you watching at the moment? I'm looking for recommendations."

He resisted the urge to rub his neck. That would add another five minutes to this hand washing. "I haven't watched TV in a while."

"Oh." She blinked, as though she couldn't quite believe it. "Nothing?"

He shrugged. "Nope."

He'd been too busy helping Harper get her apartment ready. And before that he'd preferred to spend his evenings with her wrapped in his arms, whispering softly about stupid things that made him feel wistful.

How she didn't like cheese as a kid, but now couldn't live without it. Or that she used to believe moths were baby bats, and still screamed whenever she saw one. The corner of his lip twitched as he remembered the night she had a craving for donuts, and he'd driven around town in the early hours of the morning, trying to find somewhere open and serving.

And now he'd messed it all up. Hurt her in a way he'd never intended because he'd been too caught up in his own world to think about her needs. He should have told Alice and her parents about Harper and their baby before they ever stepped foot in Angel Sands. But the guilt he felt for being alive when Sara and Jacob were dead had stopped him, the way it had stopped him living until Harper stepped into his world.

For the past few months she'd pushed the darkness away. Given him hope where previously he'd had none at all. And he'd sabotaged it all.

What a fool he was.

The buzzer went off, and he rinsed his hands and arms beneath the tap, holding them up as a surgical tech passed him a sterile towel. When they were dry, he slid his arms into the gown she was holding, then slid on the latex gloves, using the fabric of his sterile gown to pull them over his fingers and palm.

"Ready?" the nurse asked.

"Yes."

She opened the door to the theater and James walked inside, reminding himself to leave his problems in the prep room, the way he always did.

They'd still be there when the surgery was over, that was for sure. Even if he wished they weren't.

❧ 2 6 ❧

"Thirty four weeks," Ellie said as they walked into her office. "How are you feeling?"

Harper had arranged to meet James at the hospital. It made sense, after all. He was working and she'd spent the morning at the Silver Sands Resort in a videoconference with the other designers as they discussed the running order for the fashion show. With only two weeks to go, everybody was tense, and Harper was no exception. On top of that, she'd barely been sleeping at night. Her head was too full of thoughts – of the baby, of James, and of course of the fashion show. It was overwhelming.

"I'm fine," Harper replied, smiling at Ellie. "A few aches and pains, but nothing abnormal."

"Your blood pressure is a little high." Ellie frowned as she looked at the read out. "Have you been getting enough sleep?"

"When the baby lets me."

James leaned forward to check the results. From the corner of her eye she could see his brow wrinkling. "One-forty over a hundred?" he murmured. "That's concerning."

"It is. We're going to need to monitor it over the next few days. Do you think you can come in daily for the next few days? I'll ask the nurse to set you up a few appointments."

"You want me here every day?" Harper repeated, her face paling. "I don't think I can do that. I have a big event coming up in a couple of weeks. I need to be prepared." She'd just about finished the alterations, but she still needed to check the fit on her models again and make some last minute changes. Plus there was talk about changing the finale – which could mean having to make another dress to fit the theme. Taking time out for a daily hospital appointment wasn't possible.

Not if she wanted to fit in food and sleep, too.

"I can measure it," James said. "And send Ellie the read-outs daily." He glanced at Harper. "That's if it's okay with you?"

Was it? The thought of seeing him every day again sent a shiver down her spine. But it also reminded her how easy it would be to let herself believe in the fairy tale. She felt torn, knowing how much easier it would make her life, yet how hard it would be on her emotions.

"Yeah," she eventually said. "That's fine with me."

"And you've had no other symptoms?" Ellie asked. "No vomiting or headaches or unusual pain in your abdomen."

"No," Harper told her. "Nothing."

"Okay. I want to run a couple of tests today to be sure. And James, I need you to keep an eye on things when I can't, okay?" She smiled at Harper. "Since Daddy is a doctor, we might as well take advantage, right?"

"Yeah, sure."

"This big event. Is there any way you can get more help with it? I'm concerned about your stress levels."

"Not really, but most of the hard work is done." Harper pressed her lips together. "There may be one more dress to make but I'll tell them it isn't possible if needed. This little baby is more important." She patted her stomach.

"Okay. Good. And do you have a plan to wind down after this? When are you thinking of taking leave?"

"I have a few more custom orders to finish, that should take me through week thirty-eight. After that, I'm planning on taking at least a month off. Probably two."

"That's sensible." Ellie made a note on her pad. "How about you, James? Are you taking time off?"

"I've requested two weeks after the birth."

Harper turned to him. "I didn't know that."

"I figured you might need some help. Or at least some sleep." He gave her the hint of a smile.

"And how about your birth plan. Do you have it ready yet?" Ellie asked.

"I've started it," Harper told her, grabbing a printed sheet from her purse.

"A start is good. You'd be amazed how many patients I see who leave it until the last minute, which is the absolute worst time to write it out. As your obstetrician, it helps me to know what you want, and to be able to let you know if it all is even an option. Can I take a look?"

Harper passed it over to her, and Ellie scanned it, nodding as she turned the page. "It's looking good. You've got nearly everything covered." She tipped her head to the side. "You don't want your mom in the room? You'd be surprised how many first timers do."

"No. I don't want my mom there." Harper's voice was thick. "My friend Caitie's going to be here to support me, along with James. And his parents will probably be in the waiting room."

"You try stopping them." James raised an eyebrow.

"And have you packed your bag yet? We recommend doing that around now. Just in case." Ellie winked.

"I have." She'd packed and unpacked it a dozen times. Right now it was by her bed, filled with everything she thought she needed.

"Then you're one up on most women I see. Okay, so let's get to the fun stuff." Ellie clapped her hands together. "You guys want to take another look at your baby?"

"How worried should I be about my blood pressure?" Harper asked once they'd left Ellie's office. They were standing in the main entrance of the hospital. James was still dressed in his green scrubs, ready to go back to work, but he'd insisted on walking her to her car.

"It's concerning, but you shouldn't worry too much. Because it will make your blood pressure spike more. It's one of those things that needs monitoring and if there are any massive changes we call Ellie. You don't have any swelling to your hands or feet, and you aren't showing any other concerning signs. Just keep trying to relax. Maybe do some yoga or other relaxation."

"What happens if I get worse?"

"Then Ellie will want you to come right in and they'll assess you. But you probably won't. The majority of women who have high blood pressure have perfectly normal births."

"And the others?"

"Might have to have an emergency cesarean to make sure they and the baby are healthy."

Harper took a deep breath, trying to keep the panic at bay. She'd been as cool as she could in the office, but knowing there could be complications made her want to cry. "I'm scared," she said quietly.

James stepped forward, as though he was going to hug her, and she found herself stepping away. God, it would be so easy to let him hold her, comfort her, pretend everything was okay. But she couldn't do that. Not now.

She wasn't her mom. She was stronger than that.

He dropped his hands back to his side, as though he'd thought better of even trying to touch her. "It's going to be okay," he told her. "Ellie is an amazing physician. She knows exactly what she's doing. If she thought you needed more observations she'd tell you. Just do what she said, try to keep the stress to a minimum and relax as much as you can. I know it's hard for you at the moment."

"I don't want to put the baby in danger, but I need to keep working for a few more weeks. I have no choice."

"There's always a choice."

"Not if I want to keep a roof over our heads and food on the table."

He looked at her, his gaze unwavering. "I can help you with that." He sighed. "I know you don't want my help, and I understand why. But you and the baby will always have a home and food. I'll make sure of it."

There was such a sweetness to his words, it made her yearn for him. "I know you would."

"But you wouldn't slow down anyway."

She gave him a half-smile. "I'll do whatever I can. I'll speak to the event coordinator at Silver Sands and explain the situation. And I'm going to stop taking any more custom orders until the baby is born." She patted her stomach. "Nothing is more important than this baby. I'm not going to risk losing her."

He took in a sharp intake of air. The clouds came down over his face, as though he was remembering Jacob and Sara. Harper felt her heart clench for him.

"She's going to be okay," she told him. "She is. I'll make sure of it."

"We both will."

"I'm going to head back home. Do a little bit of work and head over to the studio for some yoga."

"See? You can be a good patient when you want to be."

Harper laughed. "I guess we'll see about that." She inclined her head to meet his eyes. "Goodbye, James."

"I'll call you later. We can arrange a time to take your blood pressure tomorrow."

"Sounds good." She lifted her hand in goodbye, then turned on her heel and headed to the glass doors. It was only when she walked out into the open air that she realized they hadn't talked about last weekend at all. He'd put no pressure on her to discuss Alice, or how she was feeling about the situation.

And she was grateful for that. Because right now she needed to concentrate on growing this baby, and keeping her safe until the time was right to give birth.

Rich looked surprised when he opened his door to James that night. "What's up?" he asked, his head tipping to the side as he scrutinized his friend. "Oh, hey, you wanna come in?"

"Only if I'm not disturbing you."

Rich shrugged. "Mi casa es su casa, my friend. And if by disturbing you mean dragging me away from deciding on whether to order Chinese food or pizza, yeah, you're a big distraction." He grinned. "Come on in, we can order for two."

James followed Rich into his living room. He lived in an apartment three blocks from the beach. The floor-to-ceiling windows of his tenth floor home overlooked the ocean, framing the view like it was a moving picture. The television was on, but muted, a sportscaster opening and closing his mouth as no doubt he imparted the details of that day's sporting news.

"You want a drink?" Rich asked, taking a sip from his half-full bottle of beer.

"Just a soda. I'm driving."

Rich pulled a can from the refrigerator and threw it to James. "I'd wait a minute before you open it." He winked. "You want me to order you some food? I think I've decided on Chinese."

"I'm good." James wasn't feeling all that hungry; hadn't been all day. After the appointment, he'd spent the afternoon meeting with patients, trying – and failing – to put Harper and the baby out of his mind.

"How's Harper?" Rich asked, as though he was clairvoyant.

"Not great. We had an appointment with Ellie today. Her blood pressure is elevated. We're having to check it daily."

God, he'd wanted to turn back the clock to last week. Call Alice and her parents and tell them about Harper, invite them to meet her, even. He'd made so many mistakes and it was killing him to think he'd caused Harper more stress. Because all he wanted to do was put his arms around her and protect her.

He popped the tab of the soda and lifted it to his mouth to drink the bubbling overspill. "I've messed everything up," he said as he swallowed. "But that's the story of my life, isn't it?"

Rich looked up from where he was ordering on his phone. "What did you do?"

"I didn't tell Sara's family about Harper. And when they came to visit on Saturday they discovered her in the basement."

Rich's lips twitched, as though he couldn't quite decide between amusement and horror. "Oh shit. What did Harper do?" He put his phone down on the table, leaning forward to listen to James as he recounted the events of that day.

"So you two are in some kind of relationship?" Rich clarified.

"We were, but I don't think we are anymore." James took a sip of soda, but it tasted like ashes in his mouth. "I don't know really."

"And you haven't talked about it?" Rich asked.

"We were supposed to talk today, but then this stuff about her blood pressure came up." James swallowed. "What if it's my fault? I'm the one causing all the stress. I can't put her or the baby in danger because I want to know where I stand with her."

Rich pressed his lips together. "I can see that. So what are you going to do? Wait until her blood pressure's back to normal? What if it spikes again? Or will you keep your mouth shut until she's given birth?" He looked at James intently. "Jesus, don't tell me you're never going to say anything. That would be crazy."

"I'm going to take my lead from her."

Rich blinked. "What if this is it? What if she never mentions it again? Are you going to just keep on like this?"

James's chest clenched. The thought of not being able to touch her, to hold her, to curl his body around hers again until he wasn't sure where he ended and she began – it killed him.

"How do you feel about her?" Rich asked.

"What do you mean?"

Rich smiled. "I mean, do you love her?"

He didn't need to think about it. The answer was in his heart. It was in the way he thought about her night and day, the way he wanted her so badly. "Yeah," he said softly. "I'm in love with her."

"Then for Christ's sake tell her. She's a catch, man. And for some crazy reason you're the guy who caught her. Don't let your fears hold you back. Wait until the baby comes if you want, but after that you need to start fighting for her." Rich shook his head. "I had no idea the two of you were in a relationship, but now that I know, it makes sense. I've seen you smile more in the past few months than you have for years. I've watched you come alive again, when I thought we'd lost you for good. More than anything, man, I've seen you be happy, and that makes me so goddamned happy. Don't let this thing go without a fight."

James looked at his friend through fresh eyes. They'd known each other for years, since before they'd become doctors, before he'd even met Sara. And not once had he heard Rich sound so impassioned.

"Thank you," James said, his throat scratchy. "Thank you for always being here."

"It's killed me to watch you go through this. To see you lose Sara and Jacob, and yourself. There was nothing I could do to take your pain away. Then here comes this second chance. This woman who, for some reason, wants to give you everything. And all she really wants in return is some honesty."

"I know." James took a deep breath. "And you're right. About all of it." His lips lifted in a smile. "Thanks for caring. I appreciate it."

"Show me your appreciation by not messing it up." Rich smiled back at him. "And now I'm going to order some takeout before my stomach implodes."

❧ 27 ☙

Harper opened the door to her apartment, taking a deep breath when she saw James standing outside. He was carrying a cardboard tray with a coffee, a juice, and two muffins on top. Why did he make it impossible to push down her feelings for him?

"Hey. How are you feeling?" he asked.

"I'm okay. I took a nap earlier so that helped." She stood aside so he could come in. He waited for her to lead him into the kitchen where he put the tray on her granite counter. "Excuse the mess," she said, looking at the rack of dresses that filled the living room. "It'll all be gone in a couple of weeks."

"How are the preparations for the fashion show going?"

"I think I'll manage it. We've got a run through next week and the big day on Saturday." She looked shyly at him. "Would you like to come and watch?"

"Yeah," he said slowly. "I'd like that a lot."

"I'll put your name down on the guest list." She pulled at her sleeve. "I guess we should do my blood pressure before I drink the coffee. I don't want to have any caffeine spikes."

"It's decaf."

"Even worse. I'd hate for my body to go into shock."

James laughed and took the blood pressure monitor from his backpack. "Take a seat," he said, inclining his head at one of the stools pushed beneath the counter. Gently, he took Harper's arm and wrapped the cuff around it, his fingers gentle as he pressed the Velcro strips together.

It was almost impossible not to shiver at his touch.

"Are my fingers cold?" he murmured, looking at her through his thick lashes. God his eyes were striking.

She took a deep breath and shook her head. "No. It's all good."

"Okay. I'm going to start it. You'll feel pressure for a minute."

"I know." She grinned at him. "You say that every time."

"You can guarantee the one time I don't say it my patient will start freaking out. It's part of the doctor's language. Just a little pinch... you might feel some pressure... it's important to make the patient as comfortable and as aware as possible."

She wondered what it would be like to be one of his patients. He was so calm, so capable. Almost impossible not to be in love with.

And yet she had to try.

When the machine finished measuring her blood pressure it gave a beep, the cuff slowly loosening. James looked at the monitor, his brows knitting together.

"Any change?" she asked him.

"It's a little better than yesterday but still too high. Are you feeling any other symptoms? Nausea, dizziness?"

"No."

"Any swelling of your hands or feet?" He took her right hand in his, looking down as he turned it over, before he repeated it with the other. It was strangely intimate, the way he was looking at her. He might have only touched her on her arms and hands and yet her whole body was tingling.

Stupid, treacherous body.

"Nothing more than usual. I swear my feet have grown since I got pregnant. I'm living in sandals."

"That happens sometimes."

"Will they ever shrink back?"

"It depends. But maybe it's a good excuse to buy new shoes." He smiled at her. "How are you sleeping?"

"Badly. And you?" She raised an eyebrow.

"The same." He sighed. "Is there anything I can do to take some of the burden off you? I can't sew, but I'm great at transporting stuff in my car."

She lifted the lid from her coffee and took a sip. "Mmm. You want some?" she asked him.

"I drank mine on the way."

"Was Ally there?"

"Yep. She says hi. So did Nate."

Harper smiled. "Thank you for bringing this," she said, unwrapping the muffin. "I have a feeling this little baby is going to come out looking like a blueberry."

James laughed. "We'll still love her though, right?"

Her heart clenched. "Yeah, we will."

He ran the pad of his finger along his jaw. "Harper..."

"Yeah?"

"I'm so sorry about the other week. About scaring you when you saw Alice, and not telling her about you and the baby before she flew in. I never meant to hurt you."

"I know you didn't." Harper looked up at him. "But I *was* hurt."

He nodded. "I know you were, and I hate myself for it. I keep thinking that if I'd done things differently maybe you wouldn't be dealing with high blood pressure. That it's all my fault." He glanced down at the counter, letting out a mouthful of air. She wanted to run her fingers through his hair, make that frown disappear. But she couldn't. Not if she wanted to stay sane. She needed to keep her promise to herself.

No more hurts.

She pressed her lips together, trying to sort through her thoughts. "I think I expected too much," she told him. "It's none of my business who you tell about the baby. As long as you're a good dad to her, that's all I can ask for. And I know you'll be wonderful."

"I want more than that."

Her throat tightened. How many times had she longed to hear those words? To know he wanted her the way she wanted him? But he had his own demons to fight, ones that kept pulling him back to the darkness, and she couldn't fight them for him.

All she could do was protect herself.

"I don't think it's a good idea. Not now." Her gaze softened. "Everything is so heightened. With my high blood pressure and the fashion show and the due date closing in, I don't know if my heart can take much more." She rubbed her stomach. "I need to concentrate on this little one. She's all that matters."

His throat bobbed as he swallowed. "That makes sense. You don't need any more stress. You have more than enough as it is. And I agree, the baby's health – *and yours* – are the most important things."

She waited for relief to wash over her, but all she felt was sadness. Her body ached for him, for his strong arms to wrap around her, for her head to fit against his chest as he cradled her to him.

Taking a bite of the muffin, she swallowed it down and chased it with a mouthful of coffee. But it didn't fill the hole inside her at all.

"I should go," he said, putting the blood pressure monitor back in his bag. "Unless you need me for anything else?"

"Can you check the baby?" she asked him. "Listen for a heartbeat?"

"Of course. Why don't you go lie down and I'll take a listen."

She smiled at him. "Thank you. Let's use the sofa."

James warmed up the chest piece of his stethoscope on his palm, then pressed it against Harper's bare abdomen. She was lying on the sofa, her shirt rolled up to just beneath her breasts, revealing the dome of her swollen stomach.

"Tell me if it's too cold," he told her.

"Did they teach you that in medical school, too?" she teased.

"Yep. Right after how to keep your patient from driving you crazy."

She laughed and it made him feel warm. He tried to push that feeling down, ignore it. It wasn't useful right now. She'd made it clear that whatever had been going on between them wasn't going to continue. She'd been sweet as heck about it, too. But it still hurt. Especially as it was all his own damn fault. He'd had everything he wanted, and thanks to his own fears he'd lost it all.

No, that wasn't true. He hadn't lost their baby. No matter what happened between him and Harper, their daughter would always be half his. A connection between them that nothing could break. That meant something, didn't it?

He slid the tips into his ears and concentrated on his job, moving the chest piece around until he could hear a rapid rhythm, much faster than Harper's own heartbeat. He listened to it, a smile curling his lips. "She's got a strong heartbeat," he told Harper. "Want to hear?"

She nodded, and leaned forward as he slid the ear pieces in place. Her eyes lit up as she listened to the echo of their baby's life source. "So fast," she whispered. "Such a tiny heart and so much work to do."

"It sounds like a strong one." James smiled. "Should keep her going for at least ninety years."

Harper's gaze met his and he felt it again. That urgent need to hold her, to take care of her and make her smile every day. To be with her and enjoy her company, then take her to his bed and spend the night.

"Can you see the dark line on my stomach?" Harper asked him. "And the stretchmarks? They're ugly, aren't they?"

"Nope." He winked at her. "They're as beautiful as the rest of you. And they'll fade over time, you'll hardly notice them."

He wanted to trace their jagged lines, feel her stomach contract at his touch. But instead he wiped his stethoscope down and put it away. It didn't matter what he wanted, or what he needed. Right now the only important things were Harper and this baby, and he'd do whatever it took to make sure they were okay.

Everything else could wait.

"You need anything else?" he asked her.

"No." She smiled. "I'm good."

He gently rolled down her shirt, covering her stomach back up, and offered his hand to help her stand. "Same time tomorrow?"

"Sounds good to me. I have to wait around for the postman to pick up the last of my custom orders." She looked at the gown-filled room. "Hopefully I'll be able to move around in here soon."

"Let me know if you need anything. Day or night. I always have my phone on."

She nodded. "I will."

"Okay. Take care of yourself." He couldn't resist any longer. He brushed her cheek with his hand, before quickly pulling it back.

Her lips parted and for a moment they stared at each other, the air around them crackling.

"Goodbye, James," she whispered. "I'll see you tomorrow."

"You definitely will." If that was all she had to offer he'd take it. And willingly so. The only thing worse than not being able to be with her would be not seeing her.

And he'd keep hold of that for as long as he could.

28

Being backstage at the fashion show was pure, adrenaline-fueled madness, but Harper was used to that. Having worked in costume departments on Broadway for years, quick changes didn't faze her at all. As soon as her models walked off the catwalk and through the curtain separating the staging from the dressing area she was ready for them, holding her hands out to unfasten the ties that kept their previous dresses on, then lifting the next dresses carefully over their heads, careful not to touch their clipped-in hair.

"Okay, you're done," she told Lola when she'd fixed the tiny tiara on her golden hair. "Let me just get Annabelle ready and you two can walk on for the finale."

The little girl was wearing Harper's final design. This one was all-out glitz. A tight silver bodice – strapless on Annabelle and with spaghetti straps on Lola, attached to a hooped tutu made with layers of silver tulle. Each dress was embellished with hand-sewn rhinestones, which caught the overhead lights. They were the type of princess gown that little girls dreamed of wearing, and Lola couldn't hide the excitement on her face.

"You look fabulous," Harper whispered to her as she turned to Annabelle. The model already had her arms up, ready for Harper to lift the dress over her head, covering her strapless bra and silk stockings. As Harper pulled the eyelets at the back together, Annabelle stepped into a pair of silver shoes while the make-up artist touched up her lipstick.

"Ready for the final group," the show runner shouted out.

Harper took a final look at her models, checking that their dresses were hanging correctly. "Okay. You're good to go. Break a—"

Her last word was swallowed by a gasp. She put her hand to her stomach, wincing at the sudden pain shooting through her abdomen. It was enough to make her stagger to the left, reaching out to steady herself on a clothing rack. It shifted with her weight, but she managed to stay upright.

"Harper!" Annabelle's voice was full of alarm.

"It's okay," Harper said, swallowing hard in attempt to not cry out again. "I'm fine. You need to get to the catwalk."

"Are you sure? You want me to call anybody?"

Somehow Harper managed to force her lips into a smile. "It was just indigestion. Now go, before you miss your cue."

With a final worried glance, Annabelle took Lola's hand and walked over to the gap in the curtains where the catwalk began. As soon as her back was turned, Harper let out a low moan and collapsed into the nearest chair.

What was wrong with her? She gingerly touched her stomach to find it was hard, the skin pulled taut like a trampoline. Taking a deep breath in through her nose, she held it for five seconds like her yoga teacher had taught her, then slowly exhaled through her mouth.

She could vaguely remember Ember talking about Braxton Hicks contractions. Sudden shooting pain that felt like real contractions, but were really the body preparing itself for birth. Is that what this was? Harper wasn't sure.

"Designers, your call is in two minutes," the show runner shouted. "Can you all come to the curtain."

It was customary for the designers to walk on stage at the end of the fashion show, to accept the audience's applause. But Harper found herself sitting exactly where she was, unable to find the strength to push herself back to standing.

"Harper Hayes? We need you," the show runner called out.

Another wave of pain assailed her, making her double over. She couldn't catch her breath, no matter how many times she tried to inhale. She let another moan out, deeper and more anguished.

Blood was rushing through her ears, drowning out the distant sound of clapping. Harper was vaguely aware of the curtain pulling back and the designers walking onto the catwalk, but everything else felt like it was blurring in front of her eyes.

"Harper!" The show runner ran over to her. "Is it the baby?"

Harper opened her mouth to answer, but only a groan came out.

"We need a doctor," the show runner called out. "Is there a doctor around here?"

Annabelle was there, kicking off her shoes, and scooting down next to Harper, still wearing her silver evening gown. "Honey, are you okay?"

"No," Harper managed.

"Do you want us to call somebody? Lisa's going to see if there's a doctor in the audience."

"James. He's a doctor," Harper gasped. "I want James." And then the pain overtook her again.

James clapped as the designers walked on one by one, scanning each to see if they were Harper. Her designs were beautiful, and the crowd had loved the mother-and-daughter matching outfits. He'd heard a few of them talking about putting in an order.

They'd have to wait awhile. Harper was determined to slow down for her last few weeks of pregnancy. Her high blood pressure had scared them both, but it had also brought an ease to them, too. She'd let him take care of her the best way he knew how – by checking on her each day, and making sure she was eating properly. It was strange how he felt closer to her now that they'd taken having a relationship out of the equation. It was as though his head was finally catching up with his heart and they'd both reached the same conclusion.

He wanted her in whatever form she came. Friend, lover, mother of his child. If she wanted to wait, he'd wait for as long as it took. He hadn't been in a hurry in the past three years, and he wasn't in a hurry now.

In the meantime, he'd look after her and their daughter the only way he could.

The crowd began to murmur and he looked up to see a woman with an electronic tablet clutched close to her chest. She ran onto the stage and grabbed the microphone from the stand. "Um, can you all hear me?" she asked, tapping it with her finger. "I'm looking for a Doctor James. Are you here?"

His skin turned to ice. He stood, his breath catching in his throat. "I'm here," he called out.

"Thank goodness." The woman sighed. "Can you come backstage, please. We need your help.

He was acutely aware of everybody looking at him as he walked down the aisle between the seats. There were a set of steps at the end and he climbed up them, following the woman with the tablet to the back of the catwalk.

"She keeps asking us not to fuss, but something's not right. She's doubled over in pain."

"Harper's in pain?"

"Yes." The woman nodded. "We've put her on the sofa over here."

Harper was half-laying, holding on to the hand of a woman in a silver ball gown. James recognized the dress from Harper's apartment. He dropped to his haunches, his gaze meeting Harper's.

"You doing okay?" he asked, softly stroking her hair.

She shook her head, her eyes glistening with tears. "It hurts," she whispered. "And I'm scared there's something wrong. Somebody's already called an ambulance."

He took her free hand in hers. "Try not to panic. It's going to be fine."

"Don't let go of me," she told him. "Not for a minute."

"I won't." He smiled at her. "I'm not going anywhere."

"I'm so scared."

"You don't need to be. You've got this. You're thirty-six weeks pregnant, the baby's doing great. If you end up giving birth early, she's going to be just fine."

Harper blinked. "I can't give birth. Not yet. I'm not ready." She squeezed his hand so tight her knuckles blanched. "They'll stop it, won't they? Put me on bed rest." She bit her lip. "I'll do whatever they say, I promise."

"Just try to breathe," he told her. "That's all you need to do until the ambulance gets here."

"I'm trying," she told him. "But I keep hyperventilating. What if the baby can't breathe when she comes out? What if I—oh!" she groaned, her eyes squeezing shut as she pulled her legs up against her bump. "Aaah, oh god it hurts." She pulled at his hand, bringing him closer.

"Breathe in," he whispered. "One, two, three, four, that's it. Now exhale." He looked at the model still wearing her gown. "How long since the last contraction?"

"About six minutes."

"Okay." He nodded.

"You're so calm," Harper whispered. "How can you be so relaxed?"

"Because I know you," he told her. "I know you're strong enough to get through this. So that makes me strong, too."

"I don't feel strong."

"You will. You're going to be an amazing mom, Harper. Whether it happens today or in four weeks' time, you've got this."

A tear rolled down her cheek. "I'm going to be a mom," she said, as though it was a revelation.

"Yeah, you are."

"And you're going to be a dad. Again."

"Yep." He nodded. From the corner of his eye he saw the stage curtain move. He glanced over his shoulder and saw Caitie walking over. "Is everything okay with..." her voice trailed off as she spotted Harper on the sofa. "Oh god, is it the baby?" She knelt down next to James and stroked Harper's face. "Are you having contractions?"

"I think so." Harper nodded. "They've called for an ambulance."

"It's here," the show runner shouted out. "The concierge is showing them in."

"Are you going with her?" Caitie asked James as the door opened and two paramedics walked in.

"That's the plan." James stood so the paramedics could reach Harper, and quietly gave them a rundown of her current health condition. "Can you meet us there? I know she'll want you with her."

"Of course. I'll head to my car now." She smiled at him. "I'm so glad she's got you."

He let out a mouthful of air. "I'm glad she's letting me."

Caitie leaned forward and hugged him. "I'll see you at the hospital. Keep doing what you're doing."

"I will," James said, watching as the paramedics helped Harper onto the gurney they'd brought in. He'd take care of her for as long as she'd let him.

"I hear somebody's a little impatient," Ellie said as she walked into the labor room. "How are you holding up?"

A grimace ghosted Harper's lips. "Not great. And pretty scared."

Ellie tipped her head to the side. "Being scared is perfectly normal. You'd feel the same way even at forty weeks. You've never done this before and it hurts like hell. I'd be worried if you weren't anxious."

"But it's bad for the baby."

"Let me decide what's good and bad in here, okay?" Ellie washed her hands in the sink in the corner of the room. "I want to examine you first, and ask you a few questions, then we'll talk about the next steps."

"Do you think you can stop the contractions?"

"That's what I'm going to find out." She smiled and snapped on a pair of latex gloves. "Do we have a urinalysis?" she asked the nurse who'd been taking care of Harper.

"Yes. All normal."

"That's good." She checked the monitor next to Harper's bed, concentrating on the readout. "Anything I need to know, James?" she murmured.

"Everything's as expected," he said, from where he was

sitting next to Harper, her hand enfolded in his. "Blood pressure still been higher than we'd like, though."

"Yeah." Ellie nodded. "Okay, let's take a look and see how this baby's doing." She turned to Harper and slid her hand beneath the sheet. "I'm just going to check your cervix, okay?"

Harper nodded.

A moment later, Ellie pulled back and took off her gloves. "You're five centimeters dilated," she said, throwing the latex in the medical trashcan. "How often are the contractions coming?"

"Every four to five minutes," James said.

"Hmm. Okay." She turned back to Harper. "So you're in what we call active labor. That's when you're having regular contractions close together, and your cervix is dilated more than three centimeters. Because this is your first baby, it's hard to say how long your labor will take. It could be a few hours, or could be longer, but I'd like to monitor you for the next half hour and see how things progress."

"You're not going to stop it?" Harper asked.

"Not at this point. The chances of stopping labor now are minimal, and could cause complications. We'd have liked to keep baby inside a little while longer, just to let her get a little more prepared for the outside world. But we rarely worry about a thirty-six-week-old baby. She may need a little extra oxygen, or some time in the NICU, but her chances of being born perfectly healthy are very high. As a doctor, we always breathe a little easier once a baby reaches thirty-six weeks."

"I'm going to have a baby?" Harper asked, eyes wide.

Ellie laughed. "Yeah. You are. How do you feel about that?"

Harper squeezed James's hand. He squeezed back, his fingers threading through hers. "How do you feel?" she asked him.

"I'm not the one doing the hard work," he told her. "I feel fine. And confident. And ready to meet our girl." He leaned forward to brush her hair from her face. "I'm here for you, whatever you need, I've got it."

"I need you to stay. Don't leave."

"I won't," he promised.

"And don't shout at me if I start screaming."

"I wouldn't dare." He leaned forward and pressed his lips to her brow. She closed her eyes and breathed him in. Yeah, she'd asked him to keep his distance, but right now she needed him to be as close as possible. He made her feel safe in a way she'd never felt before.

She took a deep breath, feeling her stomach tighten again. She squeezed her eyes shut as the pain over took her. "Another one," she gasped.

"Breathe in," James whispered. "Then blow out. One, two, three, four."

She felt a sudden gush of liquid, followed by a strange emptiness inside her.

"Don't panic," Ellie told her. "Your water has broke. We'll clear it up before anybody slips on it."

"That's good," Harper managed to gasp out. "Because I'm not cleaning it up."

From the corner of her eye she saw James biting down a smile.

"Ah, you're a feisty one," Ellie said. "I like that. It'll make labor much easier."

There was a knock at the door, and the nurse walked over to open it.

Caitie was standing in the doorway. "Sorry it took me a while to get here. I dropped by your apartment and picked up your bag. Just in case." She walked over to Harper's bed. "How are you doing?"

"Not great. I'm going to have a baby."

It was Caitie's turn to laugh. "I think we've known that for a while."

"Yeah, but this is the first time it's been today."

"Is everything okay?" Caitie asked, looking over at Ellie.

"It's looking good. We're keeping a close eye on her blood pressure, but everything else is where it should be. I'm going to go call up to the NICU to make sure there's a bed if we need it, then I'll be back to examine you again, okay?"

"Okay." Harper nodded. She couldn't help but feel dizzy at the speed of it all. One minute she thought she had a month until the baby was here, and now she was on her way.

Thank god James and Caitie were here. She wasn't sure how she'd do this without them.

"And just to warn you, there's a little crowd gathering in the waiting room," Caitie continued, her lips curling into a smile. "Ember's here with Lucas and baby Arthur, along with all the models from your show. James's parents showed up right after me, and for some reason my mom decided to tag along." Caitie shook her head. "And Brooke and Ally just arrived. Oh, and Breck's on his way."

"They could be waiting a while," Harper told her.

"They didn't seem to mind. It's like a party over there." Caitie grinned, and took Harper's other hand in her own. "Everybody cares about you, Harper. They want to be here to support you."

Just before another contraction took over her body, Harper couldn't help but feel good about that.

29

Damn, she was beautiful. An Amazonian, doing exactly what nature intended her to do, bringing a new life into the world to begin the circle all over again.

It was mesmerizing.

James was holding her hand, or rather she was squeezing his, her grip so hard his bones were grinding together. As her contraction ended, he wiped her face with a cold cloth, then leaned forward to kiss her temple. "You're doing amazing," he murmured, his lips close to her ear. "You've got this."

Harper inhaled deeply, her expression a picture of concentration. Her body had taken over, knowing implicitly what it needed to do, telling her when to push, to rest, to cry out with pain.

Ellie was at the end of the bed, her scrubs covered with a gown, her hands gloved as she told them of the baby's progress. "It's going beautifully," she told them. "She's halfway down. Next time you feel a contraction, I want you to push really hard, okay?"

"I don't have a damned choice," Harper gasped out. "Why

is it that men get all the fun of conception and the women get all the pain?"

"Because we're the stronger sex," Ellie told her. "They'd probably all end up dying if they had to push out a baby."

Harper opened her mouth to reply, but her words dissolved as another contraction assailed her. She tightened her grip on James again, groaning loudly as she bore down, gasping as the contraction ended.

"Do you feel that sting?" Ellie asked her. "That's the baby's head crowning. Next time you feel a contraction I don't want you to push. Just pant as loud as you can and let the baby do the work." Ellie looked at James. "You want to see the head?"

"Go and look," Harper said. "Tell me what you see."

He slid his hand out of hers and walked to where Ellie was sitting on a stool. He swallowed hard as he saw the fleshy head of their baby, covered in fine downy fuzz. "She's got pink hair."

Harper laughed. "Ow, don't make me laugh. It hurts."

"You can feel her if you want," Ellie said to Harper. "Give me your hand." She guided Harper's fingers to the crown of the baby's head. "There, that's your baby."

"Oh. Oh my god." Harper's bottom lip wobbled. "She's really real."

"Yeah, she is." Ellie grinned.

Harper's eyes met James's, and he could see how watery they were. Not just with pain, but with wonder. He felt his chest expand with emotion as their gazes continued to stay locked.

She tore her gaze away and cried out.

"Remember to pant," Ellie instructed. James took Harper's hand again, and she squeezed tightly as she blew out mouthfuls of air, groaning with pain.

"Her head's out," Ellie said. "Now we just need to help her

shoulders along. Keep panting, don't push. In a minute you'll feel a rush, that's your little girl being born. She's almost here, Harper."

"You're going to be a mom," Caitie said, her eyes filling with tears. "Such a great one, too."

As Harper's next contraction came, Ellie grabbed a towel and placed it on the bed in front of her. James watched as Harper leaned forward, grunting in pain, then her eyes flew open as their baby's shoulders came free, her tiny body cradled in Ellie's hands.

"You did it," he whispered. "She's here." Tears stung at his eyes as he watched Ellie lift the baby to Harper's bare chest. By instinct, Harper released his and Caitie's hands and wrapped her own around the baby, her eyes closing as she dipped her head, breathing softly as she cradled her child.

"She's beautiful," Caitie whispered. "Congratulations." She caught James's eye. "To both of you."

"You want to cut the chord, James?" Ellie asked. He nodded, and did as she instructed, before he turned back to Harper and their baby.

"Hey, little girl," she whispered as the baby wriggled on her chest. "It's so good to finally meet you." She looked up at James, her eyes full of joy. "Come say hello to our daughter."

———

Nobody had warned Harper about the sheer amount of activity that would go on around her in the hour after she'd given birth. Once the baby was checked for any problems and announced healthy by the pediatrician who'd been standing by, they'd given her back to Harper. She was already trying to suckle, though her lips were weak.

"It's okay," Ellie told her. "She'll get the hang of it. In the meantime, your colostrum will help her build up some immunities."

Nobody had prepared her for the emotions she'd feel, either. A whole flood of them gushed out right as the baby was born. Exultation mixed with fear and sheer exhaustion. They called the first hour after birth the golden hour, a time for her and James to bond with the baby. The fact was, she didn't have the energy to do anything else. If they'd tried to get her up she probably would have fallen over. Her legs felt like jelly.

"I'm starving," she whispered to James as he leaned over to touch the baby's hand. She curled her tiny fingers around his large one as though she was holding on for dear life, and the action made James smile.

"I'll go grab you something."

"Not yet. I want you to stay with me."

"I'll go," Caitie said, smiling at them both. "But as soon as I step into the waiting room everybody will want an update." She glanced at James. "Are you sure you don't want to go and tell them?"

He looked at Harper with soft eyes. "I'm not going anywhere yet. You can tell them."

"Okay then. I'll tell them baby..." she paused. "Um, does she have a name yet?"

Harper pressed her lips against her daughter's soft head. "I like Alyssa," she whispered to James. "What do you think?"

"I love it." He nodded.

"And I want her middle name to be Jay. After Jacob."

James blinked, his face full of emotion. "You do?"

"Yeah. One day we can tell her she's named after her older brother." Harper smiled at him. "He won't be forgotten."

James took a deep breath, as though he was trying to hold it together. He nodded, his lips pressing together.

Caitie, on the other hand, was visibly crying. "That's beautiful," she told them. "I'll tell everybody Alyssa Jay is here, weighing six pounds, and that she's a beauty."

"Are you sure?" James asked her, his voice scratchy.

"I'm certain." She smiled at him and left the room.

"Would you like to hold her now?" Harper asked James.

"That's a great idea," Ellie said. She'd been making notes on the laptop in the corner. "We encourage skin to skin with the father, too. It's perfect for bonding."

She watched as James unbuttoned his shirt, leaning over to lift Alyssa from her arms. Carefully, he pulled their tiny baby toward him, cradling her head and body as he warmed her against his bare chest.

A myriad of emotions passed over his face as he looked down at his daughter. Harper felt her eyes fill yet again as she watched him stare down with wonder, lowering his head to breathe her in.

"She's beautiful," he whispered. "Thank you."

"I'm going to leave you two for a minute, okay?" Ellie said, dimming the lights in the room. "If you need anything I'll be right outside. All you have to do is press the call light if you need me."

She'd already told them that once they'd ascertained that both mother and baby were healthy, they'd be left alone to bond. Harper nodded and smiled at Ellie as she left.

And then they were alone. Their strange, ragtag family of three. Harper felt her heart clench as Alyssa nestled into James's chest, her tiny lips opening and closing against his skin.

"I thought she'd cry more," Harper said. "But she hasn't."

"Give her time." James's eyes crinkled as he smiled. "She's tiny. She hasn't found her voice yet. But I've got a feeling she will and real soon." His eyes met hers. "Then you'll be wishing she was this quiet."

What she really wished was that she could bottle this

moment up. Yes, every part of her ached, and some parts were in a lot of pain. There was exhaustion and hunger eating at her like she'd never felt before. But that was all outweighed by the intense feeling of love that washed over her like a tidal wave. For her new baby, for James, for everything she'd ever wanted.

Why couldn't it always be like this?

"I'm glad you're her father," she said softly.

"So am I." He looked down at Alyssa again. "I'm not going to let her down. I'll always be here for her."

"I know you will."

"And you, too. Whatever happens between us, I'll always want to take care of you. Not just because you're the mother of my child, but because you're *you*. My friend, the person who brought me back to life." He lifted his gaze to hers. "Thank you for making me want to live again."

Hot, wet tears spilled down her cheeks.

"Don't cry," he said, moving Alyssa in his arms so he could reach out to wipe the wetness from Harper's cheeks.

"They're not sad tears," she whispered. "Not at all." Maybe there was a hint of regret there. A wistfulness of what might have been, if only they could have seen their way forward.

James kissed Alyssa's head and continued, "I know that you don't want complications, and I'm not planning on making things any more difficult than they already are. But you need to know you're loved. By me." His mouth curled into a smile. "You and Alyssa, you're my life now. And I'll take whatever that means. I'll be your friend if that's what you want." He took a deep breath. "Or more, if you decide you want that, too."

"More?" she asked him, her throat tight.

He looked at her through cloudy eyes. "I love you, Harper. And I messed everything up. I made you feel unwanted. Like a dirty secret I wasn't willing to share. I'll regret that for the rest of my life, because you're nobody's secret. You're too vital for that. Since you came into my life it's like you've been like an explosion of color, brightening up my dark existence. Being near you makes people smile. It makes me grin like I'm a little crazy. And maybe I am because I can't imagine life without you, not anymore."

"You don't just want to be friends?" She wanted to laugh at the strangeness of the conversation. Less than an hour since she'd brought new life into the world, she was asking her baby's father what he wanted from her. It was so topsy turvy, so different from how she imagined having her first child would be. And yet there was a realness to it that took her breath away. The same way his stare made the air catch in her throat.

"I do." He nodded. "I want us to be together. But only if you're willing to give that to me. And if you can't, that's okay, too. You taught me to live again, Harper. But now I've had a taste of life, I don't ever want to go back to the darkness. If you only want to be friends – co-parents – I'll take it." He raised a brow. "Even if it'll kill me."

She took a moment to absorb his words, feeling hope rise up in her like it never had before. "What about Sara and Jacob?"

"I'll always love them," James told her. "How could I not? But another thing I've learned is that humans are capable of more love than I ever realized was possible. Sara and Jacob will always be in my heart, but now you and Alyssa are there, too."

She pressed her lips together in an attempt to stem the tears. She wanted to believe. She did. But there was fear, too. James was a good man, he'd always try to do the right thing. How could she be sure he wasn't doing that now?

As a child she'd been a burden. To her mother, her grandmother, to anybody who had to take care of her. It had hurt to know she could be left behind so easily by her mom, always in search of the next guy around the corner. But maybe it had been her grandmother who'd done the worst damage by showing her she wasn't good enough. She needed to work harder, be prettier, to push down her natural ebullience and be quiet and graceful instead. Her grandmother hadn't wanted Harper. She'd wanted a different child.

Somebody Harper could never be.

"What if I'm not as good as Sara?" she whispered to him. "What if I drive you crazy?"

He grinned at her, rocking Alyssa in a gentle rhythm against his chest. "I love your crazy. I love the way you get so passionate about everything. I even love the way you work yourself to the bone to get things done. I'd never compare you to Sara, or compare this gorgeous girl to Jacob. I don't need to, because you're both everything I want, *exactly* the way you are."

"What if Alyssa grows up to be like me? Then you'll be surrounded by crazy."

"I can't think of anything I'd love more. I want you with me, Harper. And our baby. I want to be with you in every way. Not because we have a child together, although that's amazing. But because you're you. Beautiful, funny, and talented, but most of all, you're full of love. I can't imagine life without you and I don't want to try."

"You're making me cry again."

"I'm hoping this is the last time I make you cry. From now on all I want is your smiles."

Alyssa let out a wail. It wasn't loud, the way Harper had expected a baby to sound. More like a tiny bird than a child. But still, her sweet face screwed up as she cried, her hands curling into fists.

"She looks like you when she's angry," Harper whispered.

James grinned. "Maybe she'll be the best of both of us." He rocked her again, but her crying increased. "I think she wants you," he said softly. "You ready for her, Mom?"

Harper nodded. He stood and gently lifted Alyssa back into her arms. The baby began to snuffle against her, her mouth sucking against her skin.

"She's hungry," James told her. "Maybe we should try feeding her."

"I'm not sure how."

"You want me to call in the nurse? Or I can help you? I think I remember the basics from clinical rotations."

"I'd like you to help," Harper said firmly.

She looked down at the baby as he positioned Alyssa's face against her breast. "She might need some extra support, being so tiny," he whispered. "Wait until she opens her mouth really wide, then gently pull her on to your nipple. Don't hold her head too close. You might have to work a little to get the right position."

Harper did as he instructed, watching with wide eyes as Alyssa latched on, her mouth instinctively moving as she suckled against her. James slid a pillow beneath Alyssa to support her body and Harper's arms. "Are you comfortable?" he asked her.

"Yeah." She grinned up at him. "Look at me. I'm really doing this. I'm feeding my baby." She looked up at him. "Our baby," she corrected herself.

"Yeah, you are," he said, his voice thick. "And you're doing it perfectly."

She took a deep breath, letting the joy fill her up. "I want this," she told him, ignoring the fear that was trying to overtake her certainty. "I want you, the same way you want me. I want you to be my friend, my partner. My lover." She smiled at him. "You're not the only one who's been brought back to life. Since the day I first met you my life's changed for the better in every way. Even if I didn't know it at the time."

He blinked, hope sparking in his eyes. "You want us?"

She nodded slowly. "I do. I love you, James Tanner. And I want us to be together. A family." She smiled down at Alyssa. "If you'll have us."

He leaned forward, pressing his lips against hers in a soft kiss. "Yes I want you," he whispered against her mouth. "You and Alyssa. And I'll do whatever it takes to keep you both by my side."

30

A little while later, once Alyssa was fast asleep and Harper was taking a shower with the assistance of a nurse, James walked out to the waiting room to see if anybody was still there. As soon as he pushed the door open, he could hear the loud sounds of conversation and laughter, then he could see them – his parents, his friends, Harper's friends, too. At least twenty people were squeezed into the small room, their faces filled with expectation when they saw him.

"Um hi," he said, bemused at all the stares.

"Congratulations, sweetheart," his mom said, walking forward to hug him. "How're Harper and the baby?"

"Alyssa's fine. She's asleep. Maybe you can come in and see her later," he told her, hugging her back. "And Harper's taking a shower. When we're all ready I'll call you in to see her."

"Do you have a picture of Alyssa?" His mom's eyes lit up.

"Uh, yeah." Harper had insisted on taking one of him as he held his daughter, her tiny body cradled in his big hands. He pulled his phone out of his pocket and scrolled down, passing his phone to his mom. "There she is."

"Oh." Louise clutched the phone to her chest. "She's so beautiful. Is that blonde hair I see?"

"Yeah, though it's as fine as anything. It'll probably fall out before it grows again."

His mom passed his phone to his dad, who passed it to Deenie. From the corner of his eye he could see everybody squeezing around to take a look. Pride burst out of him at their coos and as they told him how beautiful she was.

His daughter was perfect. The child he'd made with Harper. His heart filled with love for her all over again.

For both of them.

"Congratulations, man," Lucas said, slapping his shoulder. "She's gorgeous."

"How's Harper feeling?" Ember asked him.

"Sleepy. Painful. But mostly happy." James grinned. The urge to walk back to her room came over him. To check she was still there, still okay. Would it always be like this? As though he was constantly drawn to her, like a magnet pulling him near.

"And how about you?" Ember asked, her eyes shining. "Are you holding up okay?"

Somebody passed the phone back to him – he had no idea who. There were too many people jostling around. He looked at the image on the screen, and swallowed hard. *Alyssa Jay*. He could still remember the warmth of her against his skin. "I'm more than okay. I'm damned ecstatic."

"She's so beautiful," Ember said wistfully. "And tiny, too. Look at those little fingers."

"Maybe she'll grow up and fall in love with Arthur," Ally said, leaning to glance at James's phone. "Wouldn't that be sweet?"

"No," James said firmly. "She's going to stay little forever. No boyfriends, no going out. Nothing."

Ally laughed. "Oh boy, you have so much to look forward to. Just ask Nate what it's like having a teenage daughter."

The door on the far side of the waiting room opened, and Caitie walked in, carrying a tray of coffees. Dangling from her hand was a bag full of pastries. "I'm going to take one of these in to Harper," she said. "You guys can fight over the rest." She grabbed a cup and pastry and walked to where James was standing. "You doing okay, Daddy?"

Ally laughed. "Don't ever let me hear you call him Daddy again, okay? That's reserved for couples. Or, you know… kids."

Caitie wrinkled her nose. "Eww. You know what I meant."

James shook his head. "I'm good. And Harper's getting cleaned up. She'll be glad to see you. And the pastries." He looked around the room. "She's going to need the energy to deal with these guys."

Caitie grinned. "Sadly, they didn't have any blueberry muffins, but maybe now that she's not pregnant she won't like them any more." Caitie buzzed at the entrance to the maternity ward, walking through once the door automatically opened.

"I should head back, too," James told them. "Thank you all for being here. I'll come get you as soon as Harper's ready."

"We're proud of you, son." His dad shook his hand. "We can't wait to meet your little girl."

James felt his body suffuse with warmth as he headed back to the maternity ward. He was looking at his phone again. At Alyssa. Maybe that's why he didn't see Rich standing there, and all but bumped into him.

"Hey," Rich said, slapping him on the back. "I just heard about the baby. Congratulations. Is everything okay?" He pulled at the hem of his scrubs. "I would have checked before but I was in surgery."

"Everything's great. Harper's perfect. Alyssa's perfect."

"That's her name? Pretty."

"Yeah it is." James showed Rich his phone. "That's her. Alyssa Jay."

Rich leaned forward a huge grin on her face. "You're a lucky guy."

"Yeah, I am. The luckiest." James couldn't hide the grin on his face. "She's just so tiny, you know? So perfect. All those itty-bitty fingers and toes. And her lips are just like Harper's. Her nose, too."

"Lucky for her." Rich winked. "But seriously, I'm so happy for you. Enjoy this, you deserve it." He put his arm around James's back again, giving him a bro hug. "Don't mess it up, okay?"

"I don't intend to. They're my family. I'm going to take care of them."

"Both of them?" Rich lifted an eyebrow.

"Yeah. Both of them." He lifted his hand in goodbye. "I'll catch you later, okay? Maybe arrange for a time for you to meet the baby?"

"Sounds perfect. And James?"

"Yeah?"

"Sara would be proud of you. And happy for you, too."

James swallowed hard, unable to dislodge the lump in his throat. "Thanks, that means a lot."

Caitie was waiting for her when Harper emerged from the bathroom, her body freshly scrubbed, her hair damp from washing. The aroma of coffee and pastries filled the air and made her stomach gurgle. "Is that what I think it is?" she asked.

"Decaf latte and a pastry. There were no muffins left, so I hope this is okay."

"It's perfect." Harper grabbed the pastry and tore off a chunk with her teeth. "Sorry for being so disgusting," she said once she swallowed. "But I could eat a damn horse."

"Haven't you had anything since I left?"

"Oh, I've had loads. James grabbed me some chocolate from the machine outside, and the nurse brought me a sandwich. But my stomach just feels so empty, you know?"

"It *is* empty." Caitie grinned. "You haven't got a baby in there any more. Talking of which..." She looked around. "Where's Alyssa?"

"They took her to the nursery while I showered. They'll bring her back in a minute."

"Are you keeping her with you all the time while you're here?" Caitie asked.

"Yep. I wouldn't be able to sleep if I didn't." Harper swallowed a mouthful of coffee.

"I hate to break it to you, but sleep isn't going to be on your agenda for the next few months if what Ember tells me is true."

Harper laughed. "So I hear. But I'm hoping Alyssa turns out to be the perfect baby. A really quiet one at night." She sat on the bed, Caitie beside her.

"I can't believe you're a mom," Caitie told her. "Sometimes I feel like I'm still in college, and here's you, responsible for another life."

"It feels weird," Harper agreed. "But right, too. I'm not scared of the responsibility. I'm glad I've got her. I'm so happy to be her mom. It's like I've been waiting for this all my life."

"You're a natural." Caitie smiled. "James is, too. I just saw him in the waiting room showing Alyssa's picture to everybody."

"I think he's fallen for her as much as I have." Harper traced the pattern on her gown with the pad of her finger. "He told me he loved me. That he wants us to be a couple."

Caitie caught her eye. "Of course he did. He'd be a fool not to. You should see the way he looks at you every time he thinks nobody's looking. I know love when I see it."

"You think he loves me?" Harper grinned widely. "Do you?"

"Yes I do. It's in his eyes, that's where you see it. There's a soft look he only gets when he looks at you." She pulled her lip between her teeth, remembering. "And I saw it again when Alyssa was born and he was staring at her. He's got it bad, even if he keeps messing things up."

"I keep messing them up, too."

"You just need to believe. Not just in him but in yourself. It's weird because you're so certain of yourself in every other aspect than relationships. I've never seen anybody more confident about their work than you. But when it comes to love it's like you have an Achilles' heel. As if you feel you don't deserve it or something."

Harper swallowed at her friend's words – Caitie had hit the nail on the head. "I don't feel like that anymore," she told her. "Or at least I'm trying not to. I'm going to keep working until I never feel like it again. I want Alyssa to grow up being confident in everything, and I'm going to show her how."

Caitie smiled. "I know you will. She's going to love you as much as I do. More, maybe. If that's possible."

Was it? Harper had no idea, but she couldn't wait to find out. All she knew was that here in the hospital, with her body full of exhaustion and pain, she'd never felt happier in her life. And she was determined to make it last.

"Look at her," Louise said, cradling Alyssa in her arms. "She's such a beautiful baby." She looked up at Harper, her face beaming. "You must be so proud."

Proud didn't begin to cover it. In awe was closer. Every time she looked at Alyssa she fell even more in love. With her pink skin and blue eyes, and tiny hands that gripped so tightly, she was perfect in every way.

"I am," Harper said, grinning. "Having her here almost makes up for the painful labor. And the morning sickness. And the cravings..."

James's mom laughed. "Oh, you've got a lifetime of excitement ahead of you. One thing's for sure, your life will never be the same again."

"That's what we're hoping for," James said, sitting next to Harper on the bed and sliding his arm around her waist. "I kind of like this new life."

Harper turned to look at him, her gaze soft. "I do, too," she whispered. Every word was true. It was already impossible to imagine life without this tiny little human in it. And though she was patiently letting everybody have a cuddle with her baby, Harper was already happiest when Alyssa was in her arms. Asleep and safe, her tiny mouth opening and closing like a sleeping fish.

She was everything.

Louise's phone buzzed and she rolled her eyes. "I keep getting messages congratulating me, as though I had anything to do with this little angel coming into the world." She kissed the tip of Alyssa's nose. "I told them they should be congratulating you, Harper. You did the hard work." She pulled her lip between her teeth. "Have you heard from your mom?"

Harper swallowed and shook her head. "No. I haven't told her." She hadn't told her grandmother either. Neither of them deserved to know, and she wasn't ready to spoil this day by talking to them and letting them make her feel small. Better to send a birth announcement the old fashioned way.

"I'm so sorry about your family," Louise said, carrying Alyssa back over to where Harper was sitting. Louise slid her back into Harper's waiting arms, and immediately she felt better. "I can't understand how they could treat you that way."

"It's okay," Harper said. For the first time in her life it really was. "I have Alyssa now."

"And us. You have us," Louise told her. "You're part of our family. And as James will tell you, that means you'll be spoiled a lot. We take care of our own, and that includes the two of you." She kissed Harper's cheek. "I'm not your mother, but I'll always be here for you."

Harper blinked back the tears. "Thank you."

"Hey, did somebody say family?" Caitie asked, standing in the doorway. "Because there's a huge line of people out here wanting to see you guys. It's worse than Disney out here."

Their friends were all crowding in behind her. Ember and Lucas, Ally and Brooke, along with some of the models from the fashion show and James's doctor friends. Harper turned to James and smiled when she saw his expression. He was staring at Alyssa with a look of wonder.

"Are you ready to see them now?" Caitie asked her, and Harper nodded. She was more than ready. She was surrounded by her family in the small town that she'd come to love, and she couldn't be happier.

With Alyssa in her arms and James by her side it felt like she'd finally come home.

"I think that's everything." Harper looked around her hospital room as James picked up the car seat. Alyssa was safely strapped in, her eyes wide as James held her mid-air. "Are you sure I need to be wheeled out in that?" she asked, nodding at the wheelchair.

"It's hospital policy. We don't want you falling down and suing us." Ellie winked. "As soon as you're outside the door you can stand up and walk, I promise."

Harper sighed, but sat down in it anyway, balancing her overnight bag on her lap. She was wearing a pair of soft maternity jeans and a billowy blouse, disguising her still-bulging stomach. Ellie had assured her that was normal – it took nine months to get up to this size, it was going to take a few more to get back down.

"Good luck," Ellie said, hugging Harper and James. "I'll see you in a week. But you've got my number if there are any problems – call me day or night. And you've set up your first appointment with the pediatrician, right?"

"Yep. It's all covered." James smiled at her. "Thank you for everything."

Ellie shrugged. "Harper did all the work. I just got to assist her."

When the orderly pushed them through the double glass doors, Harper found herself blinking at the brightness of the sun. Alyssa must have had the same reaction – she started to moan, and James turned her so her face was in the shadow.

"Welcome to the world, little one," he murmured. "That's the sun. You should probably get used to it. We see it a lot in California."

When they reached James's car, Harper climbed out of the wheelchair and watched as James strapped the baby seat into the back of his car. She smiled, remembering how they'd both practiced when she first bought the seat, neither of them able to work out the complex straps. Now, though, James was a natural.

"I'll head off," the orderly told her. "Good luck."

"Thank you." Harper smiled at him, and turned to James. "Do you think she's too warm in that onesie?"

"I'll put the air conditioning on," James said, taking her bag and putting it in the trunk. "You need help getting into the seat?"

"I think I can do it." Harper held on to the doorframe as she slowly lowered herself to the seat. "There, I'm in. No guarantees I'll be able to get out again."

James laughed. "I'll carry you."

"You will not. I don't want to break your back."

He slid into the driver's seat and pulled the door shut. "Okay, so where are we going?" he asked her.

"Home?" She quirked an eyebrow. "Unless you were thinking of taking us to Disneyland. Though I think Alyssa might sleep through it all." She grinned at him, and he shook his head with a smile.

"Home," he repeated softly. "But *which* home. Yours or mine?"

She looked up at him, her lips parting, but no words came out. Because the way he was staring at her took her breath away. She could see the emotion in his eyes, the hope, the fear, and the love. They matched her own. They pulled at her, like a rope lassoed around her body, forever tying her to him.

"I want you to come home with me," he continued. "Not because it's easier, or cheaper, or there's more space. But because I want to wake up with you every morning. Hell, I want to wake up with you every time Alyssa cries in the night. I want to hold you and take care of you and protect you. I love you, Harper. And I love our daughter. I want us to be a family. Starting now."

She swallowed, feeling the emotions overwhelm her. Her chest felt tight, her throat scratchy, and her eyes were stinging all over again. The fear she'd been feeling, that she wasn't worth it, that she didn't deserve this, was melted by the intensity of his stare. And she knew what she wanted more than anything else.

She wanted this. Her two loves. Her family.

He'd opened himself up to her in a way she'd never expected. Laid himself bare and vulnerable. And it touched her to her core to know he wanted her enough to risk the pain, the hurt, the rejection.

He was willing to risk everything for love.

And so was she. Right here, right now. She leaned forward, cupping her palm against the roughness of his jaw, feeling the heat of his skin leach into her own. "I love you, James Tanner," she whispered. "I want us to be your family."

He reached up, covering her hand with his own. "Thank god," he whispered, leaning forward until his lips were only inches from hers. "I was considering kidnap."

His words were warm against her mouth. She closed her eyes, smiling hard. Then she felt the brush of his lips against hers and the curl of his hand around her neck, the sensation sending sparks down her spine.

Her whole body tightened at his touch. It was gratifying to know things still worked. That she could still feel desire, need, overwhelming love. Maybe stronger than she ever had before.

"James," she murmured as he broke their kiss, his eyes still capturing hers.

"Yeah?" he muttered, swallowing hard, as though he was as overcome by the sensations as she was.

"Alyssa's watching us," Harper murmured, looking at Alyssa's face in the mirror aimed at her carseat.

He grinned. "She can't see this far. Not yet." He kissed her again, his lips curling against hers.

"She will soon. We better be careful."

"She'll get used to me not being able to keep my hands off her mom. Or she'd better." He winked.

Harper laughed, shaking her head, and took a deep breath to center herself. "We don't want her to think it's normal to make out in cars."

A look of alarm shot across his face. "No." He nodded solemnly. "We most certainly don't. She won't be making out in cars, not ever. Or anywhere else for that matter."

"It's okay, Alyssa, I'll help you sneak out when you're a teenager," Harper mock-whispered to the baby. "Daddy will never know."

"Daddy will. For sure."

Alyssa let out a cry. "She's hungry," Harper told him.

"Yeah, we should get going." He reluctantly released her.

"I think we're ready. Why don't you take us home?"

EPILOGUE

"There," Harper said, pulling the tiny hat over Alyssa's head. "Now we're ready for the beach." She looked down at the huge bag full of things she'd packed for the baby. Towels and blankets nestled next to bottles and diapers, along with a change of clothes and sunscreen to protect the baby from the California rays. "You ready to feel some sand between your toes?" she asked her.

Alyssa blinked as she looked up at Harper. She wasn't quite babbling yet, but she always looked as though she understood everything her mommy said.

"Oh look, we nearly forgot Ned." Harper grabbed the tiny teddy bear Alice had sent for the baby when they'd told her of the birth. Sara's family hadn't been back to Angel Sands since that disastrous trip a few months ago, but James had sent them photographs of Alyssa and they'd sent a card congratulating them both.

Unlike her own grandma and mother, who hadn't even acknowledged the birth announcement Harper had sent them. She was surprised to find it didn't hurt. Not one bit.

Because they weren't her family; not any more. Now that

she had Alyssa and James, she knew what the word really meant. It was about caring, loving, always putting the other person first. Something her grandmother and mother had never done.

Stuffing the teddy into the bag, Harper slung it across her shoulder, cradling Alyssa in her other arm. She turned to walk out of her daughter's room, but Alyssa lifted her hand. "What's that, sweetie?" she asked her.

Harper looked up in the direction of her daughter's gesture, her eyes catching the framed photograph of baby Jacob hanging on the wall. "That's Jacob. Your big brother. One day Daddy's going to tell you all about him."

"All about who?" James asked, walking into the room. He took the bag from Harper's shoulders and slid it over his own. "The basement's all finished. I just signed off on it."

"It's done?" Harper smiled at him, her heart leaping.

"Yep. All ready for when you want to start back at work. Everything's baby-proofed and the crib and play area are ready. I'll give you the tour when we're back from the beach."

"Thank you." She rolled to her tiptoes, Alyssa still cradled in her arms, as she pressed her lips against James's. "I can't wait to see it." She pulled back and adjusted Alyssa's hat. "And I was talking about Jacob. I said you'd tell Alyssa all about her big brother one day."

His eyes met hers, the skin at the corners crinkling. "I will." He nodded. "When she's older." He reached out and tickled Alyssa under her chin. "You all ready?" he asked Harper.

"Yep." She nodded, still smiling at him. It was strange how excited she was about this outing. Not just because it was Alyssa's first trip to the beach, although she couldn't wait to see her daughter's face when she got to experience the sand and sea. But because they were meeting all of her friends – the people who'd taken care of her during her pregnancy and made her feel so welcome after her move to Angel Sands. She'd arrived here afraid, alone, and with a tiny little life growing inside her.

And now she had a family she loved fiercely.

"Then let's go."

When they pulled into the parking lot behind Paxton's Pier, it took them a few minutes to unclip Alyssa, make sure she was covered from head to toe in sunscreen, and unpack the trunk of all their equipment. As well as the bag Harper had packed, there was a blanket for the sand, an umbrella, and a little pop-up tent where Alyssa could snooze away from the glare of the sun.

"How long are we staying again?" James murmured. "We look like we're moving to the beach for the month."

Harper grinned. "We'll probably stay for a couple of hours. I don't want her tender skin to be outside for too long. She's still only three months."

James lifted Alyssa from her arms and pressed his lips to her chubby cheek. She smelled of sunscreen and baby shampoo. He breathed her in, feeling his body relax. He loved holding her, playing with her, making her smile. His current project was trying to make her laugh. She wasn't there yet, but he wouldn't give up until she did.

He passed the baby back to Harper and took the blanket, umbrella, and beach bag, flexing his muscles to keep them upright as he closed the trunk. "I'll have to come back for the tent," he told her. "I don't have enough arms."

"Story of my life. And no worries, we'll get it if she gets sleepy." Harper kissed him. "First of all, I want to take her in the water."

They made their way along the sand, heading for their

crowd of friends on their blankets alongside Paxton's Pier. As they approached, they were greeted by loud hellos and lifted arms. Lucas stood and came over to take some of the equipment from James."

"Thanks," James said, as Lucas put the blanket down on the sand alongside the one he and Ember were using.

"No problem. Us dads have to stick together." Lucas winked. "It took me three trips to get everything from the car."

He didn't look like he resented it one little bit. In fact, he was grinning from ear to ear. James recognized that look. It was one of contentment and pride, wrapped up in overwhelming happiness. Of everything finally falling into place.

And he loved it.

He looked down to where Harper was sitting on the blanket, adjusting Alyssa's swim diaper and tiny pink sparkled swimsuit. She pulled the hat down a little firmer on her head, making Alyssa's face wrinkle up in protest.

"I'm just looking after your skin," Harper told their daughter. "You'll thank me when you're older."

He loved watching the two of them together. The love for their child shone out of Harper, somehow making her even more beautiful than she'd been before. She lay Alyssa down gently on the blanket and pulled her own shorts and tank off, revealing a grey and white striped bikini that fit her perfectly.

He swallowed hard, trying to not ogle her body. It was tough, because she was perfect. Rounded breasts, curved hips, and a stomach that still had a little bump to it, crisscrossed in silvery stretch marks.

"You look beautiful," he told her, pulling his own t-shirt off and throwing it onto the blanket.

"Thank you." Her eyes sparkled. "It's easy to feel beautiful when you look at me like that." She reached out to trace his bicep. "And you don't look so bad yourself."

"Shall we go in?" he asked her, leaning down to pick up Alyssa. She nestled her warm body against his chest. With his free hand, he patted his pocket to check that the waterproof pouch was still there, smiling when he felt the outline.

"We'll see you guys in a bit. Unless any of you want to join us?"

"Oh no," Ember said loudly. "This is your special time." She caught his eye with a grin, letting him know without words that Lucas had told her his secret. Not that James cared. He didn't plan on it being a secret for very long.

"Ready?" he asked Harper.

"Yep. Let's take our little girl for a swim."

Harper watched as James walked toward the water, his arms holding Alyssa against his broad chest. His skin was toned, tan, and it made her fingers twitch with the need to touch him. How the heck did she get so lucky? As he reached her, his eyes met hers, his lips curling into a broad smile. Alyssa kicked her legs against his chest, as though she was impatient to get this over with.

"Do you think she's going to like it?" Harper asked him, reaching out to stroke Alyssa's cheek.

"She's going to love it. Shall we dip her toes in?"

"Okay." Harper grinned as he turned the baby in his arms and crouched down, slowly lowering Alyssa until her feet were right above the surface of the ocean. He had one hand beneath her, the other across her stomach as she faced Harper, her eyes wide.

Then he lowered her further, until her tiny toes met the water. She kicked again, making the water splash. He dropped to his knees, until Alyssa was up to her waist in the water, and she looked up at Harper with delight.

"You want to swim, little one?" he asked, moving Alyssa through the water, swooshing her left and right. Alyssa hiccupped, or at least it sounded like a hiccup, but when she did it again, Harper realized it was a laugh.

"She loves it," she said, grinning.

"A water baby." James kissed Harper's head. "Hey look, do you see that?"

"What?" Harper asked him.

"There's something down there on the ocean bed."

Harper leaned down to look at where James was gesturing, and sure enough there was something down there. It caught the light of the sun, glistening beneath the gentle waves. "I think it's a shell," she said. "Or maybe a pebble." She reached down to pick it up, intending to show it to Alyssa, but her finger touched a thin metal band. She lifted it out of the water, turning it in her hand.

"It's a ring," she said, watching the diamond catch the rays. "An engagement ring by the looks of it. Do you think somebody lost it?"

"It's not lost." James's voice was scratchy. "I think it's exactly in the right place."

Harper blinked. "It's not..." her words trailed away, her breath catching in her throat. "James?" she asked, wondering if she was going crazy.

"Harper Hayes, from the moment you exploded into my life things have never been the same. I'll never be the same. You make everything better. Right. And it would be the greatest honor of my life if you'd agree to be my wife."

Harper tried to swallow, but her throat was too dry. "You want to marry me?" she asked him, still breathless.

"Yes. I want you to be my wife. I want the world to know how much I love you." His eyes softened as he took the ring from her and slid it onto her finger. "I want to shout it from the rooftops, take an ad out in the goddamn paper. Because you and Alyssa are everything I've ever wanted."

She grinned at him through her tears. "Then the answer's yes." She laughed, her head tipping back.

James turned toward the shore. "She said yes," he shouted, his words carried by the breeze. A loud cheer came from their friends sitting on the beach.

"They knew?" Harper asked.

"I told Lucas. I'm guessing he told Ember and the rest was history. The Angel Sands grapevine is strong." Still holding Alyssa against his chest, he lifted her hand, kissing the ring on her finger. "And I'm glad. I hid you away once. I don't intend to ever do it again. I want the world to know you're going to be my wife." He took a deep breath, his eyes warm. "There was a time when I thought nothing good was ever going to happen to me again. But you showed me that everybody deserves to be loved." He leaned over, still cradling Alyssa against him, as he pressed his lips to Harper's. "Thank you for making me the happiest man alive."

Harper kissed him back, feeling the joy overwhelm her. A year ago she'd visited this town and spent the night with a gorgeous man whose eyes were full of clouds. Now those clouds had disappeared, replaced by a brightness that touched her heart.

For the first time since she was eighteen years old, she felt as though she truly belonged. In a town she loved, with friends she cared about, and a family she adored. Was it possible to have everything?

As James kissed her again, and murmured sweet words against her lips, she thought it definitely was.

DEAR READER

Thank you so much for reading James and Harper's story. If you enjoyed it and you get a chance, I'd be so grateful if you can leave a review. And don't forget to keep an eye out for **PIECES OF US**, the next book in the Angel Sands series.

To learn more, you can sign up for my newsletter here: http://www.subscribepage.com/e4u8i8

I can't wait to share more stories with you.

Yours,

Carrie xx

ABOUT THE AUTHOR

Carrie Elks writes contemporary romance with a sizzling edge. Her first book, *Fix You*, has been translated into eight languages and made a surprise appearance on *Big Brother* in Brazil. Luckily for her, it wasn't voted out.

Carrie lives with her husband, two lovely children and a larger-than-life black pug called Plato. When she isn't writing or reading, she can be found baking, drinking an occasional (!) glass of wine, or chatting on social media.

You can find Carrie in all these places
www.carrieelks.com
carrie.elks@mail.com

ALSO BY CARRIE ELKS

ANGEL SANDS SERIES

Let Me Burn

She's Like the Wind

Sweet Little Lies

Just A Kiss

Baby I'm Yours

Pieces of Us

THE HEARTBREAK BROTHERS SERIES

Take Me Home

THE SHAKESPEARE SISTERS SERIES

Summer's Lease

A Winter's Tale

Absent in the Spring

By Virtue Fall

THE LOVE IN LONDON SERIES

Coming Down

Broken Chords

Canada Square

STANDALONE

Fix You

ACKNOWLEDGMENTS

First thanks always go to my lovely family. Ash, Ella, Olly and Plato the pug. I love you guys.

I wouldn't be where I am today without my agent, Meire Dias. Thanks to you and all at the Bookcase Agency for the hard work you do.

My editor Rose David and my proofreader, Mich, always work tirelessly to make my words shine. Thank you for all you do.

Najla Qamber is a kick-ass designer, and she hit this cover out of the park. You're amazing, lady!

Bloggers have always been such an important part of my book journey. Thanks to each and every one of you who shows me support in so many ways – sharing covers and release days, promoting sales, reading and reviewing books. You're the engine that keeps the book world going, and I appreciate you so much.

Finally, to my lovely facebook group members (The Water Cooler - if you want to join!), thank you! We have so much fun – you make Facebook a great place to be. You help with ideas, inspiration and most of all you put a smile on my face. Thanks for being so amazing.